VENOMOUS

L J SPENCE

authorHOUSE

AuthorHouse™ UK
1663 Liberty Drive
Bloomington, IN 47403 USA
www.authorhouse.co.uk
Phone: 0800 047 8203 (Domestic TFN)
*   +44 1908 723714 (International)*

Published by AuthorHouse 05/26/2020

ISBN: 978-1-7283-9028-4 (sc)
ISBN: 978-1-7283-9029-1 (e)

Acknowledgements

My first mention must go to my children, John and Beth. You make me proud of your achievements on an almost daily basis. I hope the production of this novel will not just make you proud of me, but also show you that any level of success in chasing a dream requires relentless dedication.

To Rachael, I say thank you. You uttered a sentence to me years ago when I first came up with the idea of writing a book:

"You were always capable."

The words stick with me and serve as my motivation to this day.

To my partner, Kirsty. I can only say that I love you very much. Your patience and co-operation with this project is unrivalled. May you share every second of enjoyment that any degree of success and happiness this project brings me.

Finally, I wish to dedicate this book to all sufferers of any illnesses but most significantly, those suffering from the varying types of Sarcoidosis, which includes my partner.

I can only hope that a mention of this condition here can

help increase awareness, of which to date so little is known and a cure remains to be discovered.

To any of those people who may come across this novel, I hope it helps you to detach yourself from your unfortunate reality for a short while. Enjoy immersing yourself into my fictional world which encompasses this novel and those that may follow!

Cheers,

I hear voices in my head
They come to me
They understand
They talk to me

Chapter 1

Ebony glanced down at her watch; the dial difficult to make out in the reflection of the sun. It was hard to believe that it could still be so hot at such a late hour in the day. The sunset was soon to descend upon them. As the landscape became bathed in an orange glow, the remaining energy-sapping rays of the sun were taking their full effect. Accompanied with the unescapable humidity, it was without doubt, an environment she had never encountered before.

She had been used to a few hot summers back home in Arkansas and was no stranger to warm climates. However, with a fully- laidened rucksack strapped to her back continuously for several hours, every step required maximum effort. She had a slender figure and it almost buckled under such excess weight.

She glanced up from beneath the brim of a sweat- soaked baseball cap. Her father, who seemed oblivious to her suffering, was gallantly leading the way and striding out ahead.

"How much further Daddy"? She uttered breathlessly, struggling with every syllable.

Her father paused. He then glanced back over his shoulder to see his red-faced daughter whose voice had just cried out in desperation, perhaps for some reassurance and motivation.

"Not too long now" he replied. "Keep at it." He circled his fists around each other in a gesture of encouragement, his face bearing somewhat of a false smile of pride in her efforts. It had little effect. By the time she had let out a sigh of anguish, he had already turned his back on her once more and was once again marching off into the distance, leaving her in his wake.

After trudging on reluctantly for another ten minutes, she stopped again. This time it was to answer the call for liquid replenishment. Her dry throat was screaming for it. Flustered, blistered, as well as foot-sore, she dug deep into her reserves of energy to pull off the padded strap from her shoulder. She dug her thumb under the strap, before managing to get a finger in to assist. With a better grip, it began to move. The fabric from the strap had felt embedded into her skin and as the strap finally began slipping from off her shoulder, the full weight of the bag became very much evident. It now felt heavier than ever It was her arm now that took the full brunt of the weight and due to exhaustion, she couldn't hold it, nor could she stop it falling heavily to the floor. As it did so, she thought she heard what could only be described as a muffled cracking sound. This could only mean one thing.

"Oh no." She exclaimed.

The overpowering thirst she had, now gave way to feelings of anxiety. A lump formed in her throat. One big enough that she imagined herself choking on it. There was a fear that whatever was in the rucksack, some of it may have been damaged. There were glass sample jars in there and the crack was very much like the sound of breaking glass.

She reached down tentatively for the main zip and whilst trying to balance haste with caution, she pulled it open in order to inspect the damage. The zip was only a quarter of the way open when she afforded herself a brief glance inside. The damage appeared to be minimal. She let out another sigh. Unlike her previous one, this one was one of apparent relief. Whilst two of the specimen jars she carried now harboured large hairline cracks down the side, their precious cargo remained both inside and thankfully intact.

"Phew." She uttered, wiping her brow with the back of her hand. "That was a close one."

She sunk her hand into the bag further, now directing her search for the drink bottle again. After a moment of rummaging she came across it, her fingers touching Its smooth surface. Her fingers tingled with the sensation as it felt so nice to touch, so much colder than anything else in the bag. Fuelled by thirst once more, she pulled upward on the bottle to free it. As she did so, the momentum dragged one of the specimen jars up with it and out through the opening of the bag. It fell to the floor and as it impacted on the sandy surface, It began to bounce and then roll off towards the side of the pathway. By the time she had caught sight of it, it was teasingly rolling down the camber before finding an eventual resting place in amongst the harsh grassland that surrounded both sides of the pathway.

She looked briefly up to locate her father. He was now some one hundred metres ahead of her. Thankfully, he had not seen the incident and the sounds of her rummaging had been out of earshot. She quickly theorised that if she could retrieve the jar rapidly enough, he would never need to be made aware of the accident. She was sure she could convince him the jar merely cracked during transit and perhaps using the incomprehensible heat as a factor in its demise. The worst-case scenario would be another cracked jar, but he had hundreds of them.

Leaving the confines of the stony pathway, she began to cautiously edge her way down the sandy embankment. Whilst it was not particularly steep, she was all too aware that the sand, mixed with a plethora of tiny stones and pebbles did

4

not offer a particularly convincing foot hold for her to control her decent. Luck seemed to be on her side for the moment as she managed to maintain her balance and the reflection of a solitary shimmer of fading light on the container guided he way to its location.

She reached her hand down towards the container, eyes firmly focussed on the prize. So focussed in fact, that not too far in the distance, in fact only a few metres away, she failed to detect the movement of the reeds of tall dry grass separating slightly in order to let something pass through. Her presence had alerted something, something that was closing in on her after it had been disturbed. As it got within a few feet of her, the movement stopped. Whatever it was, it was waiting for her next move. She began to make it

The tips of three of her fingers were now in contact with the jar. She began to stretch every sinew in order to reach her hand around the top of the container so as to ascertain a more accomplished grip. The last thing she wanted was to allow the jar to move further away from her, so whilst trying to be quick, she was aware of her need to maintain a secure foot grip. With blistered and numb fingers, the chances of dropping it again were significantly high. She adjusted her feet in order to get a better stance, smiling with confidence as she did so, feeling that there was no way now that she could drop the jar.

"I think I've got it." She exclaimed with glee.

Her smile then suddenly changed as she gave out a huge yelp of pain. It accompanied a rapid whipping sound. She then felt two needle- like objects sink into the soft flesh on the back of her hand, just between her thumb and forefinger. She quickly retracted her hand, still holding the jar. She cradled her hand inside her other, bringing her hands in close towards her chest. She glanced down in amongst the grass; her brown eyes widening in an attempt to identify the source of what had caused her such excruciating pain. She caught sight of a subtle movement of a few tall grass blades a few feet away, It was moving way from ger as quickly as it approached.

The commotion had, at last, grabbed her fathers' attention and he turned to see what the fuss was about.

"What happened? Did you fall?" He asked., looking at Ebony clutching her hand and breathing a little heavy as though entering a slight state of panic.

She didn't answer. Within a few seconds it seemed like she had passed into another world of pain. There were no tears but her face, her once beautiful olive complexion dried out and sore with the effects of the constant intense exposure to the sun, now appeared somewhat ashen. All the colour began to drain from her and she looked at her father in anguish, then lifted her cradling hand to examine her wound.

Already, her hand began to swell. Where once, the pattern of blood vessels that ran under her skin could be seen now formed an angry and raised patch of skin, turning purple in colour, in the centre of which were two small holes an inch apart. A small solitary drop of blood trickled from either one. At the same time, she began to notice an increased struggle to catch her breath. It was beginning to grow ever shallower with each inhalation. Not only that but her head was beginning to spin. She suddenly felt as though she had been seated on a fast spinning roundabout. By this time, her father was by her side, impatient with yet another interruption to their progress back to the camp. Noticing her delirious state, he looked into her eyes. They were beginning to roll back as she began blinking rapidly. He noticed her holding her hand tenderly, shielding something.

"My god. That's a snake bite." He exclaimed in horror as he lifted her hand up slightly and looked underneath at the wound.

Through his work as an entomologist, he was all too familiar with the risks that came with working in these sorts of habitats and the possibility of unfortunate encounters that could occur in certain environments with members of the animal kingdom. There were many species and sub-species that could cause humans a lot of harm, here in Africa alone. Though his interest lay with all non-venomous species, he was forever aware that in places like this, they were never far away and he knew enough to recognise the trademark signs of a snakebite. The problem being that his knowledge did not extend to recognition of a specific snake by it's very bite marks alone. Hopefully someone back at the base would know that.

"Did you see it? Did you see what snake it was"? His voice now raised in panic.

There was no response.

He instinctively removed his sweat soaked head scarf and wrapped it around her wrist to quickly improvise a tourniquet to reduce the rapid rate of swelling that was fast consuming her hand, which now resembled a purple partially inflated balloon. Whatever intoxicating cocktail was now making her way through her bloodstream was doing so with frightening speed. Her condition was deteriorating fast. She was now feeling nauseous and with a sudden heave, was soon being violently sick. It appeared she had only moments before she would lose consciousness completely as her eyes began to roll back for a second time. He was not over confident in his ability to carry her the remaining half mile back to the base camp but with each passing second, that was becoming a very realistic possibility. He now had a decision to make and one which he had to make fast. Remaining where they were could be her death sentence yet leaving her here alone while he raced to get help was even more unforgivable. Most of the snake sightings in this area were ones of highly venomous species so the odds she got lucky and had been bitten by a harmless one were sadly not in her favour. With that thought in mind, he had made his decision.

He gave the scarf a final pull to tighten its grip around her wrist, ready to help her along the path as best he could. She let out another scream of agony. After a subsequent shiver and a second brief period of violent vomiting, she began to go limp. The pain was too much to bear. As she passed out, her body fell forwards towards her father. He gripped her tightly to break her fall and in one motion, managed to somehow summon the strength to hoist her onto his shoulder, using her momentum to his advantage. His legs almost buckled. Now, with the limp body of his slim, yet very tall daughter over one shoulder and his own heavy backpack on the other, he began the agonising walk back to the base, regretfully leaving behind the rucksack which his daughter had carried, still unzipped and with most of its valuable contents still inside.

It was a sacrifice he was certainly not at ease with despite Ebony's predicament. The weight that now bore down on him was unparalleled. Lifting as he began moving, the irrational thought of the ground somehow giving way completely under his feet was something he now feared with every step. The terrain could also prove unpredictable. If he was to fall now, that would be them both doomed. In spite of such thoughts and predominantly driven by the concern that she may not even survive the next hour, he moved as fast as he possibly could back to camp.

Chapter 2

t was quarter to ten in the evening when Dr Garry Bush finally sat down at his desk for a well-earned cup of tea. It had been a taxing day. He had taken up his new position three weeks ago. In that time, he was sure he had only set foot in his new office a handful of times. Even when he had been here, his visits were only fleeting, maybe responding to e- mails or to pick up important correspondence and supplies. He had spent most of his time out on call, coming to the aid of the townsfolk who would call him to save them from unwanted elapid visitors who would frequently seek solace in their homes. He loved his work, but it required long hours and dedication.

As he began to sip his tea, the phone rang, startling him a little. With a wry smile of acceptance that even a quiet drink and five minutes to himself may well have been too much to ask, he reached for the handset.

"Dr Bush." He answered abruptly.

The voice on the other end of the phone was one of grave concern. He began listening to the voice as it rapidly related information, whilst reaching quickly across the desk for a pen and a scrap of paper to note down a few brief scribbles. What he was hearing had him fully alert once more. As the details of the unfolding situation were being relayed to him, his heart pumped faster, instigating an immediate rush of adrenalin.

"I can be there in 30 minutes." He interrupted. "Do we have the specimen concerned?"

Five seconds later, the call was over. Slamming down the receiver and grabbing his mobile on the way out, Garry rushed out the office door, tucking the crumpled-up note in his pocket, his drink barely untouched.

He sprinted down the corridor, his shoes squeaking on the shiny floor as he did so as though he was running up and down a basketball court. He reached a white door at the opposite end of the corridor. A large opaque window with black lettering entitled 'Venom Laboratory' confronted him. This was his destination.

The laboratory was dimly lit for this time of night. However, it was of no consequence. He did not need more light. He had spent hours carefully arranging all his laboratory equipment the day he had arrived. He knew exactly where everything was and could find it blindfolded if he needed to Every second was precious and so to know exactly where to find what he wanted was of paramount importance at times such at these, where every second proved vital. He opened a small glass-fronted refrigerator door that lined the wall at waist level. It was one of many that was placed side by side to take up the entire length of the laboratory on one side. Within each of these fridges sat rows of vials, each one individually marked, colour coded and labelled with a specific anti venom. Bush had even gone so far as to line them up so they all stood in perfect symmetry Even the outer glass casing of the fridge units themselves sported clear labels, perfectly lined up with one another, to denote the multiple anti-venoms' which could be found within it.

Having not been informed of the specific anti-venom he would require during the call, he reached into his pocket for the piece of paper he scribbled on before. He read it quickly then in earnest, greedily, but with due care, began loading numerous vials of the colour coded bottles into his carrier case which he had left open on the counter above. The specifically designed sponge lining offered numerous slots to safely house the delicate vials whilst in transit and once loaded, he shut the case lid, zipped it in its entirety and exited the laboratory again. He was already passing his office door again by the time the creaking of the laboratory door gave way to a light bang and click as the door sealed itself shut

As he made his way outside, he fumbled for his car keys. His fingers grasped the fob and he pressed it, his side lights flashing in response. As he climbed into his truck, his phone let off a loud distinctive beep to alert him of an incoming message. To stop and read it could cost him valuable seconds in his race against time. He also knew not reading it meant he could miss out on valuable information, vital to the treatment he was about to be placed in charge of. He glanced down at the screen, skimming its content as he inserted and turned the ignition key It was an update on the situation as requested and it did not make for good reading.

PATIENT ALIVE ALTHOUGH NOW CRITICAL. ESTIMATE MAY HAVE UP TO AN HOUR BEFORE DEATH LIKELY TO OCCUR. SUSPECT MINIMAL 8-10 VIALS NEEDED. WILL MEET YOU ON ARRIVAL. R

He had barely given the engine chance to fire into life before depressing the clutch and slamming it into first gear. The wheels began spinning rapidly as he released the handbrake, whilst simultaneously pressing down on the accelerator. The wheel spin brought about a small but controlled skid as the tyre treads attempted to grip the terrain, throwing up a cloud of dust in their wake. Whilst road conditions were good and he had adapted his skills well to meet the demands of driving over such uneven and unpredictable terrain, he still had to be wary of driving too fast. The initial side roads which led to and from his laboratory were often poorly lit during evening hours and large potholes were never to far away. He knew any accident or any type of delay on the way would undoubtedly mean certain death for his young patient that he was now racing to save.

After the first few miles of dirt track, he reached the junction connecting the side road to the main highway. He welcomed the opportunity to increase his speed, pressing down further on the accelerator pedal once he had completed the turn. With twelve minutes having passed already since leaving his office, every mile, every metre even, had to be covered faster than ever. The clock read three minutes past eleven as the welcome lights of the hospital grounds became visible in the distance. A quick glance at his watch and some quick math told him that he had completed the journey so far in just over 20 minutes. He allowed himself a brief smile of accomplishment and relief for a safe journey. Whilst he had not recalled ever completing the journey in such quick time since starting his new job, this was no time for celebration. He could look back and reflect on this achievement later if the eventual outcome should turn out to be a positive one.

As he pulled into the driveway that swept up and around towards the main hospital entrance, he immediately began scanning the car park for a place to ditch his truck. He quickly noticed that available parking spots, aligned both left and right, were plentiful. The hospital appeared to be quiet this evening. He set his sights on the spot nearest to the entrance and throwing the steering wheel to the left, the car veered abruptly left to follow suit. Once he felt he was within the confines of the markings, he slammed down hard on the footbrake. His vehicle skidded to a halt. This was no driving test after all and the concept of his truck not being located within the marked surface of the designated parking lines was something he was not intending to preoccupy himself with. It was as close to the hospital entrance as he could possibly put it and that was his intention.

Pushing the driver side door open with a kick of his left leg, he simultaneously reached over to the passenger seat, grabbing both his phone and his case and quickly exited the truck, slamming the door shut behind him. The sliding glass doors which donned the main entrance opened quickly as he approached, as if anticipating his haste to enter. Two doctors in their customary surgical scrub outfits awaited him in the foyer.

"Dr Bush"? Enquired one of the doctors inquisitively, extending his hand in gratitude.

Bush nodded.

"I'm Dr Ash. This is Dr Raj" responded the doctor introducing himself and his colleague.

"Pleasure" Replied Bush with an acknowledging nod. "Where is she?"

"We have her in a private room just off from the O.R sir. It's the best equipped room we have. Follow us."

Dr Ash gestured Bush to follow them, quickly braking into a light jog down what seemed like a never-ending hospital corridor. It led down through a series of double doors. Bush followed, making a conscious effort to keep pace with them so the doors did not swing back in his face, As he did so, he listened to an update from Dr Ash. The hospital seemed quiet as he had guessed from the car park and although several medical personnel could be seen moving in and out of rooms off the corridor at regular intervals, he was easily able to keep track of Ash and Raj as they pressed on ahead. Whilst he listened intently, his mind was firmly focussed on his first and vital assessment that he would need to carry out himself upon seeing his patient. He was therefore happy to act as a somewhat wanton follower to the doctors who were leading him through the hospital. Once he reached her, he may have to act quickly knowing that his first move could be his last if he either hesitated or got it wrong.

They had reached the final door on what must have been the third corridor they had sprinted down. Dr Ash, who was leading the way stopped as he reached the door. He swivelled round to face Bush pressing his back against the door to push it open.

"In here "Announced Dr Ash, backing his way into the room."

The door slowly opened and once fully opened fully, Dr Ash remained in position a second, allowing and encouraging Bush to lead them in. Bush obliged, with a nod of thanks and mutual respect. Then was quickly followed in by Dr Raj. They made their way directly to the large steel wash basins which lined the wall at waist level in front of him. Around the side of the sink units were several dispensers containing the standard anti-bacterial hand washes and soap dispensers to scrub in. Next to them, another dispenser distributed paper to dry their hands on. As Bush began scrubbing, he glanced up through the large glass plate into the room on the other side of the glass. It was at this moment that he got his first sight of his patient, the young vulnerable girl, not even in her teens at death's door. Once his hands were vigorously scrubbed and he had donned some surgical gloves, another colleague was on hand to supply him with a gown, holding out for him like a tailor would when fitting a suit. He placed his hands quickly through the arm holes, running his arms down the sleeves as the unmistakable slightly coarse texture of all too familiar hospital scrubs brushed his arm.

He had barely given time for the nurse to tie the gown at the base of his neck and waist, he made his way into the room.

As he entered, the first thing he was met with was the look of desperation etched on the face of Ebony's mother sat by her bed in the opposite corner of the room. She sat kneeling forward with her arm reaching forward, touching her daughter lightly on the arm. She appeared too scared to come any closer. He offered a brief smile of comfort as he approached the bedside then quickly turned his attention to the motionless body of his patient, allowing one of the other Doctors to formally introduce him.

"Mrs Meyer. This is Dr Bush who we told you about. The foremost expert in this field. Not only a skilled surgeon but with a specialism in toxicology and snake envenomation. If anyone can save your daughter, believe me it's this man."

Moira looked up at Dr Ash and gave a weak nod, more perhaps in hope than anything else.

Bush got straight down to it his by making his initial assessment. Ebony's left hand was now twice it's normal size.

Bush quickly decided that his first course of action would be to relieve instant pressure on her skin created by the mass swelling, If he didn't, it was likely the skin may split leading to a possible and fatal haemorrhage. He had specifically requested that the lower portion of her arm be covered but not bandaged tightly like the makeshift tourniquet applied at the incident site. The necrotising process had advanced significantly, although seemed reasonably localised and it was only his expertise and experience that lead him to the discovery of the minute entry wounds, now black pin size dots in amongst the dying tissues. After a moment of deliberation, as well as a confident nod to himself that he had found what he was looking for, he gently placed Ebony's arm gently back down by her side and then turned to the other doctor by his side.

"Cobratoxin. Melanoleuca, possibly Mossambica" he deliberated to himself I a soft mumble. Raising his voice, he beckoned Dr Raj over. Bush had made his diagnosis and was ready for his next course of action. With Raj quickly by his side, he quietly shared his findings;

"This is the work of a cobra. She has been injected with quite a fair amount of venom and although I have rarely seen such a damaging effect to the tissues, I am certain I know of the culprit. I need 10 vials of anti-venom number 4, stat." He barked. "My case is in there"

He nodded his head, gesturing towards the room from which they had scrubbed in a moment ago. His gesture was enough for the doctor to act quickly and was soon returning with his case.

Placing the case carefully on a nearby table, Dr Raj took the liberty of unfastening and pulling the lid up and open towards him. Running his finger across the rows of visible vial lids, he counted four across in his head and then carefully began extracting the vials one by one from their cushioned inserts.

"Are you sure it is the right one"? The doctor asked hesitantly.

Bush looked up at him, insulted by his line of questioning.

"Are you?" Bush barked, scornfully.

Raj didn't answer, evidently taken aback by Bush's defensive tone. Dr Raj sheepishly moved over to the medical drawers located under the window at the foot end of the bed. Opening the top drawer, he pulled out a syringe kit and began carefully removing the protective blue sheath from the packet. With its contents now on display before him, he began to construct the syringe, finally securing the needle in place He then inserted it through the lid of the vial which he held up after inverting it in order to extract the serum. He slowly pulled down on the plunger and the vial began to empty into the section at the base of the needle which housed the substance prior to injection. With the vial emptied in its entirety, Raj returned back to the bedside opposite Bush and immediately began loading the needle into the I cannula on Ebony's wrist. With the needle in place he quickly depressed the plunger, watching as the liquid made its way out of the syringe and into Ebony's blood stream

"First one is in" stated Raj looking at Bush in a way that suggested he was seeking some degree of praise and approval after his previous outburst.

"Good" replied Bush positively. "Get the other 4 vials in her. I want them administered at a rate of 10 mils per minute and we will see what the response is over the next half hour."

Bush finally turned to address Moira for the first time who was sat silent, trying her best to just stay out of the way and be inconspicuous.

"I'm afraid that is all we can do for her for now. You look exhausted. I would suggest you take this opportunity to have a break and maybe grab a coffee and something to eat. We can talk further after half an hour when I assess her again. All I can do till then is just wait to see if the anti-venom takes effect."

She stood, exuberating an understandable hesitancy to leave. An extra bit of persuasion seemed called for if she was to take his suggestion. He spoke up again

"Please Mrs Meyer. Take a break. If anything changes, I will be sure to send someone to get you. Meantime, I assure you someone will remain with her constantly for observation. She is a fighter. I'll give her that"

She looked into Bush's eyes. His sincerity seemed genuine and she already deemed him trustworthy. He was after all, the only person who had the ability to possibly save her daughter's life. Accepting a simple and logic request which seemed in her best interests was the least she could do. His persuasion paid off and she made her way towards the exit, quietly sobbing as she left.

No sooner had she left the room, both Dr Bush's demeanour and activity level changed again. Within seconds, he had uncovered her arm again, looking at the full extent of the tissue damage in more detail. Discarding the bandage in the vague direction of the designated medical waste bin, he picked up the scalpel from the steel tray of surgical instruments he had placed in front of him the moment Ebony's mother had left the room and began waving it slowly side to side over her hand as if he were holding a metal detector. He was weighing up where to make an incision. Both Dr Ash and Raj charged with assisting stared at each other in wide eyed alarm, surprised by Bush's intentions. They quickly turned their focus back to Bush and just as Bush began to lower the scalpel, Dr Ash broke the tense silence.

"What's happening doctor"? He questioned innocently, trying not to exude the same critical, ill- placed and pessimistic tone his colleague had used previously.

"She needs an immediate fasciotomy or else the skin on her hand is going to burst open." He explained." It is not particularly a nice thing to have to do but I have no choice. It's certainly not something I was going to perform with her mother peering over my shoulder sobbing."

They nodded in agreement.

"May we assist in any way? Asked Raj.

"Yes" came the immediate reply. Once I make this incision, the chances are there will be quite a bit of haemorrhaging." He explained. "I am going to need you to help minimise the bleeding as much as possible"

"Of course." Came the reply in unison as they stepped closer to the bed, grabbing a handful of swabbing each.

"Prepare yourselves gentlemen. This may be a frantic few minutes" warned Bush. "You are about to see why I used my charm to get the mother out of the room so I could perform this procedure. No parent should be there to witness this."

He looked towards the nurse stood by the door.

"Nurse Monitor her vital signs, particularly her blood pressure. Let me know the minute it begins to drop"

"Understood Doctor" She said, taking up her position opposite them, focussing her full attention on the readouts made available to them by the machines connected up to her.

"Maybe have some blood bags on standby too." Bush advised.

"That done, Bush looked up at Ash and Raj, poised and in position.

"Are we ready?" Ha asked, his scalpel resting softly on the proposed incision site.

On the second floor, the hospital canteen was quiet. A sole server stood behind the counter. Her fingers tapped the counter impatiently, waiting for something to do to evidently eek away the hours of a long night shift. Her head turned towards the door, alerted by the sight of the double doors swinging open. In walked Moira. With a quick look around, she approached the counter where the server waited, slouched over the counter.

"What can I get you love?" She asked Moira with a weak smile.

"Coffee please." She replied. "Strong and black."

"Coming right up." Replied the server, making her way over to the stack of cups stacked up behind her.

With the server away from the counter, Moira turned to survey her surroundings with the hope that there might be someone there to strike up a conversation with. The server did not seem in a talkative mood. She caught site of a lonely familiar figure sat in the far corner nursing a cup of something or other, staring down at its contents.

A moment later the server returned with her drink. Picking it up, she cautiously made her way over towards whom she had spotted. He was evidently aware of her approaching and as she reached the table and placed her cup down gently, he slowly looked up.

"I thought you were packing up back at the base." She enquired.

"I left them to it." Came her husband's reply. "I had to come." He added.

As she stared at him, she could not help but detect the solemn look on his face. Whilst an element of concern for his daughter's predicament seemed apparent, she got the impression that he had not been going through anywhere near the anguish she had since he had brought her back to the camp at death's door. Perhaps more concerned with his findings, she assumed.

"How is she doing?" He asked.

"Oh, she is just fine Jerry." Came the sarcastic reply. "Maybe you should go and see for yourself, assuming that is that you do not need to pack any more of your precious specimens first."

The anger in her voice was driving her to tears. She reached quickly into her pocket for a tightly folded tissue which she dabbed gently against her cheek to catch a first solitary tear. She had shed so many in the past hour or so, it was as though there were barely any more tears left to cry. From across the table, he looked at her, figuring out the right words he could say to help comfort her. There were none. Yet still he felt he had to speak to break what was fast becoming a very uncomfortable silence.

"Well look." He said softly. "I am here now."

"That's awfully big of you Jerry." She replied, again with sarcasm.

He reached forward, gently placing his hand on top of hers as a gesture of comfort and support. She quickly retracted it, placing it back in the pocket of her jacket and well out of his reach. His hand remained on the table as he slowly clenched his fist in a show of silent frustration and heart felt rejection. He then retracted his own hand completely from the table, slumping back against the back rest of his chair. Feeling his presence was more of a hindrance than a help, he slowly stood.

"I wouldn't go down now if I were you" she suggested strongly, predicting his intent.

"Why is that?" He asked, looking confused.

"They have just given her the first lot of antidote and they need to watch her carefully. I am not sure her doctors will take kindly to you interrupting them"

"I just didn't think you wanted me here with you right now." He enquired.

"Please yourself Jerry. I'm not staying long." Responded Moira.

She stood up herself now, a look on her face indicating she was dying to say something else, perhaps delver a home truth or too before she headed back upstairs.

"What I wanted Jerry, was for you to drop everything back at the base and come with us to the hospital like any decent concerned father would have done." She replied with an accusing tone.

He had no reply for that. At least not one he deemed to be productive. The anger in her tone hit him like a thunderbolt and he was beginning to feel a sense of guilt welling up inside him. So much so that it had now brought a lump to his throat. He was suddenly feeling the need to redeem himself. If he could turn back the clock two hours and have that time again, he felt certain he would have acted differently. He sat down opposite her again, the two of them remaining silent as they kept a close vigil on the clock on the wall as the second finger monotonously ticked on. She chose not to re-join him at the table, but instead paced up and down for the remaining fifteen minutes before heading back downstairs.

On the ground floor corridor, Bush himself had found a free minute to seek refreshment by way of a visit the coffee vending machine. An invite had been extended to him to join one of the medical staff who had been working on the Meyer case with him. Coffee in hand, they had headed towards the staff rest room when Bush had suddenly stopped and turned to the doctor politely declining his invite. His desire was to be as close to his patient as possible in case immediate measures needed to be taken. Placing the cup to his dry lips, he took a sip. As he suspected, not the best. With a flick of his wrist, he quickly glanced down at his watch. He had administered the anti-venom 35 minutes ago and if it was going start having any positive effect on her, it was likely that her condition would be showing the initial signs of improvement any time now. That is of course, if the envenomation was not too much for her to cope with. Maybe it just was not to be this time. He shook his head in an attempt to rid his mind of such negative thoughts. The belief in the power of positive thought is part of what had got him to where he is now in his chosen vocation. His pager now attached to his belt beeped. It was from the medic who had been left with Ebony in her room. This could be the good news he was waiting for. With one last gulp of weak coffee, he tossed the cup, still a quarter full, into a nearby trash can, and headed back hastily down the corridor hoping for positive news.

As he entered the room, an all too familiar tone came within earshot. A sign no doctor wants to hear It was the alarming monotonal noise of the heart rate monitor which had been hooked up to Ebony since her arrival. A thin neon blue unbroken line ran across the middle of the monitor, meaning only one thing. Cardiac arrest. Ebony's heart had stopped, and it looked as though she had lost her gallant fight for life. The cobra's neurotoxic venom had claimed another unfortunate victim. He was not going to give up on her yet though. Not by a long shot. He rapidly moved in to take over from the medic who was quickly beginning to fatigue from performing chest compressions in an attempt to revive her.

"Grab me those paddles." He shouted.

The doctor quickly obliged.

"Charge to 200 and stand back." Ordered Bush

Again, the medic quickly responded, passing the pads to Dr Bush to place on Ebony's chest.

Bush placed the paddles in their designated positions on top of the pads

"Shocking now. Stand clear." He announced.

Ebony's lifeless upper body jolted violently as though she were lay still on a bouncy castle with numerous people jumping around her. Having been elevated from the surface of the bed for an instant, her body flopped back down again.

The tone on the machine changed momentarily, interrupted as a brief shock wave moved silently across the screen from left to right. The silence only lasted a second or two. Once the irregular solitary wave on the screen passed, depicting a single heartbeat, it was replaced once again with the constant flat line pattern from a moment ago. Concurrent with that, the loud incessant tone returned to indicate the heart was no longer beating again

"Charge to two-fifty." Bush ordered.

"Two-fifty" confirmed the medic, twisting the dial on the defibrillator accordingly.

"Shocking again. Everybody clear." Repeated Bush

In a similar fashion to before, Ebony's body jolted up off the bed, this time more pronounced than before as the extra strength of the electrical charge reverberated around her frail body. The pattern repeated itself as the same wave moved slowly across the readout on the monitor. He knew three hundred was pushing it as far as upping the charge goes, particularly for such a young patient who had already been through such an ordeal. However if he did not take the risk, she was to die right in front of him there and then He loved snakes, but he hated when one got the better of him in this manner. He decided to take the gamble.

"Shocking again. This time give me three hundred. Stand clear." Instructed Bush.

The medic, after a moments hesitation again obliged,

turning the dial on the defibrillator a notch higher. It was obvious everyone felt the same. This couldn't carry on much longer and three hundred was about as high as they could possibly go before resigning themselves to losing her. The sequence of events sadly repeated themselves, sadly with the same result.

"I suggest you call it Dr Bush." Uttered the medic with a tone of resignation. "She has been through enough." He added compassionately.

Bush did not care to admit it, but he knew his colleague was right. She had no doubt suffered unspeakable pain to this point. Even if he could revive her now, there is no telling what the long-term repercussions of her injury would be. At the very least, he anticipated an amputation may be a possibility. She had now been clinically dead for some 4 minutes so there would be every chance of significant brain damage. He figured letting her go could be the right thing to do He practically tasted the bitterness of defeat but feared this time, it was something he would have to accept. He looked up at the clock and then checked it against his wristwatch before putting a stop to proceedings. Between clenched teeth, he uttered the words;

"Time of death, twenty-three twelve."

Handing the paddles back to the medic, he slowly moved back around the foot of the bed and with head bowed, walked silently back through the door and into the scrub room. Once there, he sat down, leaning forward to rest his elbows on his knees and bury his face in his hands. It was time to work out just what words to use to explain what had happened to her mother.

He had been alone in the room for ten minutes when the silence was interrupted by the creak of the door opening. A slender young nurse walked silently in and spotting Bush sat opposite her, walked up towards him.

"Dr Bush." She said quietly, as though trying to wake him from a long sleep. She edged a little closer, touching his shoulder gently as she did so. He looked up slowly.

"The parents have come back and are asking for an update on their daughter. What should I tell them?"

Bush paused for a second. Then he answered with a deep sigh.

"Tell them…. tell them …I'll see them in the family room in five minutes."

The nurses' tone changed from one of inquisitiveness to one of empathy. She knew that escorting loved ones to the family room could only mean one thing.

"I'm sorry Doctor." She said gently. "I'll take them there straight away."

She turned and left the room, leaving Bush a final moment of contemplation. He had delivered bad news to people in the past. He had undergone all the necessary medical training any doctor of medicine would do. Delivering bad news came with the territory. It was only after some ten years as a regular paramedic that he decided to combine his desire to treat the sick with his other passion, that for venomous reptiles and their conservation. But now, this felt like unfamiliar territory again. The wording he had been used to using in the past on how to break such news in the easiest way possible seemed to escape him. He knew he could ask one of the other doctors who had assisted him in the care of Ebony before her death to perform the deed for him. They did do it regularly after all. With a final shake of the head, he got to his feet. It was time. He was not going to hand the reigns to anyone else. This was his case, his patient, so it was his strong belief that he should be the one to deliver the devastating news.

Moira and Jerry were sat patiently waiting for him in the family room. The blinds which shielded an outside view had given him a final moment to gather himself and adopt his poker face. Whilst he knew they would be distraught and overcome with emotion as he would begin to relay events, it was important that he could at least begin to explain how he had done all he could and how hard she had fought to survive. If a simple facial expression would have given the game away from the offset, there would be no way he could attempt to console them properly.

He entered the room. Noticing straight away that they were sat separately, he slowly pulled a chair out from against the wall and turned it so he could address both of them.

"Where do I begin? Your daughter is a fighter and it is incredible the amount of resistance she put up."

They both looked up at him with a look of despair. Using the past tense as he had in his opening sentence seemed to have already indicated where this conversation was going. He had given the game away already.

"Despite all our best efforts..." He paused for a second to inhale deeply." I am afraid and very sorry to say that she passed away a short while ago"

Bush looked first to her father. Whilst he expressed a look of obvious shock, it seemed as though there was an air of acceptance of the situation. It was understandable as the odds were against her right from the start. Moira on the other hand was taking it very differently. She instantly broke down in floods of tears and sobbed uncontrollably. Bush placed a comforting hand on her knee, but she did not register his gesture. He was not sure if he should say any more. He was thinking of the correct follow on words to express his deepest sympathy when he noticed from the corner of his eye, that the door was opening again. At the doorway stood the same nurse who had come to his side in the scrub room moments earlier. Although softly spoken before, her tone now was somewhat different, that of a slightly disguised giddiness.

"Dr Bush" she said loudly. "I think you should come and see this."

Bush stood slowly. Leaving his chair where it was, he followed the nurse out of the door back into the corridor. He was both embarrassed yet grateful for the intrusion.

"I will be back in one second." He said, looking back into the room at Ebony's father." I am sorry about this and I will get someone to stay with you until I return when I can answer any more questions you both may wish to ask." With that, he closed the door gently.

He repeated what had become quite a familiar walk down the corridor. Once he re-entered the scrub room, Dr Bush was not an easy man to shock but both the noise and sight which confronted him had him dumbfounded.

Chapter 3

t was unusually hot as John Maher took his place in his favourite rocking chair on the wooden terracing that spanned the front of his house. Having just eaten a wholesome dinner made by his doting wife, there was nothing he loved more than to sit out in the shade with a glass of the finest Californian red wine he could afford and sip it slowly as he digested his meal.

Adjusting and buffing up his cushions to suit, he lowered himself slowly into his seat. A soft welcome breeze blew, making the fine grey strands of hair which swept across his crown rise up and perform a little dance, offering a light tickling sensation as they did so. He looked about to survey his surroundings, appreciative of the relaxing environment he found himself in. Just off the edge of the patio area, his garden looked immaculate. A plethora of different coloured flowers danced proudly in the fading sunlight, almost mimicking the motion performed by his own hair. Having spent all spring making an effort to get his garden looking so beautiful, he felt he had achieved his goal and he was determined to enjoy watching it flourish during the humid summer months. He was keen for his wife to enjoy it too.

"Just leave the pots Evie love. I'll do them later." He shouted back through the open doorway, hearing the clattering of pans from the kitchen.

"Nearly done now." She shouted back cheerfully.

She was right. Some two to three minutes later, she had finished with the pots, leaving them neatly stacked to drain and came outside to join him on the patio, a glass of wine in one hand and a damp dish towel in the other. Laying the dish towel in the middle of a nearby small coffee table, she took her place beside him in the chair he had pulled out for her in earnest. He looked at her proudly. He smiled as she too surveyed the garden, admiring his efforts.

"I wasn't too sure I could get this garden ship-shape by summer time but I'm reasonably happy with it." He declared modestly.

"You were always capable John. I knew you could do it in time if you put your mind to it." She replied.

They sat together a while, just sipping wine and enjoying the calm serenity of their surroundings. As much as they loved to relax and talk to each other, they also enjoyed comfortable silences where they just watched the world go by and listen to the wind or the birds. As long as they were in each other's presence, they both felt complete. So much so that they had barely spent a day apart in their last five years of marriage. That was the reason why John decided on early retirement. After years of being a landscape gardener for a very successful company, where John had spent many a day on the road, away from his beloved home, formulating and implementing plans for some of the most extravagant gardens across the United States, he had gotten very much homesick. He had worked for very wealthy companies keen to introduce a high level of aesthetic beauty to their company headquarters and at times he was away for weeks on end. After doing this for others, the desire to retire early and get his own property looking the way he wanted it to be just too much to resist. His wife, ever supportive of his decisions welcomed his choice.

"Have you heard anything from Moira?" He asked, eventually breaking the long comfortable silence.

Swallowing a sip full of wine, she placed the glass delicately back on the coaster. She turned her head to him, pushing down her glasses towards the tip of her nose with her finger.

"Nothing this week sadly." She replied. "The last I heard; things were going well. They had reached their camp and had already collected some interesting findings."

"Interesting findings eh." Repeated John with a chuckle. "Well I hope so" He continued. "They received a lot of funding for this trip so if they do not come up with the goods this time round, I fear the worst"

Evie, detecting the concern in his voice, quickly responded.

"I'll ring her in the morning." She stated, nodding her head in approval at her own decision

With the bottle of wine finished between them and tea well and truly settled, they adjourned inside and then a short while after that, retired to bed. John was very much still an active man despite his age but by the look on his face as he removed the last vestiges of clothing and reached for his pyjamas, today had taken a little more out of him than perhaps even he would care to admit. Evie noticed him struggling as she pulled back the covers and climbed into bed.

"You should take it easy tomorrow John" She advised.

"That I shall Evie love" He replied with a slight grimace as he straightened his leg out and lay next to her. "I am a little stiff."

The early rays of morning sunlight streamed through a small gap in the curtains as John began to stir. His partially open eyes glanced towards his bedside where an old-fashioned radio alarm clock flashed the time up in red. It was quarter to seven. It was already evident that he was alone in bed. His wife, ever the early riser was already up. Up for her morning read and a cup of tea no doubt. With that thought in mind, a soft whisper began echoing up the stairs, indicating she was in fact speaking to someone on the phone. Throwing back the crisp white sheets he plunged his clenched fists down into the mattress as he sat up bringing himself up into a sitting position. He let out a moan signalling the effort it took to rise up from his bed. Yesterday's work had taken its toll on his aching body as he suggested. He grimaced as he pushed down harder on the mattress for support to get himself to his feet. Evie was right. This would need to be a day of taking it easy. After a moment's pause, allowing his legs to bear the weight of his slender frame again, he hobbled his way over to the bedroom door where his dressing gown hung. His joint pain was already beginning to ease as he grabbed it from the hook. Without bothering to fasten it or even put his arms into the sleeve holes, he threw it round his shoulders and made his way cautiously out the bedroom door and down the stairs. Hearing the creak of the floorboards under the final few steps, Evie turned to him as he came into view.

"No answer." She exclaimed disappointingly. He tutted gently in response to express his share in her disappointment.

"I left a message to get back to us as soon as they can. I guess you can never get a damn signal in the sorts of places they end up in." She cursed in frustration. "I hope they are ok."

She seemed worried. She had always been the worrier in the family. The extent of her concern was evident with a brief affectionate touch of a small framed photograph of both her daughter and Granddaughter, which sat next to the telephone did not go unnoticed.

"I am sure they will be fine love." He offered with comfort.

After sharing their usual light breakfast, John returned upstairs to shower whilst Evie routinely began washing the pots. Just like the sheets on the bed, they had to be pristine. Whilst she knew John never paid too much attention to how clean things were, she was incredibly house proud. As she dried the penultimate pot, the phone rang.

Whilst it was quite often a little bug bear of hers to have a job she took pride in interrupted by the likes of a phone call, this time it didn't matter. It may after all, be her daughter returning her call from earlier. So excited at the thought of speaking to her, her heart seemed to skip a beat. She paused for a second in anticipation with her hand resting gently on the handset as it continued to ring.

"Please let it be her." She whispered looking up to the ceiling, hoping her prayer was about to be answered. She picked up the hand set and raised it to her ear.

"Is that you Mum?" Asked the muffled voice from the other end of the phone.

"Moira?" asked Evie, slightly confused by an unexpected voice she was hearing.

"No Mum. It's me, Stephanie. Came the reply.

"Ah Stephanie love" Replied Evie tenderly, her voice dropping a tone or two in mild disappointment. "I thought it was our Moira ringing. I have tried to get hold of her a few times this week and have had no luck at all. Do you think you could try?"

Stephanie did not speak to her sister that often. They were not that close since they had grown up. In fact, the two sisters had not seen each other for quite a while. It seemed every time their paths were due to cross, something always came up to prevent it from happening. Whilst they made a special effort when mum and dad lived close by, once they had retired and moved out to the coast, there never felt much need for such an effort after that. It was often work related and it was often Moira who could never make it. The result of which was an element of resentment as Stephanie often thought that Moira had no time for her, or for that matter, for mum and dad. This had upset her in the early years since they were very close growing up as children so for that bond to disappear took some getting used to. Another thing that annoyed Stephanie was that in spite of Moira never finding time to spend with the family, she was still considered the golden girl, She was the big achiever. Stephanie vowed that one day, she would take the plaudits. She was after all, very successful at what she did and was making her way steadily to the top of her company hierarchy. She couldn't wait but was remaining silent till her dreams had become a reality. She was a woman with a plan for sure.

"Of course, I'll try Mum" Stephanie answered sincerely.

"Could you try it for me now?" Evie asked, playing on her daughters' apparent willingness to please.

"Yes." She replied, trying to hide a growing reluctance to appease. Just send me the number okay."

After a few moments of small talk, Stephanie quickly gathered that her mother was in no mood to chat. It was unusual as she loved a good conversation to find out what

Stephanie was up to. They would converse to great levels and it would often culminate in the same question with her mum asking her when she was going come down to see her and John. Stephanie quickly realised that if she was going to talk properly to her as before, she would have to do her best to put her mother's mind at rest and grant her wish first.

"I'll ring you back in a bit then Mum"

"As soon as you hear something" Evie ordered impatiently.

No sooner had she hung up the phone, Stephanie heard a beep to indicate an incoming text message. It was the phone number she requested only moments ago.

Stephanie shook her head in disbelief.

"She can be fast when she wants to be." She uttered under her breath.

Retrieving the dialing tone, she began inputting the numbers into her phone. The series of digits seemed endless, forcing her to look back and forth several times to ensure she had inputted all the digits correctly. With confidence that she had done so, she pressed the green "Call" button on her phone to connect the call. A series of faint beeps and a muffled static followed as if to indicate the significant degree of effort needed to try to establish the long-distance connection. Some seconds later, she heard a strange beeping noise. It did not sound like a regular ring tone, but its monotonous regularity could only lead her to believe that it was a positive sign. If someone did answer, she was not sure who it would be as her mum never told her where this number would connect her to. The ring tone stopped, only to be replaced by a faint automated voicemail message. The voice, though muffled and distant, was a familiar one.

"Typical." She exclaimed, waiting for the beep to leave a message.

"Moira. It's Steph. Mum asked me to ring to see if you are all okay. She is sick with worry so get in touch. Love to Ebony. Bye." She blurted, without even pausing to take one breath

Hanging up, she dropped her phone back in her handbag, and began to hurry to her destination. She had shopping to do, clothes for a very important interview. The phone call back to her mother could wait. She had done her bit as the go between once more. After all, her mum had said to report back when she had heard something. As it stood, she had heard nothing as yet.

Chapter 4

41

he first thing Bush noticed as he re-entered the scrub room was the prominent beeping sound emanating from the heart monitor. When he had exited the room earlier, the last thing he had witnessed was the very same machine being unplugged. As the read out came into view, the screen told a very different story A pattern of peaks and troughs now displayed a slow but steady heart trace. The machine also emitted a two tone beat to mimic the heart sound. Whilst it was music to his ears, he was still attempting to grasp the shock of the situation. Taking a glance at Ebony, he noticed that there were still no signs of voluntary movement from her as that time, considering however that barely ten minutes ago there were no signs of life at all, he had to be thankful for anything positive he might encounter at this stage.

"How?" He sounded quietly with a confusing tone. Rolling his eyes upwards towards the ceiling, he begun to shake his head in bewildered awe. Hastily, he began to initiate the tedious scrubbing in process for a second time. He forcefully pulled down on the glove dispenser hung on the wall, once, twice, three times in quick succession to release each glove in turn. It was not like him to be in such a fluster but the situation, indeed the miracle, that confronted him filled him full of both excitement and confusion that seemed to render his hands uncooperative. Leaving the spare glove where it lay and the second glove only partially on, he entered the treatment room regardless. Given the recent developments, he figured no one would seem to mind too much about his little hygienic misdemeanour.

He counted the medical staff in the room. There were

four of them. They included both doctors' Ash and Raj, originally assigned to the case, and two nurses, one of which he recognised from earlier. None of them appeared to be doing much. Instead they all just stood perplexed around the bed, arms folded, staring at Ebony with broad smiles. The young girl who had been clinically pronounced dead less than fifteen minutes ago was now making an amazing recovery right before their very eyes

Bush was the first to emerge from this hypnotic state. It was time to get what he called his 'game head' on again.

"Ok." He said, trying to portray an image of calmness and composure. "Fill me in."

Dr Raj was the next to snap out of the daze in order to bring Bush up to speed.

"We had just unplugged the life support machine as you left and prep her for the mortuary when it was brought to my attention that the nurse here discovered a feint pulse as she moved her arm. the machine quickly turned on again to confirm. Amazingly, it was indeed true. A small, but traceable bradycardic response. As I arrived back to the patient, sure enough, a definitive series of QRS waves had begun to emerge on the monitor. Over the last few minutes doctor, these have been steadily rising, growing stronger with almost every beat. Since that moment and until your arrival just now summoned, her heart rate has climbed from just thirty-eight beats per minute to what you see before you…"

Raj pushed himself up on his tiptoes to get a view of the read out over Bush's shoulder.

". Forty-six Doctor…and steadily rising with each passing minute. Simply remarkable." He added.

"Her blood pressure? What is her current blood pressure?" Bush asked impatiently not sharing in Raj's admiration.

"It's still hypotensive Doctor at the moment. Eighty-seven over forty-five at the moment…but also gradually improving." the female nurse added with optimism.

"Should we perhaps use another vial?" asked Dr Ash offering it to Bush.

"Not just yet. Replied Bush. "Let's give it a few moments and see how she goes."

Another silence fell over the room, but the atmosphere had certainly lifted. A feeling of hope and positivity filled the room now. The medical staff passed the moments with intermittent routine checks, some concerning the readings on the monitors as well as some on Ebony herself. Two minutes of silence passed and as Bush altered his gaze from the monitor readings to see the medical staff all just exchanging glances, he could see them barely blinking in case they missed anything else. He finally spoke;

"If anyone wants to ask me for a medical explanation for what we are witnessing here ladies and gentlemen, please save it."

Bush smiled, allowing himself and the staff a moment of light hearted humour. The staff who stood with him reciprocated the smile, followed by a faint ripple of polite laughter of their own, which echoed around the room.

Meanwhile, back down the corridor in the family room, Ebony's parents had now been informed of her change in condition and it was taking increased effort to hold them back from making their way hurriedly down the corridor towards her room. Bush was less keen on leaving Ebony's side this time than he was on the last occasion, but a promise was a promise and he had promised to go back to see Moira and Jerry. Being a man of his word, he once again handed over temporary care of Ebony to the other medical staff in the room. Bush almost skipped out the door and down the corridor this time round. Last time he was due to meet up with them, he was praying it was all a bad dream and every step was one taken with hesitance. This time he was hoping it was not a dream. His and Moira's eyes met, her brisk walk towards him now becoming a medium paced run. A run which was accompanied by a beaming smile of relief and gratitude for the man she very much believed had somehow saved her daughter's life when all hope seemed lost. He had no time to say anything, barely even time to react as she threw her arms around him. He stumbled back slightly as the impact of her pushing up fully against him knocked him slightly off balance. He loosely returned the gesture, gently patting her on the back, at which point he felt her strong kiss on his cheek. She pulled back slightly, perhaps a touch embarrassed at her reaction to seeing him.

"I don't 'know what to say but…but thank you." She whispered gratefully.

"You are welcome, but I am not sure that I actually did too much." He replied modestly as she looked him square in the eyes.

"You did enough." She replied with the sincerest smile he had been given for a long time. A smile reminiscent of one from his wife on their wedding day. His thoughts suddenly turned to his wife back home in Boston. He certainly missed those smiles, so something that reminded him of such precious moments would always bring him out in a beaming smile of his own.

By this time, Jerry had caught up with them down the corridor. Seeing them share such a moment of joy such as this stirred feelings of unease and jealousy, even in spite of the circumstances. That first hug of joy should have been shared between them, in his eyes. Moments like that had always been reserved for him. He moved close towards his wife, taking her hand in his as an action of possessiveness which he clearly wanted Bush to notice. He reached out his other hand towards Bush so he could shake it. Bush politely obliged, adopting more of a serene respectful manner more befitting of a doctor than a long-lost friend.

"Thank you Doctor Bush." He said. There seemed little emotion in his dulcet tones. Nevertheless, Moira had expressed enough emotion for both of them.

She subtly pulled her hand away from Jerry's and folded them, so they were well out of his reach just as she had done in the canteen. She turned her full attention to Bush again

"Can we see her?" She pleaded.

"Not just yet. It is still early days and she has not regained consciousness yet."

Moira's head dropped slightly in disappointment. The desperation to see her daughter alive was eating her up inside. Her patience was not going to last long and only as a show of respect for Doctor Bush and his achievements, did she not push further to have her request granted

"If you wait here however, Ill pop back and see how she

is doing. Give me five minutes okay." Offered Bush as a compromise.

Not waiting for her to agree, he quickly made his way back down the corridor into the scrub room, ensuring the door was shut properly behind him. He was just as eager to check her progress almost as much as she was.

He had barely entered the scrub room for a third time when the nurse came out to confront him. In spite of wearing a face mask, Bush could see the look of surprise told by her eyes.

"Blood pressure now one hundred and three over sixty Doctor. Heart rate now at fifty-seven beats per minute." She reported excitedly.

Bush smiled at the news, following the nurse back into the room. This time, Bush did not bother to acquire any surgical attire. As he entered, he looked over to Dr Raj who was focussing his attention on the swelling on her hand.

"How is it looking Dr Raj?" Bush asked.

Raj looked up to Bush, not realised he was being watched. Not for the first time, he was shaking his head, eyes wide in disbelief.

"To be honest Doctor" he spluttered, "I'm lost for words. Just take a look."

Bush walked round the bed and stood beside him. Even though still loosely covered over after the fasciotomy before, the reduction in swelling was significant. From a darkened and angry combination of purple and black which signified a large extent of tissue damage, her hand was now emitting a deep shade of browny-yellow, reminiscent of a heeling bruise in its latter stages of recovery.

"Incredible." He murmured."

"Isn't it?" Replied Raj.

Predicting that his new train of thought may also be one shared by his colleagues, Bush decided to offer his thoughts anyway.

"Everyone" he announced. "I know what we are witnessing here is incredible, but it is important we do not race ahead and get carried with ourselves. Let's please just respond to each step of the recovery as it happens. She isn't out of the woods yet." He warned.

The team nodded in unison, setting about their tasks again.

"Therefore." He continued. "Keep a constant eye on her. At this rate, I would anticipate, although with no great certainty that she will regain consciousness very soon. Don't stich her arm up for a moment as I still wish to monitor and document this recovery for myself and I need to monitor the reduction of necrosis a little while longer before I am happy."

Again, the staff acknowledged his instructions, this time some with a nod and the two nurses with a verbal and robotic response "Yes doctor."

"Any questions?" Asked Bush, pausing to eye each member of his team in turn. "I will be five minutes."

He had barely exited the door when he doubled back, poking his head round the door in Raj's direction.

"Oh, and Dr Raj."

Raj jumped slightly, then looked toward Bush.

"Please cover up her arm again for me as it was. If she is to regain consciousness very soon, the last thing I want her to catch sight of is her own injuries ...however better they are now."

Raj gave him what was now the all too familiar nod of submissive understanding and then quickly turned his focus back to her wound before carefully re-applying the dressing as ordered.

Out in the corridor, Moira was pacing up and down, retracing her footsteps as a century would do when on guard duty. The urge to just burst through the door and catch even the slightest glimpse of Ebony was almost too much to resist. She had tried looking through the window but that offered no joy. Her husband simply just sat nearby. He occasionally glanced up towards her to try to engage eye contact and hopefully a conversation with her might ensue, but every time he did look at her, she appeared to be making a conscious effort to avoid his glance. Even a deep intermittent sigh to attract her attention went un-noticed. It had been ten minutes since she had spoken to Bush. It felt like an hour. In fact, for the last few hours, she felt as though for every hour she had been apart from her daughter, several days had passed. With another despairing glance of hope as she passed by the door to look for movement, she thought she heard something, a sound from within the room and just on the other side of the door which she now intently stared at. She was right. A dark shadow was on the other side of the door and was looking like they were about to open it and emerge. The door began to open slowly and the sight of Dr Bush appeared before her once again. Bush didn't wait for her to speak. He knew what she would ask.

"Not just yet" he pre-empted. "She is not conscious yet. However, her recovery is progressing very well. Her vital signs are improving, and the swelling has reduced significantly due to the anti-venom we administered."

With a small squeal of excitement and a repetition of small rapid clapping, Moira then clasped her hands together, interlocking her fingers in a notion of prayer. Behind her, Jerry stood up from his seat slowly and walked over to join her in an attempt to intervene in their shared moment of happiness and hope in a similar fashion to earlier. Summoning the sincerest smile he could possibly muster, he looked at his wife.

"This is wonderful news isn't it babe?"

She looked back at him scornfully; his false enthusiasm now very irritating. The look she was giving him showed clearly her lack of appreciation for both his input and the way in which he was now addressing her.

"It is Jerry. Yes." She replied coldly, yet courteously.

The door to Ebony's room opened again behind Bush. After a moment of uncomfortable silence which the three of them had shared, it was a welcome interruption as Dr Raj appeared to them

"Doctor Bush" Said Raj, looking at Bush.

The tone of Dr Raj's voice was a familiar one. A tone used commonly amongst medical personnel. It was a beckoning tone which all doctors understood to mean that details need to be given to them privately and not within earshot of patients or their loved ones. Something on a need to know basis and right now, it was deemed that only Bush needed to know.

"Excuse me one second please Moira." Pleaded Bush politely. With that the door shut again as Bush followed Raj back into the scrub room and the door closed behind them, leaving Moira stood in the corridor with only her husband for company once again. This time she did not go back to pacing the corridor impatiently. Instead she just stood there waiting, watching the door like a dog watching their owner preparing their food, asking herself how long the interruption would be for this time.

With the door now fully shut to ensure privacy, Raj began to speak.

"Great news Doctor." Announced Raj, barely managing to contain his professional demeanour. "She is regaining consciousness."

Bush grinned. They both did, evidently caught up in the emotion of it all.

"Let's go and speak to our patient then and see how she is doing shall we?" Suggested Bush.

"After you Dr Bush." Raj replied, stepping aside to allow Bush to lead. Again, they shared a smile and a polite yet brief moment of mutual laughter as they entered.

Sure enough, Ebony's eyes were now open, although struggling to adapt to the bright light within the room. She still appeared very dazed, turning her head slowly from side to side, attempting to take in her strange environment. The last time she had looked and felt like this was seconds before she had collapsed into her father's arms some hours ago. Whilst she appeared to be in no evident pain, it was obvious she was not yet acutely aware of her surroundings and Bush was keen to put her at ease in any way he could. He approached her cautiously, laying his hand softly on her forehead to help ease her anxiety. Her head stopped turning as his touch seemed to alert her to his presence. She slowly turned her head towards him with a more focussed stare as he leaned in slightly to speak.

"Ebony. Can you hear me?"

With a squint and a series of rapid blinks of her partially opened eyes, she offered him a slight nod, the motion of which he felt from under his hand.

"Do you know where you are right now?" Enquired Bush.

Bush retracted his hand as she took a slow deliberate look around, turning her head left, then right, as she had done a moment ago. Then after a moment's pause, she lifted her head from off her pillow slightly in order to look down towards the foot of the bed. Her head flopped back again into her soft pillow; her energy levels still very low. She appeared to be mumbling something but her semi- delirious state had made it ineligible at the moment.

"It's ok" assured Bush with a gentle tap on her shoulder, whilst pushing the spotlight away from above her head to reduce the glare. "Don't try to talk. You have been through quite an ordeal young lady, but it looks as though you are going to be fine. My name is Dr Bush and I am the Doctor in charge." He leaned in close to her. "But you and you only can call me Garry, ok?"

Bush grinned to re-inforce the special privilege he had bestowed on her.

"Your mum is waiting to see you and I am going to let her in shortly but before I do that I am going to check a little injury you have on your hand and repair it for you as best I can."

This time there was a more defined nod. The mere mention of her mum had triggered a response and she offered a weak smile in conjunction.

"Ok" said Bush. "I want you to turn the other way and talk to the nurse and try to keep still just for a few moments ok"

Ebony did as he asked. Just like with her mum, he seemed to have gained her immediate trust and the moment she averted her gaze, he removed the bandage for a quick look at her hand before setting to work whilst the nurse held her other hand, talking to her constantly throughout the procedure.

With the few extra moments that had passed, the healing process seemed to have gathered further momentum. The colour of her skin had almost returned to its natural colour, making the procedure even easier and quicker to perform. Only a small cu mark from Bush's incision remained.

"Amazing." He uttered, somewhat under his breath, too quiet for anyone to pick up on.

With that, he set about applying a numbing agent the area by virtue of a small injection and began stitching the flaps of skin back together as neatly as he possibly could.

His level of manual dexterity and hand eye condition was renowned amongst his former colleagues and he was now demonstrating his skills to the team here as well. With his quick and precise movements, he was done within a few moments. He stepped back to admire his handy work.

"Done." He announced, allowing himself a nod of approval.

Bush held his breath as Ebony rolled her head back towards him and then looked down for her first proper look at her hand. Her eyes widened, slightly startled by what she saw, yet at the same time, intrigued, almost proud of her scar. Her reaction was more favourable than Bush had anticipated. She lifted her arm up for the first time from by her side to take a closer look It shook slightly with the effort it took to lift it. Ever so slowly, she began moving her fingers, first one by one, then all at once. It was like watching a baby with a new toy and Bush was leaving her to it. Her fingers, whilst still noticeably swollen, now moved freely, albeit not to their full potential of flexibility. That would come with time.

Happy with her contentment, Bush left her side. It was time to keep a promise. The promise being to reunite a very relieved mother and her very fortunate daughter.

It was a touching moment to see them re-united. Bush had taken her off all the monitors now that had kept track of her vital statistics so her hands would be free to welcome her mother. There appeared to be no medical need for them now anyway. After a moment of just watching them together, Moira weeping slightly as she held Ebony in her arms tenderly, he quietly ushered his staff out of the room to give them a few moments alone. Moira's patience deserved a reward and Dr Bush and his staff deserved a cup of coffee, however tasteless it proved to be.

Chapter 5

55

warm summer afternoon had brought people in their drones to visit the animal sanctuary just outside Arkansas' principle town of Little Rock. It was common knowledge that Booker Rock Reserve now played host to the widest range of the most fascinating and rare members of the animal kingdom within both it, and its surrounding states. Thanks to the ceaseless hard work of the park owner and with the help of some wealthy entrepreneurs along the way, Booker Rock now attracted guests from across the United States. It was the Animal kingdom of the west. Sat within a 10-acre plot of majestic parkland and with an abundance of nature trails within easy reach, it was a perfect setting and evidently the place to be for people of all walks of life. Some would come for a day. Some would be seen attending day after day for anything up to a week.

The walkways offered ample space for visitors to pass each other by comfortably, offering the chance to stop at each enclosure along the way. In the interests of hygiene, they were kept immaculate with streams of maintenance men in their recognisable green outfits never more than 100 metres away, armed with a dustpan and brush or the likes of a hand-held hedge trimmer. On days like this however, with the park close to its capacity, the open spaces the park boasted were close to being overwhelmed with hordes of visitors. Even those wishing to view the likes of the Aviary, the residence of the popular Northern Mockingbird among others, were resigned to standing at the back to begin with and wait patiently to catch a view of these common species. Many of the younger visitors of course, would squeeze their way through to the front to catch a better view and the park had very cleverly accounted for this with its benchwarmer scheme. A scheme whereby two rows of benches were reserved for younger children at the front of each enclosure so they could not only obtain un-interrupted views of the animals, but also to enhance the learning experience offered to them from the special award-winning presentations, ran by the park's well-trained and well-educated experts.

The majority of the enclosures and structures which housed the varied animal genus were very easy to locate by simply following the pathway guidance system and maps provided on entry. Large colourful images of the contents of forthcoming enclosures had been carefully and expertly engrained into the path surface. There was however, one place on the reserve, one solitary building, that remained truly isolated from the rest. It was unique in every way and was kept apart to symbolise its very nature. It possessed an unrivalled number of potentially dangerous animal species known to man. It was the reptile house.

The path that led up to the reptile house was long, winding and offered a steep gradient to those who dare venture up it. Despite its elevated position, looking across the reserve, the house remained well hidden in amongst the greenery and fencing and was barely visible from ground level. Pictures and warning messages had been strategically posted both at the bottom of the route and at several points leading up to the building as if to almost dare visitors to approach. The tactic worked, since droves of people made their way cautiously up the pathway. They would often catch sight of the creative and disproportionate models of the inhabitants of the feature they were about to encounter, placed strategically along the route. First, the Black widow spider placed on the floor close to the fence. Then a little further up the path, visitors could encounter the model of a scorpion, more specifically, that of the Arizona Bark Scorpion, the only venomous species native to the United States, clinging to the trunk of a large tree. There were others also, as the pathway meandered this way and that. The end of the approach way culminated with the entrance under a large archway, around the top of which was written the name of the attraction, the aptly titled VENOMENON. Appearing behind the bold and bright wording was the embossed image, gold in colour, of perhaps the most feared and well-known snake known the world over. The King Cobra. Its menacing image had it poised in its strike position with both hood and fangs on show. Pictures on a nearby notice board allowed interested visitors that had not been scared off already to get to view a series of still photo shots taken of the shows and presentations that the reserve had set up in order to entertain and educate people about these elapid members of the animal kingdom. Whilst the pictures did not give anything away as to the show's exact content, they revealed enough to further entice enthusiasts, those daring and otherwise.

It was quarter past two and although a forty-five-minute presentation had only just finished, queues were already beginning to form for the showing scheduled an hour later. The show at quarter past three was the show of the day since the show featured the highlighted and most daring content of all, known as the 'Cobra's kiss'. Only once a day was this particular show featured and it was certainly the most popular. Pundits paid dollars more at the gate time and time again to see this and purchase the premium ticket. A ticket so treasured, as well as hard to get hold of at peak times that anyone in possession of one felt like they had been given the golden ticket to Willy Wonka's Chocolate Factory. However, so risky was the task at hand involved within the show, that very few people had the skill and nerve to take this task on. Luckily, one of those people worked here at this very park. His skills came at a cost to employ him to the park, which is why the tickets did also.

In the rest room, deep within the bowels of the building, Shesha sat alone, as he often preferred to do. Whilst he was neither a complete social outcast, nor a colleague disliked by the other members of the park staff, he was one who seemed to prefer his own company. By the very nature of what he did and his character in general, he did not really fit in that well with the younger generations that made up the majority of the other staff he worked alongside on a day to day basis. He did not mind. He knew the value placed on him by those who mattered and took pride in, and to an extent, took advantage of the non-expendable position he held. Without him, this place would be nowhere near as successful. Such as it was that his colleagues had often been told to be as courteous and cooperative with him as they possibly could by their superiors. Although they often seemed content enough to be around him, work with him and indeed converse with him when needed, all seemed very wary of him. They were certainly aware of him being the golden boy of the park as far as the owners were concerned so whilst they did not bear him ill will, they were disgruntled by the level of favouritism showed to him by the hierarchy. He could do pretty much what he pleased, within reason, He knew that more than anyone.

As time for each show approached, he never appeared nervous. He never paced the corridor looking tense in any way or exhaled deeply to express any degree of in trepidation. He merely sat, statue like, motioning occasionally to nibble on the unrecognisable contents of the lunch box he brought with him. His poker face gave little away but those who would ever get close enough would see the sparkle of satisfaction and excitement in his dark brown eyes that he got from what he was about to do. He had done it time and time again and with an unmatched level of daring consistency. As the people began filling the seats around the wooden stage in the centre of the showroom, little did they now they were about to witness something the likes of what they had ever seen before.

With lunch finished, only five minutes remained until the show was due to start. A quick glance through a small oval window that allowed visual access into the show room confirmed Shesha's expectations. Another sold out show. Not a single seat remained on all four sides surrounding the stage area. People sacrificed their own personal space as they sat almost like truck herded cattle, practically rubbing shoulders with strangers next to them. There were of course no small children amongst the crowd. The park had reserved the right to place an appropriate age restriction of age twelve and above for fear of the psychological impact might have on young children. This of course only added to the excitement of those present, so it was an action that the park had seemed to have benefited from on two counts.

Shesha stood at the doorway, awaiting his cue to enter. A

moment later the lights in the main showroom dimmed and a deep narrative voice began to echo through the address system to introduce the show. Firstly, the deliverance of a few simple house rules for the spectators, all of which had been drawn up by Shesha himself with the full and predicted support of senior personnel as expected. If his show was not conducted his way, it was not to be conducted at all and he had made that clear from day one.

With his name announced, he reached for the handle to the door, As it slowly opened, he began walking slowly but nonchalantly out onto the main staging area, passing in between the assigned gaps in the seating and up the wooden steps at one corner and finally onto the wooden platform. This all took place amidst an eerie silence from the onlookers. Shesha disliked applause and had specifically insisted on quiet throughout his performances. Prompted by the narration, he reached down towards a soft bag, fastened together with rope at the top. It had been placed discretely and partially shielded by one of the four corner posts that supported the platform roof. He slowly dragged the bag up onto the stage and into the middle of the floor, taking great care to hold only the top of the bag where the rope was keeping it tied shut. Looking up and around at the spectators, he dropped the bag, circling it a couple of times, first clockwise, then the other way. He then reached down for the knot that tied the bag and quickly released the tension around the opening to the bag. Once done, he then let go of the bag. As it flopped back down, there was now every opportunity for what was inside to escape of its own free will. Shesha left the bag alone. After a few steps backwards, he began slowly walking round the edges of the platform, head held aloft, eyes mainly focussed on the sac on the floor which he circled with the mannerisms of a patient vulture circling its next meal. He still found the occasional moment however to offer a hard, cold unblinking stare to those who watched him from the safety of their seats.

He had begun retracing his footsteps for a second time when a slight movement from the sac prompted him to pause. Whatever was in the bag had most definitely detected an opportunity for freedom and release from its dark prison. Staring at the opening at the bag, Shesha crouched, hands held wide as if welcoming a small loved one towards him for a loving embrace. The head of the snake was now visible to him as well as to a large portion of the audience around him, its long-forked tongue flickering rapidly to taste the air around it. A few low tone gasps could be heard as the snake began to reveal itself in its splendour. Half way out of the bag, it stopped for second, its tongue now constituting its only movement. Whilst only half way out of the bag, it was clear that this was quite a large specimen. Its striking patterning of yellow bordered, light- centred black diamonds gave all those watching an idea as to what kind of snake they were looking at, at least those who knew anything about snakes for what emerged before them was the notorious and largest most venomous snake in the whole of North America. The Eastern Diamondback.

Spectators listened as the narrative voice continued to inform them of the long list of fascinating facts and characteristics beheld by this member of the viper genus. As if on cue, the snake began to cautiously move forward again towards where Shesha was, still crouched in admiration observing its every slither. With information as to the potential size that snakes of its kind could grow to being relayed to onlookers, it was now evident to everyone that this was most definitely towards the upper end of that size range. Having almost exited the bag completely now, its chunky frame now seemed to dominate the centre of the platform. Its distinctive tail finally came into view as its true enormity was now revealed to all. It was indeed some two metres in length and its stout muscular body had even those viewing from the back of the seats stood up in awe.

Shesha never spoke or blinked. His quiet high-pitched tone was never really suited to speaking to large crowds. He would let others do that for him. This again, was one of his own stipulations placed on the terms and conditions of his employment. All he wanted to do was show off his beloved reptilian family. He handled and coaxed them with tenderness and although he often teased them in order to show their stealth and impressive attributes to dazzle the crowds, he remained in control at all times. He never once took his eyes off them and was always sure to reward them for their work afterwards. In this case, the reward for the rattlesnake was often a nice plump rodent of some description. He would tend to include the feeding into this portion of his show as a final act as it often made it easier to coax the snake back into the bag. if it was in the process of a well-earned feed, its mouth and fangs would be occupied by the consumption of its prey.

A few random claps could be heard, the sound of which echoed around the room. Hearing them, Shesha pointed immediately to a sign on the wall that read 'No Applause during the show'. With the gesture similar to that of an orchestral conductor abruptly finishing a concerto, he signalled to all the crowd for silence whilst his eyes remained focussed on the snake. Like trained dogs, the clappers responded as such and the silence returned as quickly as it was once broken, the guilty party, very much humiliated into an embarrassed silence.

More portions of the show followed with more daring demonstrations of Shesha appearing to play with, as well as taunt the numerous creatures on show. Then, the moment came with five minutes of the show to spare. The lights dimmed in the theatre a little further, almost to the point of there being no light at all. Shesha was merely a silhouette now and could barely be seen on stage. A faint noise of an object being pushed towards the stage on a squeaky wheeled trolley was suddenly within earshot of the crowd. A ramp had already been positioned to easily manoeuvre the large box onto the stage. Once up the ramp, the shadows of two members of staff could be vaguely seen placing a large chest in the centre of the platform. One of them then came around to the front and crouched down at the front of the chest. With a soft jangle from a large set of keys, he placed one in the large gold-plated padlock that secured the chest and began to slowly turn it. It clicked as the locking mechanism triggered. He stood, and with a quick nod towards Shesha, promptly exited the stage, re-joining his colleague at the back of the theatre and out of view.

One solitary spotlight now shone on the chest, casting an eerie orange glow on the lid. Then another spotlight clicked on, this one from the other side of the stage but again focused on the lid. Shesha approached the chest. As he passed around the front, he discreetly removed the lock completely from the chest, tossing it gently off the platform and onto the surface below.

The narrative voice which had been a constant feature of the presentation had now adopted a much deeper tone to his voice. A voice once quite light hearted and informative and teacher- like now came across as spooky as though it was directly taken from the trailer of a horror film. It was quieter too. The impact was evident as the body language of the audience seemed to change. Some looked around as if the voice was eminating from a presence just over their shoulder in the darkness. Some began fidgeting in their seats in preparation for what was about to happen. Those that had read the flyer would probably already know, but it did not seem to stop people readying themselves in some fashion or another.

Approaching the chest once again, Shesha flipped the lid open, peering inside to view the contents. There it was. Awake, partially coiled, head resting softly across its scaly abdomen. The shine of the spotlights dimmed slightly as he reached in to grab a gentle yet sure handful of the snake which lay before him.

"I give you….. the King Cobra." Announced the narrator.

Prompted by the introduction, Shesha lifted the Cobra from its chest, but rather than removing it completely, he draped its impressive frame over the side of the chest, allowing it to glide comfortably of its own accord over the side and down to the floor. Sensing the vibrations of Shesa's retreating footsteps, the snake, all two and a half metres of it was quickly free of the chest, its customary hood not yet retracted. This made it yet somewhat undistinguishable from many other species on show, at least to the untrained eye. That quickly changed as it spotted a human presence within close proximity. Although it was Shesha that it had detected, someone whose touch and handling it was perhaps accustomed to, its natural instincts had kicked in. Picking its spot strategically to allow maximum scope for vision and movement, its body began to rise up from the surface. Concurrent with the raising of its head from the floor, its hood was now fully and menacingly spread wide as a warning. It stared him out with its spherical eyes which shone like prisms. Shesha moved, first shuffling left, then right. The snake, not one to be out manoeuvred followed his every step, turning the entirety of its upright tight necked body in response. Tipping its head back slightly, it stopped for a second patiently awaiting the next movement. Upon sensing the source and locality of the vibrations were coming from a source within striking distance, the cobra elected to strike, throwing its body forward with stealth like speed and accuracy. Its warning had not been heeded. It's strike found its target.

Shesha watched as barely a foot away from his right leg, the lightning strike of the cobra embedded its venom filled fangs into the soft sponge filled body of a large puppet held by a single tuft of hair on the top of its head. Moving his way deliberately around the platform in order to give the open-jawed crowd repeated chances to see the impressive arsenal of the snake, Shesha enticed the snake to repeat the action on numerous occasions. The cobra duly obliged, striking again, then again, each time with paralleled aggression and efficiency. Each time it was the puppet was hit, the force of impact sent it swaying back and forth. After some dozen strikes or so, Shesha cast aside the puppet, its ragged surface stained and saturated with venom from repeated strikes. It now lay by the side of the staging area close to where Shesha had tossed the lock earlier. It was time to allow the snake a moment to just simply show off its striking frame and perhaps then to settle a little. He didn't move. The snake didn't move and they both remained like that for what appeared to be at least a minute or so. Then slowly, Shesha dropped to his knees. He and the snake were now at eye level as the snake lowered itself to stay in line with him. On his hands and knees, Shesha ever so slowly began to edge towards the Cobra. With a few very deliberate crawling movements, he was now well within striking range once again. Should the Cobra strike now, it would most definitely succeed landing a fatal bite on its intended target. This time of course, that target was no stuffed puppet.

Little more than a foot now separated their two heads. Shesha paused again, still sharing an unblinking stare with his elapid cohort. Shesha tilted his head down slowly to the right, almost resting the side of his face on his shoulder, yet not daring to look away. As if in a trance, the Cobra leaned to right to mirror him. Shesha tilted his head the other way. The cobra did likewise. This pendulum game continued for several repetitions until finally, raising his head upward slightly, Shesha leaned in, kissing the cobra on the top of its head, not once, but twice for good measure. The cobra didn't flinch. Whilst it remained hooded up, it seemed to accept, almost encourage Shesha to show it some affection. Backing away cautiously, he slowly regained his feet and the distance now between him and the snake grew again. The snake then began to lower its head towards the floor as though Shesha's treatment of it had seemed to have had a calming effect on it. Retracting its hood slowly, the snake sank further down until its abdomen rested once again on the platform surface. Shesha took his opportunity and grabbing the snake behind its head, he lifted it from the floor. With a slow and gentle winding motion he moved his other hand up the snakes' body a foot or two and lifted the Cobra high enough for its head to clear the edge of the box. It seemed to take the hint and slowly made its way back into the comforting darkness of the chest and out of sight. Closing the lid, the snake was returned to safety. With the exercise complete, the show was over.

As normal lighting levels resumed within the arena and the spotlights were turned off, the crowd began to rise in unison. There was no cheering, yet a chorus of rapturous applause filled the room. With a simple and quick turn and bow to all four sides of the platform, Shesha expedited his exit from the platform, disappearing silently out the door from which he once came. The two assistants who had loitered around to await the conclusion of the show were now making their way back to the platform in order to re lock and remove the chest. Picking up the lock from the floor, one of the assistants secured the padlock back in place, pulling down on it firmly to check it was secure. As the majority of the crowd exited the doors off to both sides, a few remained, as if holding on to the idea that there might be something else worth seeing before they left. They watched the chest being put back on the trolley and being slowly wheeled away out of sight. One done, they too left, leaving the arena bare. Just an eerie silence was all that remained.

Shesha too was leaving. His task done for another day. Gathering his belongings and placing a dusty tired- looking brown baseball cap loosely on his head, he moved silently through the corridor towards the staff exit door at the rear of the building. He opened the door slowly, peeking out to see if anyone was nearby. Not that he was sneaking out but the last thing he wanted was to be spotted and hounded by spectators from the show, hence the use of the side door. Assured that all the crowd had dispersed, he pushed the door open and walked out into the early evening air. Passing a small head high window, he took a quick glimpse through it and gave a pride filled smile at the large array of tanks which lined the walls, some of which contained the showcased species he had just used for his show.

"Goodnight my friends." He whispered. "See you again in the morning."

The park was now quiet in comparison to how it had been an hour ago. Droves of crowds were now reduced to trickles of people taking one last look at the enclosures on their way towards the exit gates. Still, Shesha kept a low profile. With his head partially bowed and the collar of a flimsy plain jacket pulled up over the side of his face, he made his way briskly towards the gates, passing by the enclosures unnoticed. Although he did not fear recognition and deemed it somewhat inevitable at times, it made for a happy end to the day if he could make it out of the park and home undisturbed This included a degree of anonymity from those that worked at the park also. This was one such day. He had things to attend to back home where the other half of his little unique family had no doubt missed him.

Chapter 6

wo days had passed now since the traumatic events of the snake bite. Ebony woke from a peaceful and painless sleep, happy in the knowledge that if the doctor was to give his approval, she would be allowed home by the end of the day. Not quite home as she knew it or had hoped for, but at least out of the hospital. She yearned to spend some quality fun time with her mother, and they had decided on a small mini vacation together for a few days upon her discharge from hospital. Bush was more than happy with her recovery. In fact, he was astounded at the rate of it. Only a few remaining bruises and the occasional bout of numbness now remained as a reminder of her ordeal. A scar on her left hand from the procedure he performed was likely to be the only physical marks she would be left with as a lasting visual memory. Bush had pleaded with her to stick around for a few days in order to run a few final tests. Having made her aware that her recovery had seemed to have gone against all medical logic and explanation, he was very keen to stay in close touch with her. He wanted her help and co-operation to try to figure out what had happened and answer some questions no-one really knew the answers to. Ebony seemed happy to have been labelled as a medical phenomenon and so happily agreed to help Moira gave him her number so Bush was confident they would stay in contact.

Ebony rose to her feet, stretching, then moved over to the sink to freshen up. She had been transferred to a regular ward now and so had a little bit of company if she wanted it from the few patients which she shared the ward with. Her main friends though were undoubtedly the doctors and nurses that were assigned to her care. In the short space of time that she had been there, she had gotten to know almost every nurse on both the day and night shifts. They all certainly knew her well. Those not directly involved with her treatment also were all to familiar with her story. She was made to feel a little like Harry Potter in that sense. She was known simply as 'the girl who survived'. News of her story had travelled fast through the medical staff at the hospital. On her walks to the canteen, doctors and nurses alike often stopped and would ask her how she was feeling, some even asking to have a look at her wound, what there was of it. Even those staff in a hurry would still tend to pass her in the corridor offering an admiring smile or a friendly nod of the head as they passed. She felt like royalty here now. Yet still, she was dying to leave. Leave for good.

She quickly brushed her teeth, humming to herself as she did so. It was so nice to be up and about and she was in such high spirits that she was taking pleasure in conducting even the most mundane of tasks. It seemed like the best way to try to pass the time this morning. She had a few hours to kill before the discharge papers were to be signed and ready to pick up so she would have to occupy herself with something. The communal television room offered little in the way of both comfort and entertainment. Some kind of a world news channel which would be of no interest to a nine- year old was about the only channel that was fully audible above the static. The only other channel seemed to air endless re-runs of old dramas and the occasional sit-com. Again, not really her type of programme. Books were also scarce, magazines even more so. As she took her seat in the reception area in order to do some people watching, she reached into her cardigan pocket to retrieve her phone. A click of a button revealed the time.

"Two hours." She said to herself. "What on earth can I do for two hours?"

Sensing her boredom, a familiar member of staff approached her from the main desk. Someone who had become somewhat of her friend since she had been given the freedom to move around within the hospital building. Every time she had sat out here, this same person had always kept a constant vigil over her and often found any moment in between work tasks to speak to her and try to keep her busy.

"Good Morning Ebony. How are you today?" You must be thrilled and excited to be leaving today I bet?" She asked with a broad smile.

"Yes. Mum will be here soon." She replied, smiling back and fidgeting with excitement.

The receptionist paused for a moment and then crouched down beside her.

"You look a bit bored now though. I'll tell you what. How about you come with me for a short while" She suggested." I have some things I need to deliver to the wards, and I need someone big and strong to push my trolley for me. I think you would be perfect for the job."

Ebony nodded gleefully, almost jumping off her seat.

"Come on then." She replied, extending her hand for Ebony to take.

Ebony knew her mum would not mind. Since her admission, she had learnt that the lady in question had been talking to her mum quite frequently and had promised her, during their chats, that she would keep an eye on Ebony whilst she was still here as a patient, and particularly when her curious nature got the better of her to bring her out of the confines of the ward itself. Sue, the receptionist had always attempted to find some excuse for breaking off from work to indulge in a little bed-side manner. Such was Ebony's celebrity status, she had found herself sat on the staff table, often occupying the seats of the top residents and consultants, with Sue sat with her. The staff never seemed to mind though. Ebony also often met up with Dr Raj who would be happy to give up his seat in exchange for a chance to get a good look at her hand and have her re-live her memories of what she remembered from that fateful day.

With the errands run, they stopped by the canteen for one final visit. The choices on offer at this time of morning were not in abundance as the remnants of breakfast were being cleared away frantically to make way for the lunchtime menu. But that didn't matter. There was after all, only one thing she wanted.

As she approached the counter, another familiar face came into view from the storeroom at the rear of the kitchen. Ebony spotted her immediately.

"Rosa." Ebony shouted with a wave.

From the other end of the counter, a small middle aged tired- looking lady, dressed in kitchen whites from head to toe and a food stained apron looked up towards her. Rosa was the tea lady and although she was not normally accustomed to delivering food to the wards. She too had made friends with Ebony and her mum and so would use her breaks to sneak the occasional treat to Ebony in her room. She knew Ebony had quite taken a liking to the shortbread biscuits that she made. The only problem was that they were quite popular with other members of staff also, particularly the nursing staff who tended to have a bit of a sweet tooth. So it was then that Rosa would sneak one under the counter for Ebony just to see the smile on her face when she had the opportunity to take it to her. It was a slightly risky action to take, but she felt it was worth it after what Ebony had had to endure over the last few days. After all, this would be the last time she would get to do it.

Ebony approached the counter and Rosa shuffled over to meet her. After exchanging a brief heartfelt smile, Rosa reached down beneath the counter, disappearing out of view for a second. She soon re-emerged holding something in her hand, the end of which was discreetly tucked under her oversize sleeve. With a quick glance round to catch sight of any prying eyes, she reached her hand over the desk, motioning Ebony to do the same with an accompanying wink. Ebony responded and Rosa discreetly placed the contents of her hand into Ebony's outstretched palm. She knew what it was.

"Put it in your pocket quickly my darling." Rosa whispered mischievously. "Auntie Rosa might get told off if people found out I had saved it for you again."

Ebony quickly obliged with an equally mischievous grin and a chuckle of her own.

"Now let me come around there and give you a big goodbye hug and kiss because I'm going to miss you after you go today." Said Rosa with sincerity.

"We all will." Sue added.

Rather than remaining where she was and waiting for Rosa to take the long walk down to the other end of the counter and around the till area in order to make her way back round towards her, Ebony set off running down the customers' side of the counter to meet her. When she got close, she opened her arms ready to embrace her. Before Rosa could attempt to stoop down, Ebony had already wrapped her arms around her in what felt like a vice like grip, filled with affection and typical child-like enthusiasm.

"Ooh dear me." Exclaimed Rosa, reacting to the jolting impact of the hug with a slight backward stagger.

Such was Rosa's stature, that the top of Ebony's head came to rest just under her neck and with her arms trapped within the hold which Ebony had on her, she was only left with the option of placing an affectionate kiss on the top of Ebony's head. Ebony loosened her grip slightly and Rosa was able to free her arms and wrap them around Ebony's back to pull her closer, at the same time taking care not to squeeze her too tightly. She was still after all, seen to be a recovering patient in the eyes of all that worked there.

"Please make sure you write to me to tell me how you are getting on." Pleaded Rosa.

Ebony nodded, still with her cheek pressed up against Rosa's chest. Then she let go, took a step back and with a solitary tear of sorrow which trickled from the corner of her eye, offered Ebony one final wave. With that, she turned and made her way back into the kitchen whilst Ebony retreated, treat in hand, back to where Sue from reception patiently waited.

"Come on you." Sue said in a playful and slightly impatient tone as Ebony skipped past her and through the door and out into the corridor.

It was time to return to her room for her belongings. Moira was due soon and wanted Ebony ready to go. They had to get straight to the airport if they were to make their trip.

"Ebony." She shouted.

Ebony stopped immediately and turned.

"I just have one more quick stop here to make before we go back to your room for your things." She explained. "Can you just wait here a moment for me?"

Ebony sighed slightly with impatience, somewhat typical of a child whose moment of excitement had been unfairly and agonisingly delayed without reason. Sue sensed her impatience

"This is where I get the papers from to say you can go home."

Ebony's sense of discontent and impatience quickly gave way to acceptance and she now seemed much happier to wait around for a moment longer.

"Don't worry" Sue reassured her. "This will only take a second."

It was indeed a brief stop and they were back on their way down the corridor again within minutes, this time walking side by side. Ebony's eyes kept averting to the large brown envelope clutched tightly in Sue's hand.

"Is that it?" Asked Ebony, loosely grabbing the bottom corner of the envelope as they walked.

"Yes. That's it." Came the confident response. "Your mum just has to sign this and then you are free to go."

Approximately thirty minutes' drive away from the hospital was the nearest hotel. The districts' only hotel and the hotel at which Moira had been staying at since leaving hospital the previous afternoon. With Ebony's short-term recovery complete, there had no longer been either the room or necessity to confine herself to the relative discomfort of the hospital in attempt to get some sleep as she had done for the first thirty-six hours or so. She could now rest easy again during the night knowing that Ebony had plenty of people looking out for her whilst she spent her final day there.

A few issues checking out and a rather uncomfortable telephone conversation with her husband, had meant a small delay to Moira's departure from her hotel. Eventually however, with the barely audible toot of a car horn and grabbing her heavy case and dragging it out behind her, she climbed into her awaiting taxi and headed out towards the main road towards the hospital.

As she settled in for the thirty-minute journey to the hospital, she stared out the window thoughtfully. She began to plan in her head the events for their forthcoming trip. She was so keen to make up for lost time, not only for the past few days, but for a long time before the incident too. Whilst she had never been obsessed with her work, she had now come to realise that it had taken over her life. Time spent alone thinking, during the last couple of days had made her see that changes had to be made to her work- life balance and she was keen to make such changes with immediate effect. This little break for the two of them was testimony to that.

Moira's car pulled up outside the hospital entrance with perfect timing as Ebony was making her way with her bags packed towards the reception area, accompanied by one of the nurses.

"I'll wait here Mrs Maher." The driver advised Moira.

"Thank you." She replied gratefully. "I won't be a minute or so."

"Take your time please." Replied the driver, reaching for a paper which lay beside him on the front seat.

Moira strode gallantly through the doors as they slid open to welcome her and straight into the waiting arms of her daughter. They exchanged a loving hug and a smile.

"You all ready to go sweetheart?" Her mum asked.

She most certainly was. All her belongings were packed in a small carry case with her jacket draped over the top which lay in wait on one of the chairs behind the reception desk. They approached the desk together.

"Good morning Moira" Came Sue's cheerful voice echoing loudly from across the desk. "I have the papers for you here to sign." She added, offering Moira a handful of neatly stacked papers and a pen.

After a quick skim read through the papers. Moira located the signature box at the bottom of the discharge sheet and scribbled her name in childlike fashion. Handing back the pen and pushing the papers back towards the far edge of the desk, she turned her attention back to Ebony who stood by her side.

"Say goodbye sweetheart. It's time to go. Let's go and have some fun, shall we?"

After saying their last goodbye's and thank you, Moira grabbed hold of the bag which now sat by her feet.

"We will keep in touch" Promised Moira, looking back over her shoulder as they began to make their way towards the exit for the final time. The car was still there waiting, it's rear door left courteously open for their imminent arrival with the driver still immersed in the reading of his paper. As she walked round to the other side of the vehicle, Moira hesitated for a second, looking up to take one last look at the building from which she had just left. A feeling of relief took hold of her and she afforded herself a wry smile and an exhale of satisfaction and content knowing that she was leaving in the best possible terms. The people in the hospital she would miss for sure, but the place itself, she could not wait to see the back of. Yet she watched it disappear until it was no longer in sight through the drivers rear view mirror.

A long ride to the airfield was beginning to test Ebony's patience once again. Every turn which she anticipated to be the last only seemed to reveal more endless non- descript lanes, beside which lay endless acres of random shrubbery and arboreous landscape.

A sharp and unexpected turn off the main arterial route brought them into an opening. A series of modest looking white buildings confronted them, with a low perimeter fence that trailed off into distance. Above the level of the fence, the tails of several small aircraft could be seen parked at random intervals. This was no major aircraft hub, merely a regional airbase but it was the nearest airfield for one hundred miles, offering the only connection to the outside world and a lifeline to researchers and scientists alike, who needed to transport large amounts of expensive and heavy equipment for expeditions such as the one Moira and Ebony had travelled here for two weeks ago. They had of course travelled over with many other members of Moira's research team. They however, including Ebony's father. had already returned home earlier that day in order to get back to analyse and present their findings. Whilst Moira was quite keen to catch up with her team at some point soon, she was looking forward to the next few days even more.

They headed for the largest building of the few. Even though it outsized the others, it seemed to only offer the basic amenities that an airport can possibly offer. There was a solitary desk upon entry, manned by a stern looking broad-shouldered gentleman, armed solely with a stamp and ink pad who could be seen off to one side. Above him, hung a scrawled chalk board sign indicating his purpose. To further emphasise his presence, a large badly drawn arrow hung down on another board pointed directly to where he sat.

There was no queue and Moira approached the desk with Ebony close behind. She promptly handed over a small series of papers and 2 passports. The surly gentleman took them from her, without even any eye contact, opening each passport in turn. With one very quick look at the papers and then a fleeting glance at Moira and Ebony, he reached for his stamp. He handed the documents back and quickly pointed towards the one small check in desk at the other side of the room. Passports in hand, they headed towards it.

The check in procedure was thankfully a quick one. With a solitary sticker placed on the flight cases and a simple signature verification on what looked like an old- fashioned class register, they made their way through a set of double doors into what could only be a departure lounge. A very simplistic whiteboard confronted them detailing any flight activity for the day. There was not much planned and it was easy to recognise their flight on the listings. Next to the board sat a well- dressed airport official, sipping from a mug of a hot beverage. On a small table by his side rested a clipboard, a walkie talkie device and a marker pen along with a stained scrunched up cloth. The sight of the drink seemed to spark a thirst in both of them that needed quenching before their flight

They began to talk of their plans upon reaching their destination. Ebony reeled off a long list of things she wanted to do. Each one of them she mentioned accompanied by an excited "ooh- ooh" sound. She had reemed off some fifteen items in total by the time she stopped for breath, or an occasional gulp of juice. They were keen to tick off as many things as possible. Moira folded the list and placed it in her back pocket, prompting Ebony to finish her drink. Just as she took a last gulp, a loud voice emanated from the now open double doors in one corner of the room. It was the man they had encountered when they entered the lounge.

"Anyone for Pakor Air 82 to Panaga?" Shouted the voice with a strong regional accent.

"That is Pakor Air 82 to Panaga. Step forward please." instructed the voice in loud broken English as well as in several local dialects.

"That's us." Announced Moira, standing up and readying herself to join the queue of eager passengers who had already formed an orderly line at the door.

"Panaga" whispered Ebony repeatedly to herself, changing the emphasis each time on each syllable as though creating some wonderfully entertaining phonetical word game in her head. Her playful utterances continued as they approached and then boarded their flight and it was only when the aircraft doors were sealed and the two giant wing mounted propellers began to turn. She signed off her game with a little chuckle and focussed her attention on the view from the window. The aircraft began to lurch slowly forward to make its way to the end of the runway.

With the mountains, ancient rain forest and vast cavernous regions soon visible below them, the aircraft banked sharply left, smoothly passing through occasional gatherings of cloud that seemed to caress the wing as they floated over it.

"Finally." Moira whispered to herself, relaxing back in her seat. She looked to her side to see Ebony drifting off to sleep.

Chapter 7

With a solid infra structure now in place and a suitable stand-in organised, Bush found himself on a plane home back to Boston. Just like his patient and her mother, he needed a break too. He felt a tinge of guilt about leaving so soon after only just taking up his post, but the need to return home for a few days was too much to resist. His first month of a six-month placement had been the most hectic month he had ever experienced.

Ebony's case alone would have persuaded many a doctor to take a few days of respite. However, Bush had simply not stopped all month. Even stopping work to take time to eat properly had gone awry. This eleven-hour trans-Atlantic flight was without doubt the longest he had sat down for some considerable time. By now sitting back and relaxing did not feel right.

"Ladies and gentlemen. We have now commenced our final descent into Boston's Logan International Airport. The Captain has now switched on the fasten seat belt signs, so we do ask at this time that you return to your seats, fully open the window blinds and fasten your seatbelts. May we also ask that you ensure all your trays are stowed away and secured in their upright position and that any baggage is placed in the overhead compartments above you or well beneath the seat in front of you. We would like to remind passengers that operating any electrical equipment such as lap-tops and other hand- held devices is now prohibited until you are well inside the terminal building"

Bush glanced up at the cabin attendant as she continued her announcement.

"The cabin crew will now pass through the cabin for one

final check before we land and we do hope you have enjoyed your flight with us today and hope to see you on board one of our flights again in the near future."

With that, the attendant put the phone back in its bulk mounted holder and slowly strode through the cabin, the other attendants quickly following suit.

The skies were cloudy over Boston and despite the size of the wide- bodied jet, the wind and low cloud base was not making the final approach a particularly smooth one. It reminded Bush of the small roads and pathways he had driven his truck down over the past month or so. Such was the case that he barely batted an eyelid as the turbulence took its full effect. Other passengers around him were not quite as calm

The aircraft soon touched down beneath a murky Massachusetts sky and began to taxi towards the terminal.

"Ladies and gentlemen" Came the familiar voice again over the address system. "Welcome to Boston International Airport. The local time here is now a little after 5pm in the evening. Please remain in your seats until the aircraft has come to a complete stop and the seatbelt signs have been turned off. On behalf of the Captain and the rest of the crew, I would like to wish you a safe onward journey."

Bush followed the instructions to the letter, unlike some of the other inpatient passengers whose seat belts could clearly be heard clicking open around the cabin.

"Idiots." Bush muttered to himself. "What do they hope to achieve?"

He was himself very keen to disembark but knew nothing positive could be achieved by reaching for his things now. The whirring on the engines soon ceased and within moments the door was opened for passengers to get off. Bush felt the cold air from ten rows back and reached for his jacket, putting it on before reaching up to grab his bag. Giving his thanks to the crew, he followed the drones of passengers into the airport building and headed for the baggage hall.

Although he was returning for recreational purposes, his close friend and colleagues at the institute for toxicology in the city had kindly laid on a car to pick him up at the airport and as he came through the double doors into the arrivals hall, he was soon sought out by a well- suited chauffeur who took his bag from him and asked him to follow him outside. Bush did so with a gratuitous smile. Hailing a cab at this time of day, in poor weather conditions, would not be easy so having a car laid on was a very convenient and welcome gesture. It was good to be home, even if only for a few days.

As the car left the airport, Bush begin to envisage the scene that might await him on his arrival home. That familiar smell of freshly brewed coffee, maybe with the sound of the television on in the background. The best sight would be that of his beautiful wife, Kirsty, ready to welcome him with a smile and a kiss.

Thanking the driver, he lugged his case up the flight of steps leading to the main door. After a moments' fumbling for the right key, he located it and put it in the lock, turning it quietly but quickly to escape from the rain. Once inside the main hallway, he eagerly pressed the lift button, shaking the rain from his overcoat. His flat was on the top floor of a three-storey apartment block, so he had no intention of using the stairs. The lift seemed to take an eternity to descend back down to ground level and Bush waited impatiently, so much so that he pressed the button twice more as the lift made its way down. A feint ping indicated it had reached the ground floor and no sooner had the doors begin to slide open, he pushed his case inside, then manoeuvred himself in next to it. The ascent was as equally tedious in terms of its speed.

"Finally!" He exclaimed as the lift made a second ping sound and the doors slowly slid open again at the third floor.

The familiar sight of the art décor which lined the corridor walls brought a welcome smile to his face. He located his own apartment key and moved slowly down the corridor. His wife was expecting him but not on the earlier flight, so he did not want to spoil the surprise. He had planned to surprise her even more with dinner reservations made for the following evening at her favourite restaurant.

Turning the key, he grimaced in the hope that the locking mechanism didn't cause too much noise and alert her to his presence before he had even entered the door. Besides, there was another reason to make as little noise as possible on entry. He didn't want to disturb his new born son from his slumber.

His son, Theo had been born shortly after he had left and leaving his heavily pregnant wife at home with his birth imminent had been perhaps the most difficult decision he had ever made. Had it not been for the understanding, and persuasiveness of his wife and the incentives offered to him to secure his and their long-term financial future, he would most certainly have stayed at home. However, with such a close network of close friends and relatives close by to look after Kirsty in her final stages of pre-natal care, he knew she was at least in good hands and would not be short of company until he got home. Her own sister had agreed to even be her birthing partner which made Garry very happy. Not only was she a nurse anyway, but the three of them were very close.

A smell of freshly brewed coffee filled the air on entry. The apartment was both welcoming and warm. He could hear Kirsty shuffling around in the kitchen and so as not to startle her, he left the door on the latch for the moment. He hung his coat up in the hallway and eased the door open into the kitchen to see her pouring a cup of coffee from the machine. He smiled, ready to surprise her.

"I'd love one thanks baby."

Kirsty stopped pouring, placing the pot shakily back on counter, her hands trembling at the sound of the familiar voice from over her shoulder. She slowly turned. The tears of happiness had already begun to flow by the time she had crossed the kitchen to embrace him tightly.

"That's what I have been waiting for." He said softly, his cheeks still pressed between her shoulder and her neck.

They pulled apart slightly, now looking deep into each other's eyes. She kissed him passionately, eyes shut, savouring the moment having missed his touch.

He pulled back again smiling, with only one question on his mind which he just had to ask.

"How is he?" He enquired with the affectionate tone of a true proud new father.

"He is great. He has been a little restless today with a touch of nappy rash but in general, its been great since the first moment he came home." She reported. "Give him an hour though please darling as I have only just put him down for a nap."

She looked at her watch, then stared into space as though calculating something in her head.

"He will be ready for a feed in about three quarters of an hour anyway. Maybe I had best grab a nap in the bedroom. They do say the mother should try and sleep when the baby does."

She walked across the living room towards the bedroom door, turning back to Garry.

"Care to join me hubby?" She asked with a teasing glance over her shoulder.

"Would Bonny ever say no to Clyde?" He replied rhetorically, quickly in pursuit. She giggled as she kissed him playfully as he crossed the threshold of the bedroom door, reaching behind him to push the door firmly shut.

The next forty-five minutes seemed to pass ridiculously quickly. The sound of a baby's cry could be heard from the room next door, faint at first, growing in prominence with each passing second.

Kirsty sprung up from the bed, eager to attend to him.

"Let me." Garry said, placing his hand on top of hers to stop her leaving.

She smiled, appreciating the chance to continue lying down to rest.

Garry sprung up, excited to be tending to his child. His son may have been crying but it was the first time he was to lay his eyes on him and pick him up to hold him. It didn't bother him at all that little Theo was exercising the power of his lungs.

"Nappies are in the store room, milk in the fridge." Shouted Kirsty through the bedroom door, left slightly ajar in case he needed to ask anything from the next room.

"Got them." He shouted back.

For a first nappy change, things went quite well. He felt proud of his achievement as he fastened the final press stud between his legs.

"It's feeding time little man, yes, it is. Who wants din-dins?" He asked playfully in his best baby-like voice. He rocked his son in his arms as he began to settle down as if he knew his baby cries had been answered. Carrying the prepared bottle in one hand and Theo in the other, Garry retired to the living room and plonked himself down in his favourite chair. He had missed his favourite chair and was comforted by the feeling of the cushion still bearing the shape of his posterior. He teased his son's lips with the teat of the bottle. His little mouth opened with acceptance and he began feeding.

With his free hand, Garry reached for the remote control to the television. Turning it on, he flicked through the menu to the sports section and picked one of many pre-recorded basketball games Kirsty had kindly recorded for him. This was his ulterior motive for gladly volunteering to take the night shift in terms of feeding and changing Theo. He wondered how many games he could get through to catch up on the half a season he had missed before he too fell asleep. At least three he predicted to himself.

With Theo asleep again, as well as Kirsty napping in the bedroom, he settled in for a good night's viewing. He had put Theo back in his cot, leaving the door partially open to monitor his movements. Instead, in his left hand now was a nice refreshing ice cold bottle of beer and in front of him, a large bowl of pretzels. The perfect game time combination as far as he was concerned.

Half way into the second game, he took his first glance at his watch. Twenty past ten. It had been a long day travelling, yet he was wide awake. The dreaded jet lag had hit him. A part of him wanted to continue watching but after the thrashing he had just watched his team endure in the previous game, in addition to the thoughts and flashbacks from dealing with Ebony's case, he was not enjoying it as much as he had anticipated. The beer was going down a treat however and he soon found himself on his fourth bottle. With each sip he took, another unanswered question entered his mind. He was still ecstatic she had made a full recovery, but he had to question how it came to that. There was no reason why she should have even survived. Previous patients suffering similar snake bites had been lucky to walk away with serious disfigurement of a limb, often included an amputation of some sorts. Yet with Ebony, there was nothing. A small scar as a reminder of an incision he himself made on her hand was all. He stood, taking a quick look at Theo lay still in his cot. Then he walked over to his unpacked bags and fished around for the files he had brought home, specifically her file which contained a detailed report of everything that had happened during his time with her. Maybe there was something in there that might answer at least a few of the questions he had.

Opening the folder, he began to scan every page like a detective examining his evidence. The admission report revealed nothing he didn't already know but he read through it again anyway to make sure. One thing did arouse his interest, but it only proved to deepen the mystery further. He looked closely at the time scale between her being admitted and the time before he had administered the first dose of anti-venom. He calculated it to be about forty- five minutes. This was well within the time frame it would take a serious envenomation to prove fatal. Yet it was not un-heard of that victims could still survive a little longer than this.

"Hang on though." He said to himself. "How long did it take her get from the base to the medical centre?" He asked himself. He looked further into the report, but no further evidence could be found to shed any light on this. He would have to wait till tomorrow to answer this query. The thought plagued his mind as with further rational thinking, he also had to consider the time taken to get her back to camp. If this time frame was anywhere near the two-hour mark, it dawned on him that no one would manage to sustain a cobra bite and live for that long without emergency medical treatment.

Garry would have a further wait to obtain any results from the toxicology department regarding several of Ebony's blood samples he had sent to them at several intervals during treatment. The ones he was particularly interested in were those just after the anti-venom was delivered. Had the bite not been as severe had he thought despite its superficial appearance? Had the anti-venom been that concentrated that it just happened to have had a far more positive effect than anyone had expected. One thing was for sure, he had certainly instructed the right type of anti-venom to be administered. He took a great deal of satisfaction in knowing that. He would just have to be a little patient and play detective for a while longer. This had by no means, become an open and shut case. With one more cycle of feeding, changing and soothing his son back to sleep, he retired to the bedroom, confident that despite all the unanswered questions, he was tired enough to grab a few hours of sleep.

With a much-needed full nights' sleep behind her, Kirsty awoke early to attend to Theo. She felt more alive than she had felt in weeks. It was amazing what an uninterrupted nights' sleep would do. She had left Garry to sleep and by the time he woke it was a little after eight in the morning. Again, the scent of coffee beans drifted throughout the apartment. Not being one for lying there to contemplate his next move, Garry sprung up from the bed. A slight dull ache reminded him of his over zealous drinking the previous night. Aside from that, he felt good. No longer jet-lagged at least. Kirsty turned to him as he entered the living room, yawning. His hair, normally so neat and tied back in a pony tail, now scraggy and sticking up in all directions.

"Ooh. The sexy look." Kirsty joked.

He smiled.

"I'll feel a lot sexier after a cappuccino, a shower and a shave." Came his reply.

With a stroke of his son's soft baby cheek as he fed, along with a good morning kiss for his wife, he took his coffee into the bathroom with him and began to run his shower. It seemed every time he was alone now, his mind formulated more questions about the case. A hot shower proved no different, though it did leave him feeling refreshed. Many of the questions were of the same nature as those that came to mind the night previous. At least today he would get some answers. He needed the answers. He did not want anything to distract him from the enjoyment of a romantic night out with

Kirsty, so finding out what he could would pacify him for the time being. He shaved, got quickly dressed and grabbed a slice of ready-made toast before preparing Theo for his morning walk. He had missed walking around the neighbourhood too and was keen to see a few local friends during his brief time back at home. Kirsty knew little of Ebony's case and it was Garry's intent to keep it that way. He always tried to separate business with pleasure and besides, every time they did speak, he was far keener to hear of her progress during the latter stages of her pregnancy. He loved that she supported his work and was interested in what he had been up to, yet was keen to forget about it when he was at home. It was just a shame that this was not working out for him quite so well this time.

Several puddles along the sidewalk reminded Garry of the torrential rain from the previous evening. By the looks of it, he had escaped the worst of it. Today was much brighter. The sun shone sporadically through the clouds as Garry strode down the block. A small supermarket was first his destination in order to purchase a newspaper. He was keen to catch up on what had been happening whilst he had been away. Then from there, it was on to the café for what Garry considered to be the best coffee in the state. Finally, he was set to drop off Theo with Kirsty's sister Elizabeth. She had kindly agreed to take Theo for the majority of the day and overnight so Garry and Kirsty could spend some quality time together.

It was great to see everyone again going about their day to day activities. He missed this. All of a sudden, for a moment or two, his time in Mozambique faded into a slightly more distant memory, as did the notion of him having to go back after a few days. Everyone made a fuss of Theo as expected, as he was gently pushed around in the pram. Garry, having got his paper, was enjoying a brief sit down outside the café before moving on to Elizabeth's house some four blocks away. It was after dropping his son off there that he was intending to ring the base in Mozambique and the toxicology lab here in Boston where his long-term work and life's research was based. Then he could get some answers.

An hour, and a predictable third cup of decent coffee later, this time made for him by his sister-in-law, Garry left Elizabeth's house. No sooner had he reached the end of her driveway, he was quickly on his phone, hoping to obtain a signal. Ringing someone in the heartlands of the African wilderness was very much a hit and miss thing. Luckily this time, the signal seemed strong and he got through within a minute or so. He paced slowly as he waited for an answer. Then, a faint voice could be heard. It was a voice of some one who knew it was Garry calling them.

"Dr Bush. Is that you?"

"Yes" Affirmed Bush." I need you to find out a couple of things for me regarding the Maher case."

"Of course, Doctor Bush." Came the obedient reply of his assistant.

"I need you to find out how long it takes on foot from the incident site where the Maher girl was bitten to the base where they were located. Ask anyone who knows that particular trail well."

"Of course Doctor. I'll get right on it." He replied with urgency.

"Good. Call me back as soon as you know."

With that, Bush hung up and began redialling. Keying in the last number, he put the phone back to his ear.

"Toxicology, Kath speaking." Came the voice from the other end of the phone.

"Kath. It's me, Garry. I'm ringing for the toxicology results on the Maher girl I sent you last week."

"Hang on one second Garry." Said Kath.

Bush could hear the background noise of chair wheels sliding across the tiled floor, then a series of light tapping noises as she began to access the information on her computer. She began to chat as she waited for the computer to respond.

"May I say well done on this one Garry. It seemed like quite a close call. Such a good job you were there on scene so quickly to administer the right anti-venom. She owes you her life."

There was a short silence as she tapped a few more keys.

"I'm sending you the results now Garry."

Garry's phone bleeped almost instantaneously with an alert to an incoming e-mail. While he began to access it, Kath began chatting again.

"Naja Mossambica I see. Its been a while since I did a tox screen that came up with the Mossambica. Such a large envenomation too. You must have been amazed that it took up to only ten vials to rid her....."

"What did you just say?" Garry interrupted abruptly. What he heard stopped him in his tracks.

"I said how amazed you must have been that it took only ten vials to save her. With the amount of venom, the injected, I would have expected more than fifteen would."

"No no. Before that" Garry interrupted again.

"Oh. You mean using the Mossambica polyvalent. Yes, I was a little surprised when I first saw the results I have to admit. It seemed strange that the snake didn't at least warn her off with its customary venom spitting first. Prior to the first vial, a few signs did seem to indicate that it might have been the Melonoleuca. As I said. Your decision saved her life Garry…. Garry…Are you there? She asked, getting only silence.

"Yes… I'm here. Thanks Kath. Speak later."

Bush could barely get his words out. He hung up the phone without even saying goodbye. The realisation of what he just learnt hit him like a thunderbolt. He began to shake slightly as a lump formed in his throat.

"It was the Melonoleuca" He said to himself. "How on earth could I have prescribed the wrong anti-venom?"

He sat for a moment on a conveniently placed bench nearby. He had to sit down before he fell down. The tension in his body was building further and he could feel the adrenalin pump round his body as he continued to digest what he had been told. Then the biggest question of all came to the front of his mind. It scared him a little to think about the answer.

"If a different anti-venom was used, how in the blue blazes of hell did she not only survive, but come back to life and then fully recover?" He asked himself, dumb- founded. He scratched his head in confusion. This only raised more questions

A message came through for him from his assistant he had spoken to moments earlier. Taking a deep breath, he began to read its contents

'THE CAMP WAS APPOXIMATELY 30 MINS ON FOOT FROM THE PROPOSED SIGHT WHERE SHE

WAS BITTEN. IF CARRIED, CAN ONLY ASSUME IT MUST HAVE TAKEN HER FATHER AN HOUR TO GET HER BACK TO BASE CAMP'.

"That's well over two hours before any at all anti-venom" he calculated in shock and surprise "There is no way she should have survived this for numerous reasons."

He was back on the phone again to his assistant. He did even not bother saying hello this time.

"Go to my case. It's in the lab. Second fridge along" Bush instructed.

"Yes Doctor." His assistant replied meekly, sensing the urgent tone in Bush's voice. "Right away."

He was back within moments with Bush's carry case. The very one he had used at the hospital with Ebony, still untouched after his visit and luckily for him, as yet unpacked.

"Open it!" Ordered Bush.

The assistant did as he was asked, first unzipping the lid around the top and then flipping the lid up and allowing it to drop over the back of the case. Having done that, he turned his attentions to Bush again on the end of the phone.

"What is it you wish me to tell you Doctor? The assistant asked. "I have the case open in front of me."

"Tell me how many vials are missing and from which row."

Bush held his breath, waiting for the answer. After a quick calculation, he got it.

"There are eight missing Doctor. "He stated confidently. "Eight vials from the fifth row."

"Are you sure?" Asked Bush. "Take one out from that row and read me the description on the label."

Again, the assistant complied, slowly removing a vial and holding up to the light, began to read.

"Polyvalent Anti-venom serum. Naja Mossambica. Apply ten millilitres per minute until symptoms begin to subside."

Bush's worst fear had been confirmed. He had used a different anti-venom to what he had intended. Then it dawned on him. It was Raj who actually administered the anti-venom. It was Raj who he instructed to extract them from his bag. How could he have selected from the wrong row of vials?

Before he could accuse Raj of any degree of negligence, there was one more thing he had to check.

"The top of the bag where the lid is. "Enquired Bush. "Did it open towards you or away from you? "He asked, now awaiting the reply he fully anticipated."

"Away doctor," Came a confused response. "Is that right?"

"Yes, yes. That's fine." Bush responded, now having fathomed out exactly what must have happened.

"Finally, take a vial from row four and read me the label. Just the snake types this time." Asked Bush solemnly.

Again, the assistant reached into the bag and carefully located and extracted a single vial from the requested row and began to relay the desired information. Bush spoke the same words in tandem as a sign of resignation to the truth

"Naja Melanoleuca."

"Thanks." Said Bush quietly. Then hung up without another word.

He stood and after a moment, slowly began the slow walk back home. He would come back to this this another time. He had a dinner date to get ready for.

Chapter 8

Jerry woke up late. He was used to hearing the hustle and bustle of Moira and Ebony running about the house by half past seven getting showered or ready for work and school respectively. They weren't due back till tomorrow from their trip, so it had been a very quiet few days at home alone. A look at the clock revealed it was now five past eight. He shot up in horror. Today was a big day and he had a big appointment in the city with his boss and a group of constituents responsible for funding his recent trip. His task today was to present his findings and dazzle them with what he and his team had discovered.

Sacrificing a shower due to time constraints, he quickly headed to the bathroom and soaked his face in cold water. With a brief brush of his teeth, he made his way back into the bedroom and reached into the wardrobe, grabbing for the first suit he could lay his hands on. He was soon dressed, but not to his usual standards for such occasions. Grabbing the wider end of a tie from the rail, he pulled it sharply as he made his way out of the room. He rolled it up round his hand and stuffed it in his trouser pocket as he grabbed his coat and keys. Slamming the door behind him, he headed out to the car. Consumed by the rush, it was only then that Jerry realised he had left his presentation material inside the house.

"Shit." He cursed in frustration.

He banged the steering wheel in anger and exited the car once again, fumbling for his house key whilst hotfooting it back up the driveway to the porch. He had at least prepared his material the night before and so it was that it only took a few extra seconds to go back inside and grab what he needed. With both hands full, he placed a series of small folders between clenched teeth, gripping them tightly as he closed the door behind him once more. He leaned into the car and placed his things behind him on the back seat then turned and bowed the head of his tall frame to get into the drivers' seat. The engine fired to life with the first turn of the key and he quickly reversed off the drive, without even so much as a look either side to see if anyone was imminently about to pass the threshold to the driveway along the sidewalk. Slamming the car into first gear, he sped away down the avenue, the noise of the engine audible for everyone on the entire street to hear. The clock on the dashboard now read twenty- three minutes past eight. It was at least a twenty-minute journey into the city when making good time and without any significant traffic congestion. He only hoped that today would be one of those days. He had to make the office by nine o'clock. It was going to be close.

Luck appeared to be on his side as he sped through series after series of green lights. Barely two blocks away from the office was where he encountered the first unwelcome volume of traffic. Whilst it did not look like it would delay him long, it was now 8:46 and he was still yet to park and make it up to the eleventh floor before he had reached his final destination.

As he quickly parked up and turned off the ignition, a last glance at the dashboard clock read one minute past the hour. He was officially late and as he bolted over the carpark with all his material to hand, his mind had the image of his boss pacing the eleventh-floor corridor, or humbly apologising to the associates trying to assure them he was on his way. Neither was a pretty picture and he knew he would suffer the consequences verbally afterwards. His boss was a reasonable but a powerful domineering type gentleman and in thirty years of business, there were two things he hated, tardiness and having to apologise and look humbled in front of others. Even those who may have been his superiors.

The elevator was partially full as he entered. There was no apology from him as he attempted to attain a better grip of his belongings, hitting numerous fellow occupants within the confined space as he did so. With a comfortable grip acquired, the elevator pinged to signal its arrival at the next requested stop. His floor. The eleventh. He looked out, ready to see his boss stood there impatiently, arms folded, perhaps pointing to his watch angrily. There was no sign of him in the corridor. He made his way quickly down the corridor to the conference room. Large windows stretched down from floor to ceiling on either side of the door to the conference room and so he knew he had been sighted before he even had made it into the room to offer his apologies personally.

"Not off to the greatest of starts Jerry." He said to himself as he reached for the door, gesturing to one of the gentleman with a greeting nod who had now spotted him.

"May I apologise for my late arrival gentlemen?" He said, opening the door.

The two gentlemen said nothing. One of them reached up to cover his mouth from a solitary cough with his clenched fist. The other sat there motionless, stone-faced. If anything, Jerry would guess that his look was one of disdain.

"Evidently another hater of tardiness." Jerry thought to himself. "Great."

"I see you made it then Jerry, finally." His boss said in a disgruntled tone.

"Yes Sir. Please allow me a moment to prepare." He pleaded.

Receiving no answer from any one of the three gentlemen sat before him, he began to lay out his presentation equipment, consisting of a series of rolled up maps, his lap top, and a small collection of containers, each with a specimen inside. The specimens varied in colour, size and sub species of mainly beetles and butterflies and seemed impressive to the eye. Though the size of the collection did not appear to be impressing the two gentlemen in the slightest. They seemed to have very few questions for him and even the most interesting of facts he relayed were met with a simple nod or the odd 'mhm' sound. He was sure he had spotted a few looks of disappointment between them also.

"Thank you, Jerry," His boss said, standing as his presentation drew to a close.

"Grab yourself a coffee or something and we will call you back in a short while. We have a few items to discuss regarding your findings."

Jerry nodded, happy for the break and definitely in need of refreshment. Looking a little flushed, he made his way quickly out the door to escape the intense and intimidating atmosphere. It felt So intimidating that it had caused Jerry to hesitate several times, particularly on the few occasions where he had made proper eye contact with the two very serious looking gentlemen that side beside his boss around the table.

Jerry made his way to the rest area. A small designated alcove aligned with vending machines which dispersed a wide array of snacks and drinks. He sat in the corner reflecting, wishing to be a fly on the wall back in the conference room for the next thirty minutes or so. In the time he sat there, he found himself going through three cups of coffee, yet ate nothing. His stomach was churning with the nerves that overwhelmed him. The consequences could be quite severe for him if he had not impressed the partners with his findings.

After being made to wait forty minutes, his boss entered the alcove himself, heading straight to the coffee machine. Allowing it to fill, he picked up the cup and turned to retrace his steps. He glanced down at Jerry as he passed.

"Do you want to follow me Jerry?"

Jerry stood and closely followed him back to the conference room. He quickly noticed that the two gentlemen from before were no longer present. He took a seat next to his boss, who quickly got to his feet again as he began to relay feedback from the two partners. It did not make for good hearing on the whole.

Jerry walked out of the conference room thirty minutes later with two words ringing in his ears. The last two words his boss spoke and the two words no employee wants to hear. Jerry didn't even bother picking up all his belongings, grabbing only his coat and his lap-top before heading down the eleventh-floor corridor and summoning the lift for what would now be the final time. Once down to the lobby, he handed in his pass key to the security desk and the guard accompanied him out of the building up to the main barrier at the entrance to the car park. His car had been a company car and thus, he had been told to relinquish the keys with immediate effect. Dejected and lethargic, he began the slow and humiliating walk to the bus stop to catch the first of two busses it would take to get back home.

As the bus came into view, the rain began to fall. It was slow at first but by the time the bus had lurched its way forward through the congested traffic and into the heart of the city towards the depot, it was torrential. Having not taken into account the possibility of surrendering his car, Jerry only had a light jacket with him. It was soaked within moments of him getting off the bus. By the time he reached the stop for his second bus, he could feel the saturation on his shirt as the material began to cling to him. His once tidy hair now clung to his face as drips began cascading down his face. An uncomfortable fifteen minutes passed before the welcome sight of the bus came into view. It was warm on board as the bus was full and he hoped that the journey might give him chance to dry out a little. An elderly gentleman sat beside him as the bus left the stop and whilst he seemed vaguely familiar, Jerry was in no mood for conversation. At the same time, despite his discomfort due to his soaked attire, he was in no mood to go home yet either. Instead, the decision was made to pay a trip to an old bar in the centre of town. It was a good twenty-minute walk from home but it was as close as the bus would get him to home anyway and his desired destination was only a stone's throw from the bus stop.

He had not been in there for about a year or so. He and Moira used to go in quite frequently for a drink, to socialise, even the odd game of pool from time to time with friends. The thought of going back in there now was a little daunting after such a long time away and he knew he would have to perhaps explain his absence to the regulars who had got used to seeing him and Moira in there. He could not have predicted the work commitments and relationship issues between him and Moira at the time that would have stopped him visit regularly. Still, in spite of the teasing he felt he would have to endure, the idea of going in there was beginning to lift his spirits slightly. He spent the remaining thirty minutes of the journey reminiscing, thinking of all the regular people they used to see in there, hoping they might still frequent the establishment as they once did. He remembered a particular barmaid that he used to know and flirt with every chance he got and hoped she still worked there too. With things between him and Moira the way they were, he felt like a degree of flirting would be both enjoyable and justified.

He got off the bus and with a quick check in his wallet, made a detour towards the bank first. The rain had eased and although not dry, the journey had warmed him up a little. His coat would have plenty of opportunity to dry for an hour so over a chair in the bar or perhaps up against a nice warm radiator.

Cash in hand, he strode with purpose and renewed enthusiasm towards the pool bar. It was five past twelve so he knew they would have just about opened up. Turning the corner, he immediately spotted the large neon lights which extended from just above the modest wooden door entrance, right the way to the top of the two-storey building. During hours of darkness when the bar was open, this huge neon sign would be lit with blue and green and could be seen for almost a mile up the road. However now, it was off and only a now open sign pinned on the outer door was the only indication that customers were free to enter. With a deep exhale, he pushed the door open and walked in. A second door confronted him, even less well maintained than the outer door, which led into the pool room. He used to sit in there when he and Moira went in, so it seemed like a good place to sit this time and enjoy a few drinks.

Throwing his coat over a random chair, he acquired a bar stool and sat down. The place had not changed much. Everything was more or less where it was when he last came in. From the green tiled walls, right down to the fading flower patterned, heavily scuffed carpets, everywhere he looked brought the memories flooding back.

"I just hope the beer is still good." He said out loud, not expecting to be heard in what appeared to be an empty room at the moment.

"The best in town." Came the reply.

A female appeared from the other side of the bar. A woman in her mid- forties, dressed in a plain white top and blonde wavy shoulder-length hair who Jerry recognised as the girl he was thinking of earlier. The flirty bar maid he had always had a thing for. They recognised each other instantly.

"Goodness me." She said. revelling back in shock. "Jerry Maher. Where on earth have you been these past twelve months?"

"Busy with work. Out in Africa mainly." He replied apologetically.

Sensing his guilty tone, she paused for a second before replying.

"Well, it's great to see you Jerry. I hope this means you and your lovely wife Marcy will maybe start to come in again like you used to. What can I get you?" She asked, reaching for a glass from beneath the bar, not taking her eyes off him as she provocatively leant forward.

Jerry returned her flirtatious look with a smile, not bothering to correct her mistake with his wife's name but instead making the most of the view of the bar maids cleavage which she had purposely flaunted.

"You haven't changed a bit love." Jerry complimented." Let's start with a double Jack Daniels and coke and go from there shall we?" He added.

The minutes soon turned into hours, the doubles into trebles and the place began to slowly fill with regulars, only some of which Jerry recognised. It did not stop him striking up a series of conversations about anything that crossed his mind and it was not long before he was sure he had told everyone in the entire bar that he had been fired earlier that day, almost as if he was proud of it. Jerry continued to drink and play pool well into the early evening. It was only when he seemed unable to grasp the glass and his lack of co-ordination resulted in a couple of minor accidents such as the breaking of a stool as he attempted to perch himself on it, that the bar staff decided it might be best he left for home, encouraging the idea by refusing to serve him any more drinks.

"Are you okay getting home darling"? Asked his flirty bar maid friend from earlier, who had stopped behind for a couple of drinks after finishing her shift.

Jerry tried to answer but his words would not come out right, instead manifesting themselves as a strange series of blended illegible sounds, not too unlike a record being played on the wrong speed. She figured there was no way he would make it home, if indeed he knew where home was in his present state. Hailing a taxi with a shrill voice at the curb-side, she put her arm round him and helped him like an invalid into the cab then climbed in after him. Jerry did not quite know what was happening but was in no fit state to put up any degree of resistance. Instead he lay there in the taxi, taking up the majority of the back seat with his head flopped against the door, with his barmaid friend sat squeezed in next to him.

They reached their destination. A little flat on the outskirts of town. Then, after paying the driver, she leaned over and gave Jerry a few gentle face slaps to wake him up as best she could. With a delayed response and eyes almost shut at this point, Jerry sleepwalked his way up a small driveway, led by hand by his female friend into her flat. Once inside, she helped him to move towards the sofa and nudged him backward, so he slumped onto it. The sudden comfort of something soft behind his head to support it meant he was out like a light. With a sigh of resigned disappointment, she reached for a large throw from over the back of the sofa and laid it over him gently as his sleep grew deeper and his breathing grew louder. From her sigh and the way she had looked at him all day, she might have been hoping the end of the night might have turned out a little differently, hence her reason for staying behind to wait for Jerry. However now, it was pretty much evident that any chance of a sexual encounter with her estranged married friend, was out of the question. With that, somewhat under the influence of intoxication herself, she staggered across the living room to her bedroom, closing the door behind her and fell fully clothed onto the bed.

Jerry woke to the smell of burnt toast. Peeling the cover down from round his neck, he looked down at his shirt. It was untucked, creased and now somewhat stained with something he could only guess could be alcohol of some sort. He gave a repulsed look as he inhaled his own scent, then nearly heaved as he tested his own breath by licking then smelling the back of his hand. He was alone in the room but did notice that through a crack in the bedroom door, one single bear arm drooped over the edge of a mattress, the rest of the body hidden under mismatched covers. He began to piece together the events of the previous evening and as he focussed on a picture on the wall, it quickly became clear where he was, and who had brought him there. He looked back in the bedroom. Not a single movement. He contemplated his next move for a moment, thankful that he could think reasonably clearly after last night's drinking. He decided that he should return home and shower and change first of all. After that, if he still felt fresh enough, maybe head back down town to the pool bar to say thanks for a great night and possibly apologise for anything he might have done that might have been a little out of sorts.

He quietly dressed and made himself look as presentable as possible for the journey home. He quickly scribbled a short note on a small fridge-mounted notepad which simply read

'Nicola. Thanks for last night. Jerry x'

Then he quietly exited the flat and closed the door carefully behind him. It was good to be out in the fresh air and it seemed to clear his head within moments. With the vivid memory of an enjoyable evening now at the forefront of his mind, the rest of the previous day's events had been pretty much forgotten. He knew he would have to deal with the aftermath of being sacked and any repercussions it might bring about, but not now, not yet. For the next few days, his new objective was to relax, take some time to himself and enjoy a bit of a social life again. Maybe even he and Moira could grow close again by spending more time together.

As it turned out, when he got home, a message on the answering machine had been left for him by Moira. He pressed play as he began to take off his dirty clothes, throwing them in the laundry basket one by one.

"Jerry." The message began." With everything that has happened with Ebony recently, as well as us two having our problems, I have decided to extend our holiday and take Ebony to my parents' house for the week. Maybe we can talk about things when I get back. See you soon."

Jerry paused as he listened, trying to pick up on Moira's tone. It was pretty much emotionless. It neither indicated anything positive nor negative might come of it. Then his mind switched. He remembered they were due back today. His only reason for deliberating whether or not to go out again down to the pool bar was because they were coming home. Now they weren't, there was nothing stopping him. He had all night. No. He had all week to himself to do as he pleased. With that in mind, he quickly showered, changed and dressed into something more comfortable and casual and headed out again. He had been told there was to be a band on later that night. That was a new feature on a Friday night. Maybe he might stick around for that too

Upon entering the bar again, this time a little later in the day than he had done the day previous, he noticed a couple of other regulars from past times. Quickly getting reacquainted, they were soon in the swings of drinking and numerous rounds of pool, some of which were played for winnings of up to 50 dollars each. Jerry enjoyed pool and when sober was quite competitive. As a second day of binge drinking began to take hold, he began to win less and have to pay out more. Only the re-emergence of Nicola on the bar for the evening managed to deter him from losing an absolute fortune at the table. He was keen to thank her for her help and hospitality and quickly made his way over to the bar to buy her a drink. As the night unfolded and the band came, played, then went, the two of them exchanged constant glances. With her shift ended, he found himself once again in a taxi with her, heading back to her flat. This time however the night unfolded slightly differently as Nicola's hopes for the previous night were well and truly turned into reality.

Chapter 9

Two Years Later

t was approaching the end of the summer break. Ebony wasn't looking forward to enrolling into college, but the time had come regardless. She had just spent a very relaxing week with her mum at her grandparent's house and did not want to leave. The only person who spoilt Ebony more than her mum was her grandparents, particularly over the last two years which had been tough. First had come her near-death experience which for Ebony, was something she seemed to keep re-living through her dreams even now. Then there was the separation of her mother and Father a short time after. She didn't really have a very close bond with her dad, but his presence was still missed at times. Moira on the other hand, was glad to be shut of Jerry and rebuild a new life for them. Had it not been for a job offer she couldn't turn down at home, she was certain the two of them would have moved out here to be a lot closer to Moira's parents. Jerry had been reduced to a worthless alcoholic dead-beat living in a small bed-sit above a launderette in town so the further away from Ebony he was, the better it was for the both of them in her eyes. They had not parted on good terms at all and heated arguments had become commonplace until Moira had enough and told him to leave and never return.

John had offered to drive them home. It was a good two to three-hour journey across state and he wasn't one to put his foot down at any point in his vintage Cadillac. Ebony passed the time reading and playing on her phone whilst Moira and her father enjoyed a little sing song to the varied songs played on the radio, itself a very old-fashioned looking accessory.

There were no digital read outs or auto tuning buttons. There wasn't even a cassette player. Just two dials and a needle to indicate the frequency it was tuned into. That was the way John loved it. Old fashioned and simplistic. That's why he loved driving his beloved car and was happy for the excuse to drive them home. Sadly, the weather was not quite good enough to have the top down and 'drive free' as John called it.

In the distance, the tall buildings of the city eventually came into view. As they grew close, John turned off the main interstate to take one of the more minor roads towards the suburbs. He did not like driving in the city centre anyway and so was happy Moira had at least bought the house on the outskirts of the city. The area they were passing through became more residential now and some five kilometres from home, they drove past a newly built splendid looking series of buildings all closely knit and encompassed by tall blue railings. It seemed familiar.

"Is that the college Mum?" Asked Ebony, pointing out the window.

"That's it." Confirmed Moira with a sense of pride. "Supposed to be a fine institution so I've heard."

Ebony's anxiousness meant she did not quite share her mother's enthusiasm for the place. Instead, she just stared in awe at the magnitude of the place. It was so much bigger than she had been used to. The car soon lurched around another corner and on to the penultimate avenue before home. Feelings of familiarity sadly did not bring about any real sense of comfort for either of them. Instead, more of a resignation that the summer holidays were over and it was time to get back into a routine for both of them, Moira for work, Ebony for the start of college. They turned again, onto their own road this time, its tall trees hanging over wide grass verges that ran intermittently down the entirety of the street.

The car pulled into the driveway and came to a halt with a high pitch squeak. Ebony got out first, catching sight of the two twins playing over the road. Although slightly younger than Ebony, she found them fun to be with. The boy was cheeky and mischievous and had always made Ebony laugh. Despite his misdemeanours, he had the innocent looks along with the puppy dog eyes that just made people want to grab hold of him and hug him rather than chastise him. His sister was very much the opposite in character. Very much the goody two shoes of the family. At age 8, she had the maturity of an eighteen-year-old so when Ebony had run out of energy chasing around after Jack, she would sit down and maybe read a book or do some drawing with Jack's sister, Amy.

The whole family were sitting out on the front lawn, where Ebony couldn't help but notice the presence of a large inflatable paddling pool. Jack was sat in it, wildly thrashing about in the water, very much in his element. Amy was sat nearby on the grass with what looked like a collection of imitation kitchen accessories with her. She played happily, surrounded by her collection of dolls throwing her own rendition of a tea party. Everything seemed relaxed and fun and Ebony thought it might be a good idea to join them.

"Can I go over and play at Jack and Amy's a while mum?"

Moira looked over the road to see the fun they were having for herself. She wished she could join them but there was too much to do at home. There was no reason to prevent Ebony from a final last few hours of enjoyment before it was time to turn in though. Like the typical teenager, she would only get under Moira's feet while she was sorting things out anyway.

"Sure. But just an hour or so ok?" Moira replied.

"Okay mum." Came the reply, barely audible as she began skipping down the pathway down to the roadside.

"Ebony?" Moira shouted after her.

Ebony turned.

"Aren't you forgetting something?" Moira asked, hinting with a brief gesture towards her grandad, still sat in his car.

She quickly came back up the pathway to wear his car was parked. Leaning in to the driver side window, she kissed John quickly on his cheek.

"Love you gramps. See you soon."

By the time he had chance to reply, she had vanished. John smiled, shaking his head slightly. He turned to Moira who was unloading the last bag from the back seat of the car.

"That girl. She's growing up so fast love. Be sure to let me know how she goes on at college tomorrow." He insisted.

"Will do dad." She shouted as he wound up his window in preparation for leaving. Moira stood on the porch to wave him off as the car slowly rolled back down the driveway. As he backed out onto the avenue again, John sounded the horn at Ebony who was already making herself at home on the lawn opposite, joining in with Amy's little tea party. Ebony waved at her Grandad as he moved off silently into the distance.

Two hours passed and the daylight began to fade. A light breeze had picked up which forced Jack out of the pool. He shivered slightly and went to sit on his mum's knee who was sat on a deckchair by the door. She wrapped a huge towel round him to dry him off, simultaneously cradling him in her arms. As if on cue, her husband stood and began to deflate and empty the pool. As Amy tidied her things away, Moira appeared again, walking over to Ebony to summon her inside for something to eat and settle down for the evening.

"Hello Moira." Greeted Jack's mother. "How was your holiday?"

The two of them exchanged a friendly hug.

"It was just what we needed to be honest." Replied Moira.

"Fancy a beer before you go back?" Jack's mother asked, pointing to a cool box full of bottles.

"No thanks Pam. I'd best get Ebony back and settled. Big day tomorrow for her. Plus, I'm back at work." She added regretfully.

She turned to Ebony.

"You ready sweetheart?" She asked with a smile.

Ebony stood and said goodbye to Amy, who stood also to give Ebony a hug. Ebony returned the gesture, wrapping her arms around Amy's small frame.

"Ow" Amy exclaimed. "Not too tight."

Ebony loosened her grip immediately, offering Amy a heart felt apology as she did so. Amy didn't reply. Instead, she retreated quickly to where her mother stood with Moira with a slightly fearful look towards Ebony and held her mother around her chest. Ebony suddenly felt wracked with guilt,

"Don't worry about it Ebony." Insisted Sue. "She gets a little grouchy when it's time to come in."

Ebony gave a weak smile. She began to shake her left arm slightly as a slight feeling of numbness took hold. It was something she had been told to expect from time to time by Dr Bush and guessed that was the reason she had squeezed Amy a little harder than she thought she had. Despite the numbness, it seemed she didn't know her own strength at times.

By the time they had made their way back over the road, the feeling of numbness had died off and with a nice tea to hand soon afterwards, the incident with Amy was all but forgotten. They settled down on the couch together watching television until they both began to yawn.

"Time to turn in I think sweetheart?" Suggested Moira.

"I guess." Came the reluctant reply.

Ebony lethargically got up from the comfort of the sofa and followed her mum upstairs, turning out the light to the hallway on the way up. Ebony made her way into her bedroom. Her covers had already been pulled back and her pyjamas lay neatly on her pillow. In true teenage fashion, she threw her clothes for that day into a pile at the bottom of the bed before reaching for her pyjamas and putting them on. She then climbed into bed, placed her glasses on the bedside table and switched off the light. The door was slightly ajar and Moira peered in on her way back from the bathroom.

"Sweet dreams" Moira whispered.

That night, Ebony's dreams were to be anything but sweet. Instead, the most vivid and graphic images haunted her nightmares to an extent that they had not done previously. She had only really suffered flashbacks to date, which she didn't really have time to make any sense of. The flashbacks and flickering images were always accompanied by a low eerie whispering sound, as if somebody was trying to communicate something to her. This time however, her sub-conscious was in overdrive, allowing Ebony to see things with much more clarity than in the past.

She found herself sat on her neighbour's lawn again, where she had played alongside Amy. It was night time and there was not a sound to be heard. The silence was soon to be broken. Out of the corner of her eye from across the lawn, she caught sight of something near the porch. Her eyes widened with curiosity. Whatever it was emitted a bright green glow. It was both as small and bright as a laser beam and it shone right at her. She lifted her right arm up, opening her palm to protect her eyes from the piercing light. She allowed herself a sporadic look between her spread fingers, only to see that the single light she had seen had now separated into two bright lights. They were side by side and now slightly larger than before. Large enough to notice that they had begun to take shape, an oval shape. An oval shape which came to a sharp joining point at both the top and the bottom. They resembled a set of eyes, very demonic in appearance. A set of eyes that were watching her relentlessly. Whatever possessed those eyes was moving closer to her yet still, the eyes were the only thing she could still see in the darkness. Then came the audible sound again which she had become accustomed to hearing in her dreams. It was almost recognisable now as a single word repeated slowly over and over, albeit a word she had never heard before. Through the increasing feelings of fear, she still tried to focus on the sound in an attempt to finally identify it. It was the loudest it had ever been so this was her best chance yet.

The two eyes which peered at her now had ceased to grow in size. Whatever was growing nearer to her seemed to have temporarily stopped. Instead of moving in a forward motion, it now began to rise up and tower over her, only stopping when it got to about three feet above her head. After a moment of silence, she heard that same word again. Whatever was in front of her was speaking to her. Yet before she could fully understand what she had heard the noise changed to a loud hiss. Ebony sat there, defenceless, frozen in fear and sweating profusely as whatever this thing was lunged towards her with stealth and speed. As what appeared to be an open mouth, which seemed large enough to swallow her whole, was about to engulf her, she closed her eyes, preparing herself for what might happen, her last image being that of two dripping needle-like fangs, some six inches in length bearing down on her. She waited for the impact. None came. No pain at all. She dared to open one eye; her body still tense with fear. She was alone again. The laser- like eyes had disappeared. Her mind switched back to the voice she heard and as she repeated it over and over again in her head trying to make sense of it, she heard a small child's voice from next to her.

"Ow. Not so tight." The voice said.

Ebony looked down to her left side, recognising the voice instantly.

She screamed loudly as she looked down at the young girl's head which her left arm had been wrapped around. Though the girl's eyes were open, they were lifeless, rolled back to the top of her sockets. From the corner of each eye, streams of blood trickled down her cheeks. The same was true of her nose as blood began to run from each nostril and over Ebony's hand that still tightly gripped her head. She screamed a second time, letting go of the girl's lifeless body, her skull crushed under the pressure of Ebony's vice-like grip. Ebony got to her feet in order to flea the scene as quickly as she could. She immediately fell, having tripped over something. After rubbing her ankle, she slowly rose to her feet and looked down at what it was she had tripped over. At her feet lay the fragments of a small bulb, shattered into numerous pieces. She quickly realised that, along with the other things now strewn across the floor, it was her bedside lamp. She must have knocked it off during her nightmare at some point as now it lay well and truly broken on her bedroom floor. An unfortunate reminder of her night tremors.

The rest of the night passed by without incident, meaning Ebony managed to get some degree of un-interrupted sleep. As her alarm sounded on her phone, she reached over to de-activate it in order to maybe grab an extra fifteen minutes or so. As he de-activated it, Moira passed by her bedroom door and noticing her movements, entered to rouse her.

"Up we get lazy bones." She joked, gently nudging Ebony on her shoulder as she leant down to pick up her pyjama top, discarded during the night and still slightly damp from sweat. She looked at Ebony, whose face remained buried in her pillow.

"Another night tremor?" She asked with concern.

Ebony nodded without even lifting up her head.

"You know we can see someone if they are getting too bad? "She suggested, expecting Ebony to once again decline the offer, as she had so many times before.

Ebony shook her head. This time with her face emerging from the pillow

"No. I'll be ok." She replied with optimism

Ebony got out of bed and headed off to the bathroom to shower, leaving her mother to watch her wonder off down the landing, a concerned look on her face. She had been very keen for Ebony to take up the offer of professional help to help her sleep better at night. She did not want to push it on her too forcefully though as she knew this was Ebony's own way of trying to simply get on with her life. She had done remarkably well so far, and her nightmares were about the only reminder of the events of two years ago. The separation from her husband had not been an easy one either so Moira could only assume this was also a contributory factor to Ebony's state of mind too.

By the time she was ready for college, there was little chance for breakfast. They both grabbed a cereal bar from the cupboard and made their way to the car. The plan was to come into college with Ebony to go through the enrolment procedure, sign the necessary forms, see she was settled and knew where to go, then disappear off to work herself. On the car journey, neither of them spoke a word, each of them contemplating what lay ahead that day.

The two of them marched into the college. It was as impressive from the outside as it was inside. Huge stair-like structures allowed access to long corridors. Each corridor seemed to house a series of varied shaped windows and a series of doors, all identical in colour and in what seemed to be exact symmetry to the opposing side of the corridor It was like a maze. Looking up at all the levels and staircases, Ebony half expected them to start moving left and right, similar to what they do at Hogwarts. Looking back down to the ground level and it was all so open planned that it made the place appear even larger than it actually was. A huge reception desk stretched right the way along the back wall with various points of enquiry dependant on their purpose. They took their place in the line behind a small group of parents, stood with their sons or daughters at the section of the desk marked 'ADMISSIONS'.

Upon reaching the front of the queue, they presented the clerk with Ebony's registration documents, then waited nervously a few moments while they were taken away and checked through and eventually, handed back. After a moment of tapping away on her computer, the desk clerk looked up at them.

"Thank you, Mrs Maher and Ebony." She then turned her attention to Ebony alone. "Your form room is 2A on the second floor. If you would like to just go on up and your class tutor will be there to meet you. Welcome to Clinton State College." With that she bowed her head and began filling in some more details on a form which sat in front of her. It was plainly obvious she had nothing more to inform them of, so in order not to hold up the queue forming behind them, they stepped aside, Ebony throwing her bag over her shoulder in the process.

Moira turned to Ebony to give her some last words of encouragement before leaving. Ebony sported a brave smile but the nerves still shone through.

"Enjoy your day sweetheart. I'm sure you will be fine once you have settled in a little and made a few friends within your class."

She kissed Ebony lightly on the cheek, then set off out the door, leaving Ebony to find her designated classroom.

After ten minutes ceaseless searching she found the door marked 2A. As she entered, she noticed the classroom was almost full of students who had arrived before her. Like with the few that had entered before her, the noise in the classroom dropped as she entered. This was what she expected as her new class mates began to weigh her up. She could feel every pair of eyes staring at her. She made her way to the nearest desk she could find. A seat on the third row and right in the middle of the classroom. She had hoped to find a window seat to at least offer her a small sense of freedom and whilst she was not in any way claustrophobic nor xenophobic, her present location made her feel anxious and very defensive, surrounded on all four sides by strangers. For a moment, she just wanted to run. Run out the door and not come back. She didn't. Instead she sat there as if frozen in time, barely daring to make a move in case it attracted undue attention. The delay of the teacher entering the room had not helped and so when he did finally enter moments later and the attention had become centred on him, she slowly began to settle, her heart rate returning to a normal pace. Unaware that her nervous disposition had attracted the attention from a small group of girls sat in the corner behind her, she listened intently to the tutor as he ran through a few fundamentals about college life and what the pupils should expect from their time there.

Ebony thought the time to go home would never come. What should have been an exciting day had just turned out to be a tedious one. A series of formalities every freshman has to undertake such as a guided tour of the building, led like tourists from corridor to corridor, stairwell to stairwell. There was an odd hello or exchange of welcoming smiles from a few of her classmates but nothing she might consider to be a friendship forming. At least today, she did not have to put up with the bus journey home. With it being her first day, Moira had been given special permission to pick her up. Her car was a welcome sight in the car park, and it forced a smile from Ebony. Her first of the day. As she walked towards the car, she heard a small harmony of female voices call to her in unison.

"Bye Ebony." They said, culminating in a series of giggles that implied that they were mocking her in some way.

She turned around to see who it was. It was the small group of girls from the back of the form room. They had constantly giggled and sniggered throughout the address given to her earlier by the tutor and she now began to believe that maybe all that might have been directed towards her also. Not wanting to appear rude, she waved softly in their direction, then got into the car. Spotting her seemingly positive interaction, Moira smiled as Ebony looked over at her.

"Some new friends sweetheart?" Moira enquired with enthusiasm.

"I'm not sure yet." Came Ebony's reply. "I hope so."

"Are you sure you are going to be ok with getting the bus to and from school from tomorrow morning?" Moira asked, negotiating her way out of the car park.

"Yeah. Fine." Ebony replied briefly, distracted by people watching as hordes of students scurried out of the main gates.

In truth. She was not looking forward to the prospect at all. A hundred or so people packed in like sardines for twenty minutes and open to any and all pranks that might happen whilst they uncomfortably invaded each other's personal space twice a day was not her idea of a fun time. If she had felt uncomfortable and irritated before whilst in the classroom, she began to expect more of the same in the morning on the ride to school. How right she was.

That night, Ebony's dreams came back to haunt her once again. Unlike the night before however, they were not so graphic and certainly not as frightening. Rather than images, she was being plagued by voices, one of which kept calling her name softly as if the sound were caught on a breeze. The other voice was the one she had heard many times before. The one that the demonic green- eyed creature had whispered to her the previous night. The same word that she had to date, not been able to decipher. This time however, the word seemed clearer and though it was not the voice of a human, for the first time, what was said was recognisable.

She woke briefly to reach for her phone in order to note the word down before she forgot it. She then saved it with the intent on looking into its meaning when she got to college later that morning. There was a good library there and plenty of opportunity to do a little bit of research. With a sigh of satisfaction, a feeling of peace and contentment came over her and she lay back down on her pillow and quickly fell back into a deep sleep, not to be disturbed again until the alarm on her phone woke her for college once again.

Chapter 10

t had been two months Since Shesha had finally retired from his position at the reserve. His mornings now consisted of long solitary walks and pursuing his hobbies as anyone recently retired would do. Above all, it gave him chance to spend more time with those he cared for, those he called his family. They were often asleep during the daytime as for the majority of the time, they worked tirelessly during night time hours so the mornings were very quiet, leaving Shesha to do his own thing.

As a routine, he would often wake and immediately adjourn to the kitchen in order to make himself a cup of refreshing tea. One of his kitchen cupboards was always fully stocked with a plethora of herbs and spices, most of which were perhaps unknown to western civilisation and were not easily obtainable from your local supermarket. Some had to be ordered from miles away and took weeks to arrive. However, there was a small shop nearby that stocked a few of his favourite ingredients. Though he did not go in there regularly himself, he was well known by the shop owner and it was commonplace to see him send one of his two daughters in there at least once a week to collect his order. The shopkeeper would even have his oversees orders delivered to his shop, so everything was to be kept together. He seemed a kind old man and very willing to please, according to Shesha's daughters who ran the errands for him.

Shesha turned on the radio in the kitchen, ready to lower the volume if needed on account of his girls who may have used it before him to listen to music the night before. He had almost been deafened on a few mornings with the level of decibels that blasted out from the radio as he turned it on. It was quite surprising how the music had never woken him up.

The radio switched to the news and Shesha began to listen to the reporter with interest. Turning it up slightly, he sat at his small kitchen table with his freshly made concoction and listened intently.

"We are here at Booker Rock Reserve where the third in an alarming series of animal abductions has taken place. The abduction was believed to have taken place late last night from one of the buildings on the reserve which housed a series of the most venomous animal species on the planet."

The newscaster went on as Shesha took a sip of his tea, interested but undeterred by the nature of the broadcast.

"Both police and staff here at the reserve are baffled as to how the snake, an almost two-metre-long King Brown snake, was able to be smuggled without detection past park security which has remained tight since the two previous abductions last month. Park executives have issued a statement and offered a reward to anyone with any knowledge or information leading to the safe return of the three snakes. Experts are warning, should you encounter any of the three snakes missing from the reserve that they are extremely dangerous and not to go near them. Should you see them, please call the reserve on the dedicated number listed on the website, or the local sheriff's office."

Shesha stood, a blank look on his face. There was no panic, no air of concern that these snakes were among those that he had worked with for years and cared for on a day to day basis. That time in his life had passed after all and it was well within his rights to consider this to be someone else's problem now. All he could do was send well wishes to his former employers and have faith that wherever the three snakes were, they were in good health.

He moved over to the sink and rinsed his cup, leaving it on the side for later. He was meticulous in the fact that he always used the same cup in the morning and afternoon for his tea. The tea always tasted better to him in that one particular cup. He then reached up into the cupboard for a file which appeared full of paper cuttings and similar articles which he had saved and took it back to the table. He opened the file began leafing through it. The first few pages were dedicated to his time back home in India when he qualified to become a chemist and a professor. Among the pictures of him with tutors and friends was a protective sleeve containing several certificates of his achievements. Then he came to a section of the folder which he had lay out like a scrapbook. A series of paper cuttings which denoted the rise in popularity of his show at the Booker Rock Reserve. One had a photograph of him with the owners holding a huge certificate awarded to the park for a best live show at a public event. Another was a clipping which gave details of his first ever scheduled show. Whilst he enjoyed reminiscing for a moment, his focus was on the articles he had collected more recently. Those had put to the back of the file. As he smiled, he pulled out one particular cutting and began to read over it again as he unfolded it carefully, smiling with admiration as he touched each word as he spoke it aloud;

The article was dated back two years ago. It concerned a young girl who had survived a terrible encounter with a venomous snake in Africa. A picture of her innocent face filled the top half of the article with the detailed report below. He read it slowly and then placed it back in his folder, but not before stroking his nimble fingers over the picture of her face.

"Poor girl." He said to himself looking into her sorrowful eyes, his tone full of sympathy.

He closed the folder and placed the file back from where it had come from and then set about his regular household chores, all done slowly but very methodically and with attention to detail. After an hour or so, it was time for a break. There were others in the house who could take over later and whilst still in good health, Shesha grew tired quickly. After making himself a second cup of tea, again using his large blend of herbs, he retired to the living room and to his favourite arm chair by the window where he began to read his book. He quickly became absorbed by its content and did not even look up until he heard the sound of voices from down the corridor. It had been some three hours of reading and someone else in the house was finally awake.

After a few moments, there was a creaking sound in the corridor. Someone was indeed up and heading towards the living room. Whoever it was slowly opened the door and entered quietly, surveying the room to see if anyone was there. As Shesha spotted her from his armchair, he lowered his book and greeted her smiling.

"How are you Ebony?" He asked.

"Ebony?" the girl asked, looking a touch confused. "Who is Ebony uncle?"

Shesha shook his head in realisation of his error.

"Sorry Coral." Shesha said with red faced embarrassment. I trust you are well rested?"

"I am Uncle. Thank You" She replied walking closer towards him in his chair and extending her arms to him to embrace him lightly, yet lovingly as he sat.

"Has your sister awoken yet?" He asked.

"I believe so." Came the reply.

Shesha watched as Coral, or Caroline as she was officially known, moved into the kitchen and headed towards the refrigerator.

"It's on the third shelf down." Shesha called out to her, predicting exactly what she was looking for.

She looked at him with an infectious smile, pushing her long blond hair behind her ears. He had looked after Caroline for four years now and had seen her blossom into a beautiful, yet feisty at times, teenager. She groomed herself immaculately and bore the appearance of a real-life model. At eighteen years of age, she was also quite independent. Shesha had been quick in giving them their respective new names shortly after getting to know them. He had felt it brought them closer far quicker and had helped them gain a certain degree of closure on events of their troubled past. Coral was also very loyal and with Shesha to thank for her care and guidance over the past four years, attending to his needs was still her priority and was at his side ready for whenever her help or company was requested. She had had a tough few years before meeting Shesha, especially due to the traumatic death of her parents five years ago.

She pulled out a large carton from the fridge and unscrewed the lid. Grabbing a nearby glass which Shesha had left out for her, she poured the slightly viscous lemon-coloured liquid into the glass until it was nearly full. Placing the carton on the side with the likelihood of wanting more, she began drinking from the glass. Evidently thirsty and enjoying the refreshing taste, she consumed its entire contents in seconds.

She looked towards Shesha who stared back smiling at her.

"Have some more by all means. I have made plenty." He said, returning to his book for a moment to finish off the page.

Coral reached for the carton again and poured herself another glassful. She began gulping it down again, a little slower this time, taking a moment to catch her breath and savour the taste a little more. Finishing off the final mouthful from the glass, she placed it by the sink and returned the remainder to the fridge from once it came in order to keep it cool. The drink had been nothing like she had ever drank before and though she didn't really like it at first, it had grown on her to the point where she now drank little else. It gave her the energy she needed for her regular gym sessions as the gym was the one place she could not seem to keep away from. Shesha was constantly making new batches for her and her sister claiming it contained essential medicinal ingredients to keep them both healthy and strong. He even promised one day that he would teach them the secret to making it as it was quite a long and complicated process and a family secret. He had also told them it was an ancient recipe and that if the recipe and method were to be given out to the wrong person and consumed incorrectly, not only would it not have any beneficial qualities, but it could cause more harm than good. It was to be treated like a medicine, but a medicine to be consumed in far larger quantities than an average over the counter cough mixture. So, for that reason, the girls just left him to it, never really enquiring as to its contents or how to put it together. It was never in short supply and that is all that bothered them.

It was at that moment that the other sister entered the room. She was equally as beautiful in appearance to Coral but in a much plainer sense. Unlike Caroline, Diamond sported much shorter hair and black in colour. She was very much similar in stature to Coral and in many ways shared the same personality traits, particular when it came to her devotion to Shesha. She too would do anything he asked of her. The one thing she did possess was a winning smile, able to win anybody over with the slightest grin. Being slightly younger than Coral however, she did seem a little more dependant towards Shesha than her older sister. Her kind nature meant she was much more vulnerable, perhaps even naive at times, to influences from the outside world and tended to spend much more time with Shesha than her older sister did, seeking his guidance at regular intervals. She was however fiercely loyal and defensive towards those she loved and had an aggressive streak which she would display to those who hurt or offended those close to her.

"Get yourself some juice before you do anything else please Diamond." Shesha instructed, noticing her heading towards the cupboard, undoubtedly in search of some breakfast. She had far the better appetite of the two of them. Hearing his request, she quickly diverted her attention to the fridge, grabbing the same glass Coral had used beforehand. She opened the fridge door and after a quick scan of the contents, recognised the large container of liquid she was searching for.

Like her sister, she greedily filled the glass and poured it down her gullet under Shesha's watchful eye.

"Not so fast Diamond. It's true quality is in the taste also. Savour it."

Diamond's final gulp was taken a little slower. Placing the glass down, she smiled then gave a small belch. She looked apologetically at Shesha who offered her a discontented look.

"I apologise Uncle."

"You will enjoy little in life Diamond if, by your own doing, it is over with too quickly" Shesha retorted calmly.

Diamond turned to Shesha, nodding in appreciation at his words of wisdom.

"What do you have planned for today Uncle?" Coral asked, re-emerging from the bathroom.

"I need some supplies later if you would be so kind as to both go and get them for me?" Shesha asked humbly. "I have something I must put together later and the rest of the family needs feeding before you two have dinner later on this evening."

"Yes of course Uncle." They both replied, their voices almost an echo of each other.

"Then we must sit down and talk about something very important. I have foreseen there may be somebody who requires our help and guidance. Guidance of a similar sort that was given to you some time ago. Should that be that case, I ask for assurance that you two will do your part to help me complete this task and welcome her into our lives."

He looked at them both sternly, waiting for an answer.

"Of course, Uncle" Coral replied.

"We will help any way we can to welcome this person as you welcomed us" Diamond reinforced with enthusiasm.

"I am glad Diamond as there is something I need you to do for me first of all."

With that, Diamond attentively sat down in front of Shesha whilst Coral made herself scarce by going for her regular afternoon gym session Diamond's blue eyes looked right into his, nodding occasionally as he began to go into more detail regarding his wishes and instructions. When he had finished, she smiled from ear to ear and clasped her hands together in a controlled excitement at the responsibility she had been given, evidently keen to start straight away.

"That sounds wonderful Uncle." She exclaimed. You can never have enough really true friends."

She stood, leaned over to hug Shesha gently in appreciation for his faith in her, then proceeded to the kitchen to make some lunch before taking a rest on her bed once again.

Chapter 11

t was Sunday and Ebony was pleased not to be going to college. Friday night had brought about only sporadic periods of sleep, her head haunted by voices, some of which had become familiar in respect to her previous dreams. Some of them however, had never been heard before. One of these new voices, soft and quite high in pitch, seemed to come from a human rather than a reptile and seemed to be calling her name, as if beckoning towards her. It did not seem threatening towards her, yet it was unsettling and eerie in terms of its repetitive whisper.

It had become increasingly more difficult to get a good night's sleep now. She had found herself sat outside in her grandfather's favourite spot on the porch, wide awake in the middle of the night on several occasions whilst staying with her Grandparents the previous week. She felt the same then as she did now. Not only wide awake, but a very acute sense of her surroundings and with an inexplicable urge to search for something but she did not quite know what. What she did know is that she did not want to lie still in bed. She was far too restless for that. She glanced down at her phone to catch sight of the time. It was quarter past four in the morning. She slid out of bed and grabbed her dressing gown. Slowly sliding her feet one by one into her slippers, she crept out of the bedroom door, down the landing and down the stairs without so much as a whisper. Making her way through to the kitchen, she paused for a moment at the window to the back door. A soft rain could be heard and the drops of dew on the back lawn twinkled as they caught the light from the security lamp over the top of the door. Grabbing the key, she slowly, yet purposefully, pulled on the handle with just enough force for it to open. As it did so, she stepped out onto the flags, her senses heightened by both the drop-in temperature from the cool night air and the sounds and smells that lingered in the dark of night. A rustling in the undergrowth caught her attention. It was coming from under the bushes somewhere at the foot of the garden and she instinctively lowered her body down to a crouching position to get a better look. Without even realising, she was now on her knees on the edge of the grass, the rain soaking through her pyjamas. It did not phase her in the slightest. She just watched the movements from under the bushes, her eyes wide open, trying to spot the source. The rustling ceased for a moment, as though whatever it was had become aware they were being watched or stalked by a predator. Ebony was not fooled by its silence. She still detected its presence. She sensed it somehow and she felt a tingle in the roof of her mouth. Ebony then began to lower herself further to the ground and soon her pyjamas were soaked from her chest downwards with a mixture of already fallen rain which coated the grass surface and the torrential downpour which had ensued. It did not deter her from lying completely on the grass, head upright and resting her elbows on the lawn. Her chin was only a few inches from the surface so as to be at eye level with whatever creature lurked in the undergrowth. Using her fingers to grip the grass along with subtle side to side hip movements, she slid her way towards the back edge of the lawn. It was then that she got her first glimpse of what she had detected. A small rodent, similar to a possum quietly sat up against the fence. It was easily visible but still not within touching distance of Ebony. Ebony shifted to her left slightly, not taking her eyes off the creature, then edged slightly closer. Something in her head was telling her to reach out and grab it whilst she still had chance. Then, in the second in which she had to contemplate the option, the rodent vanished, burrowing its way through a small hole in between two fence panels where the wood had decayed and eroded over time.

All of a sudden, Ebony became fully aware of her environment again and her predicament. She was now dirty, wet, and also getting very cold. She also felt something else. As she got up slowly from the lawn and made her way back towards the door, a sense of frustration and anger crept over her. Nothing overwhelming, yet a real sense that she had missed out on an opportunity. With the thought going through her head of what she could possibly have done had she caught the creature; she closed and locked the back door again as quietly as she had opened it and proceeded to strip off all her soaked night attire. Throwing it directly in the wash, she crept naked back up the stairs toward her bedroom, grabbing a conveniently placed bath towel off the banister on the way. Feeling only slightly more at ease, she lay back on her bed, puffed her pillows up and grabbed her glasses in order to read from and play with her phone until the time came to get up for college.

With the onset of daylight, a degree of fatigue began to set in for Ebony. She really had become a night owl lately. Whilst this pattern of activity was fine for the weekends and holidays, it certainly was not going to be conducive to college life. She groaned in disapproval at her mother's calls from downstairs to get ready, only eventually doing so in order to stop her being asked every thirty seconds or so. By the time she had gotten ready and been practically forced out the front door, lunch money in hand, she had only ten minutes to make the walk to the school bus stop some four blocks away. The rainfall she had encountered earlier that morning now returned with a vengeance. Within moments, drops of rain began running down her face. She had her blazer on but that offered little protection. She began running for the bus and as she rounded the final corner, she was relieved to see it just pull up at her stop. She queued behind the two remaining students left outside in the rain to board. As she waited for her turn to get on, she glanced through the window to see just how packed the bus was. Whether deliberate or not, she noticed most of the senior students had taken up positions towards the rear of the bus with all the younger students from lower year groups crammed like sardines in the front section. One thing was for sure, there was no chance of a seat. Ebony's stop was the penultimate stop on the route, so the chances were that the bus was always going to be full by the time it reached her in the morning.

With the one consolation in mind that it was better than being rained upon any further, Ebony got on board and tried to free herself a bit of a spot in a small alcove behind the driver's cab. It wasn't comfortable at all, but she had in fairness, expected worse. Any feelings of content soon disappeared when some two hundred yards down the road, the bus pulled up for its final stop before school and a final group of around eight students attempted to force their way on board. With her personal space now well and truly invaded, Ebony began to feel increasingly more anxious with every second. The doors to the bus swished shut and it slowly crawled away from the stop with what seemed like one centimetre of space left on board. Ebony was now semi- crouched, firmly pressed up against the back of the driver's cab and almost pinned to it with two large school bags, worn very inconsiderately over the shoulders of two slightly older and taller female students in front of her. Her head began to pound with the noise levels on board. She longed to scream in a beg for silence and to have the freedom to use her arms so she could push the bags away from her face and chest. She felt well and truly cornered and somewhat threatened. This was not the best time for another bout of numbness to occur in her arm but that is exactly what was beginning to happen. Fortunately, whilst she was unable to use her right arm to help restore some feeling, she did have access to a small portion of a seat edge which she now used as an improvised scratching post since this time, a strange tingle or itching sensation could still be felt beyond the numbness. She rubbed it against the seat edge with all the strength she had under the circumstances until it began to hurt. Had she been able to look at her arm at this point, she would have been able to detect not only the nasty abrasion caused by the scratching which had removed at least one layer of skin on her forearm, but also, she would have realised that what lay below was a completely different type of skin surface to her normal one. Her sodden blazer and now very clammy shirt meant this had gone undetected for now.

The journey was unbearable, worse than any experience she had had in terms of overcrowding. As the doors mercifully swung open and the unfortunate soles who stood up against it were practically pushed out onto the sidewalk, it took every ounce of resistance Ebony had to swing out violently in order to create some room to move. Room to even breathe. She somehow resisted. Instead her exit from the bus instigated a need to run to somewhere much quitter. A huge tree sat in the gardens of the college and it offered long overhanging branches which Ebony figured might offer shelter whilst she composed herself for a short while. So it was then that whilst all the other students poured into college, Ebony simply rested against the thick trunk of the tree until she was the last student left outside. Then and only then, did she decide to slowly walk towards the main entrance, straightening her shirt and securing her tie in place as she did so. Her arm still stung slightly where she had rubbed it but she would have to wait for morning recess to attend to that.

The morning lessons seemed to pass with a blur. Ebony felt that she had not digested a single word or learnt a single thing in the last hour and a half. Thankfully the lessons were not practically based so she was able to just sit and draw little attention to herself whilst at her desk. At times she even nodded off for a few moments whilst the tutor harped on about this and that. Normally, she would have been far more attentive, but such was her need to catch up on her sleep, her mind would not focus on any verbal stimulus at all. The bell at the end of her second lesson was the only thing that had aroused her since she had walked into the building that morning. She had managed to keep her arm covered at least and now at last, she would have chance to examine it for herself. She quickly folded her books up and unceremoniously dropped them back into her bag. She waited for the melee to clear and then stood up from her seat and headed out the door onto the second-floor corridor. It was very chaotic, with herds of people coming towards her as she headed for the stairwell. She was fortunate enough that most did seem to stick to the correct side of the corridor so any collisions with other people seemed unlikely despite the numbers of students pacing about.

Having negotiated the stairs, she began to seek out the restrooms. Following the series of wall mounted signs, she was soon on the right trail and as she grew close, she caught the scent of disinfectant or similar cleaning products commonly associated with maintaining water closets. She entered the outer door to the toilet, glancing either way down the corridor as she did so in order to see if she was alone. For the moment at least, that seemed to be the case. She was pleased to see that the bathroom was both spacious and clean and large cubicles offered a good level of privacy. Instead of a cubicle however, she opted for the sink area. Above the sinks hung a series of shiny spotless large mirrors. Placing her bag down by her side, she slowly peeled off her blazer and began unbuttoning her cuff button in order to roll back her sleeve. As she rolled her sleeve back, she got her first look at her forearm.

It proved to be a very brief first look as noise quickly had her roll her sleeve back down again and she began to swill her face under the tap in order to exhibit non-suspicious behaviour to anyone who might be looking to enter. No one did. She waited a further few seconds and then unrolled her sleeve again. The scratch she now saw was long and looked inflamed and stretched along the backside of her forearm adjacent to her scar. She took hold of a small edge of a piece of skin which appeared to be loose. Thinking it might just flake off after a second, she began to gently pull on it. Rather than flaking, it was growing in size as it detached itself from her arm. A piece some six inches in length had been peeled off and it was completely intact. She rubbed her arm to remove the last few flakes of skin and gently rubbed her thumb across the new layer of skin which now showed beneath. Whilst it looked like normal human skin, its texture was now somewhat different. Her thumb detected very slight yet frequent ridges between small circle- like patterns of smooth and silky skin. It was almost like a scaly pattern she had uncovered. It was nothing like she had ever felt before, or indeed seen on a human appendage. She had no time to examine it any longer. Her apparent increased level of awareness now detected the faint vibrations of feet approaching the door to the bathroom. With that, a faint smell of perfume wafted up her nostrils. She rolled her sleeve down quickly as the door opened. Three girls walked in, giggling as they did so. Spotting Ebony putting her blazer back on, they slowly walked towards her. She recognised them as the three girls sat at the back of the classroom on her induction day. Whilst their smiles seemed welcoming, Ebony suddenly felt uncomfortable surrounded by the three of them. It was similar as to how she felt when she first entered the classroom with everybody watching her on her first day.

"Well hello there Bony." The largest of the three said as she stood right next to her. The others stood close behind, now laughing at the mocking and name calling which had begun.

"It's Ebony." She corrected timidly.

"OK Bony." The girl repeated. Then she stopped and put her fingers across her mouth like someone who had just realised they had just given away a secret of sorts. From behind her closed fingers however, it was still evident that she was taking great pleasure in her verbal bullying tactics. A mischievous almost evil smirk was very much evident from the up-turned corners of her mouth.

"I am Alexa and these two are my little groupies, Nat and Kim."

She briefly turned to them.

"Say hi to Bony girls." Instructed Alexa, not taking her eyes off Ebony.

"Hi Bony" Both girls said together in unison, their voices filled with a giddy sarcasm and laughter.

Alexa turned and smiled at the girls and then turned her attention back to Ebony. She seemed to tower above Ebony as she stepped even closer towards her. Not only was she taller but she was also in possession of a much fuller figure that did not seem befitting with her age. Her long wavy mousey brown hair which cascaded over her shoulders made her appearance seem even larger and Ebony now felt very much threatened. The pounding in her head returned, as did an overwhelming desire to retreat. She attempted to step away slightly but felt a firm hand on her shoulder from behind which stopped her in her tracks.

"Not so fast Bony. Me and the girls just want to help you settle in."

Ebony looked towards the girls. They nodded with false intent and enthusiasm.

"Now. We have Math this afternoon, right?" Alexa asked in a much friendlier tone.

Ebony nodded, conscious of the fact that Alexa's arm

which was around her shoulder now appeared to have hold of her with a much tighter grip.

"Well, the girls are just going to check that you have all you need for the lesson. We are good like that aren't we girls?"

She spun Ebony round to face the other girls, her arm still firmly around Ebony's shoulder. Meanwhile, the two girls had taken it upon themselves to pick up, open and now empty the entire contents of her bag out onto the bathroom floor. Ebony just stared, not daring to do or say anything. The thought went through her head that after her bag, the girls, along with Alexa might physically turn on her. Such was the case that her mind now began to conjure up any ideas about how she might go about defending herself.

"All here!" Nat announced as she tossed the bag on the floor again.

"Now perhaps a little personal grooming service. We need to look our best for class don't we Bony?" Kim asked as she fished around in her blazer pocket for something. She pulled out a cylindrical container and flipped off the top and then began applying it to her lips. After quickly rubbing them together, she offered it in Ebony's direction.

"I think this shade will suit you Bony" She said with a laugh. "I'm not very good applying make-up though am I girls?" She added.

"Terrible" Alexa replied, as she grabbed the back of Ebony's hair firmly, tilting her head up for Kim to apply the lipstick in any manner she saw fit.

Just then, the door swing open to disturb proceedings. Alexa quickly let go of Ebony who took a couple of welcome steps back from Alexa, her faced daubed in make-up.

Although the girl who entered only seemed as big as what Alexa was, she came across with a degree of authority and superiority in her demeanour towards the girls. She was definitely not intimidated by them and though shorter than all three of them in size, did not appear intimidated in the slightest. Seeing what was going on, she spoke up, addressing Alexa directly.

"I'm pretty sure you three have some better place to be during recess. Am I right Alexa?" She asked, giving the impression of her being a school prefect.

The girls didn't answer. Instead, they just quietly filed out of the bathroom one by one and away down the corridor, appearing slightly disgruntled at the disturbance, yet unwilling to confront the girl despite out numbering her. Alexa was the last to exit and offered the girl a cold stare as she brushed past her before catching up to her friends in the corridor.

With them gone, Ebony's apparent saviour looked back towards her, her blue eyes bathed in sympathy. Without speaking, she slowly walked towards Ebony, crouched beside her and began picking up her scattered belongings from off the floor. Ebony gazed at her and they exchanged a smile. The strangers smile was a warm one and indicated no malice which in turn, was enabling Ebony to slowly release the tension she felt moments earlier

"I am sorry that you had to go through that. It normally takes them three a little longer into the term to target a victim to bully." She explained, as she passed Ebony a handful of her pens.

"How do you know them?" Ebony asked, gratefully taking the pens from her.

"I was a target of hers last year. It did not last long though. The big girl, Alexa came here as a result of being kicked out of another college a couple of years ago. She is very good when it comes to bullying and intimidation and physically, she is quite strong. She is not too clever when it comes to learning though but you wouldn't be if you force people to do your homework for you. That's why she is back in first year again."

Ebony placed the last of her books back in her bag and stood up, mirrored by her friendly helper. Someone she immediately perceived to be a person she would like to get to know a little better.

"What's your name?" Ebony asked, extending out her hand in friendship. "I'm Ebony." She added.

She took Ebony's hand with affection and almost cradled it between her own two hands, both cold and yet very smooth to the touch. The gesture generated a warm feeling inside for Ebony and her smile grew with the sensation as she felt an immediate bond forming between them.

"It's so nice to meet you Ebony. What a beautiful name"

Ebony looked down slightly to disguise her blush.

"I am Diana, but I let my real friends call me Diamond."

"Diamond. That's a really nice name. I like it a lot." Ebony replied in admiration.

"Thank you Ebony." She replied humbly. "My uncle chose it for me. I would say let's go somewhere and chat, but I think the bell is about to go for lesson. I hope we can catch up at lunch time though for a chat." She suggested, accompanied by that warm and charming smile Ebony saw moments earlier.

"Love to" Ebony replied.

Diana turned to head out the bathroom door, leaving it

to close slowly in her wake. Ebony's smile remained and with the first feeling of confidence that she had found a friend, she too exited the bathroom. Things were looking up at the thought of finding the first person she could actually talk to. She needed a good reason to come to college in the morning. Perhaps now she had it.

The unusual context of the maths class had led to a trip to the library to use the computer suite. As Ebony took a deliberate place at the back of the line behind her fellow students, she reminded herself of the task she had set herself that morning. This might well be an opportune moment to use the computer to seek out the origins and meaning of that whispered voice which plagued her sub-conscious and dominated her dreams. She began to whisper it to herself as they set off down the corridor, going through numerous alternatives as to how to possibly spell the word she had heard in order to come up with an effective search. As she entered the suite, a number of derivatives danced in her head, all of which seemed as likely to be as accurate as each other. She would need a little bit of time away from prying eyes in order to stumble on the right one.

She strategically picked a desk in the far corner to sit at. One which offered the most privacy when it came to the location and angle of the screen. Her heart began to pump a little faster as she turned on the monitor and the computer began to load. She would still have to go along with the lesson plan and follow the tutor's instructions left for her and so she elected to do this first, theorising that if she could get ahead of the class, it would give her time later in the lesson to pursue her own investigation. Maths was her strongest subject so she was reasonably confident she could complete the task quickly.

Her fingers were long and thin and she had excellent hand eye co-ordination. Ideal typist fingers. Her mother's lessons from a young age on how to touch type were now very much coming to fruition. She carefully began to divide her attention between the two tasks, ensuring that every time the tutor approached her side of the classroom, it would be the maths assignment that would be displayed on her screen. When the tutor was satisfied that she was working hard on it and turned away, she quickly switched screens.

She typed in her first guess. It brought up nothing relevant. Whist the computer searched for her second option, she quickly switched back to her classwork, sensing that someone might soon be peering over her shoulder imminently to check on her progress. Pen in hand, she looked upward to feign the appearance of someone deep in thought. Her tutor approached. Soon convinced that she was still heavily immersed in the task at hand, he soon moved away again, his attention drawn to a series of unnecessary giggles from the other side of the classroom that had broken the silence. She looked back down at her screen, switching it back once more. The computer had stopped buffering and it's search was complete. Nothing again. She was about to enter a third option when she noticed a small icon which caught her attention. A click on the icon revealed a possible suggestion. A suggestion that seemed to be a very realistic possibility.

Do you mean NAJA? The text read.

Clicking 'YES' with her mouse button softly, she again returned to her maths work for a moment to disguise her activities. She did not have as long to wait this time. Again, checking her teacher was still occupied and the other students were keeping themselves to themselves at their own desks, she flicked back once more to a page which now displayed a ream of text and factual information. She skimmed her eyes over the page. At the top of the page was a much larger version of the word she had encountered. She began to read the text below.

"NAJA

A genus of venomous elapid snakes known as Cobras." It read.

That was all she needed to know but still she scanned the rest of the page out of curiosity. Half way down the page, was a small stamp- sized picture on the screen. It was that of a Cobra, its hood fully extended, its eyes gazing forward directly out from the screen as if looking directly at the reader. If she did not know better, she would swear the image was moving and projecting itself out of the page in an attempt to get closer to her, similar to the eyes she had encountered in her graphic nightmare a couple of nights earlier. She sat there a moment, just staring at the picture, in particular at those eyes. Then in her head, she heard the soft whisper again of the word now on screen, its true meaning now uncovered. Now it was if the image on the screen was the one whispering the word to her. She blinked a couple of times in disbelief as she watched the cobras tongue protrude from its mouth. She was more in a hypnotic state now, as though she had spent the last ten minutes looking through a kaleidoscope. The same voice then whispered her name and without thinking, she promptly replied.

"Yes." She whispered at the screen.

"Yes what Ebony?" Came a much louder, more human sounding voice from nearby.

"Mmm... Yes. I think I have finally figured it out Sir." Ebony quickly replied disguising the true meaning of her outburst.

"Good. Just in the nick of time too. Right boys and girls. Please shut down your computers, ensuring first that you have saved and then sent the work to me on the e-mail attatched to the question sheet..."

Ebony sighed with relief, praising herself with her quick thinking as the teacher continued to round up the lesson. Moments later, the bell sounded for lunch. Ebony stood, still a little taken back by what just happened, yet content with the fact that she had at least discovered the meaning of the elusive word that had plagued her for days on end. She left the library and boldly strode to the canteen in the hope of bumping into Diana again. She wasn't to be seen so Ebony left the canteen, headed out the main exit and headed towards the big tree she had found that morning. It seemed an ideal spot to gather her thoughts and make sense of what she just witnessed in the computer room. Although she wasn't to see Diana again that day, she felt her presence, almost like an angel sat on her shoulder. With that feeling of comfort being carried around inside her that warmed her soul, her day was possibly the best she could have hoped for. Even another potential encounter with Alexa and her bosom buddies didn't quite seem as worrying as she thought it might have done. With a spring in her step and after her final lesson of the day which passed uneventfully, she decided to walk home. The chance of further rainfall was significant due to the greyness of the clouds above, but she didn't really care. She was feeling content and she didn't want another uncomfortable bus ride to destroy that.

Chapter 12

One Month Later

The temperature on the wall mounted thermostat was touching eighty degrees and with the windows having been shut all night, it meant that the bed sheets were drenched in sweat and had to be peeled from Jerry's legs. He was in neither the mood, nor the condition to attempt such a task at the moment. He simply lay there, lifeless, suffering the effects of yet another successive night of heavy drinking, along with an intoxicating blend of recreational drugs which he was now hooked on. Though he lay face down with his eyes shut, only semi-conscious, he gripped the bed under the illusion that it was actively spinning round within the confines of the room. In reality, this was impossible. The bedsit he now resided in, on the few nights where he hadn't managed to talk himself into the bed of the many females he knew, did not possess enough space for the bed to even be moved more than forty –five degrees. To maximise any space, Jerry did not even have a cupboard. What was once one of a fine set of suitcases now harboured all of his clothes and lay constantly open in the corner of the room. This meant him even having to shut the case on the rare occasions that he wanted to close the bedroom door.

Besides the bed, empty bottles lay scattered around, some upright, containing the soaked ends of cigarette butts, with others lay on their sides, allowing the last drops of stale and flat ale to drip onto sticky linoleum flooring. The floor was decorated in stains ranging in colour, concentration, size and degrees of pungency. The remains of anything from spilt milk to curry sauce could be stood on with any wrong placed footstep.

With his arm draped over the edge of the bed. He reached down blindly, his fingers attempting to grasp one of the upright bottles he knew he had there. Despite his condition, his waking thought was that of another mouthful of beer. It had worked in the past in order to help him begin to function for the day. His mouth felt incredibly dry as a result of the humidity in the room and prominent state of dehydration. He fumbled around and finally managed to co-ordinate his finger movements just enough to grasp the top edge of a bottle top. He pulled it up to the bed and delicately rolled onto his side with a groan of someone who had not gotten out of bed for a month. With half open bloodshot eyes, he tried to focus enough to examine the contents of the bottle lifting it up so the bottom of the bottle was almost inverted. There seemed just enough in there for one mouthful. He tipped the bottle back further, emptying the contents into an eager open mouth. The taste was both flat and the temperature of the remaining dregs of beer were luke warm. Not refreshing, even by Jerry's current low standards. It only fuelled his thirst further. He had managed to sit up, motivated by a search for other remaining alcohol containers of any description. There were several littered around the place, yet none offered him the opportunity of more than a teasing drop or two which would drip from the lip of the bottle at an annoyingly slow pace. There was only one thing for it. Get dressed and head down to the off license to replenish his stores. He leant over on his elbow, supporting himself as he peered over the bottom end of the bed. Surveying the scene, he managed to locate and grab his trousers, followed by his shirt and pull them up onto the bed in a bundle. The funk of stale beer seemed to occupy every particle of material and his shirt was almost creased beyond recognition. Gathering together any degree of self dignity and self-preservation he had remaining; he tossed the shirt back on the floor in search of a more presentable option. A white lightly stained t-shirt and a jacket was about the best he could find through his blurred vision as his eyes adjusted to the light.

Driven on by the mission at hand, he made his way over to the mirror in his bathroom. He glanced at himself in the mirror, seeming pleasantly surprised at what stared back at him.

"Still looking good." He assured himself, pointing towards his reflection in a narcissistic fashion.

Scooping up several handfuls of running water from the tap, he proceeded to sweep his wet fingers through his straggly and greasy hair. Satisfied it was more than good enough and resembled something like what it had looked out when he had gone out the previous afternoon, he grabbed his jacket from off of the arm of the chair and with a slight uncoordinated stagger, made his way out of the front door, closing it, but not locking it behind him.

It was warm outside and the sun made him squint a little in order to gather his bearings. He fished in his pockets for the remainder of any change left over from yesterday. Pulling out all he could muster from deep down into his pockets, he realised quickly with regret, that he was far short of the money needed to purchase the goods he desired. So much drink and drugs over the past twelve months or so had also meant that all his finances were depleted. The only way he seemed able to attain funds at present was a combination of borrowing money here and there, mainly from the women he slept around with, or winning the occasional twenty dollars through games of pool, when he was in a condition sober enough to play properly. Sadly, any winnings soon found their way back into the till behind the bar or into the hands of local drug pushers which he had dealings with that were still claiming to offer him 'mates' rates' as they put it.

With a handful of dirty fingernails, Jerry scratched his head, contemplating his next move. He thought of visiting Karen to ask for a spare few dollars, but it was a Sunday. She would have slept in after a night shift. Any attempt to wake her would most probably be futile and had he managed to bang on the door hard enough, it would have brought about a very unwelcomed response. The option of any charitable friend down at the pool bar sprung to mind but it was only eleven in the morning and it did not open until two o'clock on Sunday. There were probably very few now who would lend him the money, since anyone he had borrowed money off had seen no sign of a payback, despite his promises. His options were somewhat limited and he paused for a moment or two outside his front door until he came up with an alternative.

Three hundred metres down the road, the owner of a small non-distinct off license was just opening. Weekends had gotten surprisingly busy and so opening at eleven was something the shop owner had decided on in an attempt to bring in more revenue and please his regulars, an ever-growing list of people since a local competitor had moved out of the area. As a result of both the time and the nature of the shop, it was the only one open on that particular street, which despite its size in comparison to the rest, made it stand out. It's shiny well-maintained windows gleamed in contrast to the dull grey shutters which encompassed the shop door on both sides. No sooner had he opened, a handful of people had already entered to obtain everything from a small bottle of milk to their Sunday broadsheet newspaper. Jerry took a look through the open doorway before he entered. A few people were still milling around the shelves, looking for this and that. A young mother with a somewhat troublesome young son could be heard, desperately trying to use the lure of a chocolate bar of sorts to trade for a moment of peace from him. A tall man was on the other side, discreetly eyeing the top row of magazines, no doubt plucking up the courage to choose one and overcome the embarrassment of approaching the counter with it. Jerry entered, walking towards, then slowly past the man as he sheepishly made his selection, pushing it in behind a local paper from a lower shelf to save face. Jerry smiled to himself at the man's discomfort and slowly moved his way to the back of the store where a surprisingly wide array of alcoholic drinks were on offer. Though his range of choices was quite wide, his selection was quick. He reached for a premium 4 pack of beer that had fast become a favourite of his. Next to the prepacked multitude of bottles, there were also a series of individual cans stacked on top of one another. With what Jerry was planning to do next, this seemed like a much more convenient option. He placed the multi-pack back on the shelf.

Jerry began pacing slowly up and down the aisle, trying to look as inconspicuous as possible, awaiting the right opportunity. With his head slightly down, scanning the shelves, he averted his glance upwards, looking around the perimeters to check for any degree of surveillance which the shop keeper had in place. Thankfully, none seemed apparent. He noticed the woman who was still trying to appease her child approach the counter with several items of confectionary. Despite her apparent generosity towards him, the young boy still played up. The shop keeper seemed to take pity on her and attempted to console the child also with a kind offer of his own, offering him a lollipop of sorts over the counter which he seemed to gladly accept. The mother smiled at the shopkeeper's generosity and that it seemed to calm the young boy a little. They were now engaging in small talk.

This was Jerry's best chance. Holding his pockets open in turn, he loaded a can in each one. Grabbing a third, he slowly approached the counter and queued behind the young woman whilst she thanked the shopkeeper for his generosity.

"You are most welcome. Have a nice day." The shopkeeper wished the woman as she gathered together her things and took the hand of her somewhat more content child and led him out the shop door.

"Will that be all Sir?" Asked the shopkeeper as Jerry placed his solitary can on the counter top.

"Yes thanks." Jerry replied, sorting the correct change from the coins in his palm.

With a feeling of satisfaction that overpowered any degree of guilt for his petty crime, Jerry exited the shop as discreetly as possible. Once outside, he quickly opened the can and took a first refreshing swig from its cool and refreshing contents. He felt better almost immediately, something like himself again. He marched back the short distance to his bedsit and letting himself in through his unlocked door, plonked himself down in front of a modest size portable television set as he worked his way through the first of his three cans. It was too early to consider where the rest of the days drinking would take place yet.

As he flicked through the channels, he came across the station which broadcast both the regional and local news. Whilst it was not his programme of choice, it was the channel which his television was able to pick up with minimal interference in terms of reception and static. After a short and insignificant feature, the programme turned its attention to a different storyline. It was a story that eighteen months ago, would have been very close to his heart. He listened as an enthusiastic newsreader began to detail a report.

"A team of local scientists claim they have recently discovered a new species of beetle. On a recent expedition to South America, the team encountered the creature in the foothills of the Andes and having brought it back to the United States for further investigation, were surprised to find that it did not match any known description of the three hundred and fifty thousand on record. The project leader, Danny Carruthers said the team are overjoyed at their findings and aim to revisit South America again soon to learn more about their discovery, hoping they can do everything in their power to protect this species from becoming extinct."

Jerry knew the name Danny Carruthers well. He had teamed up with him and Moira on numerous occasions to work on certain projects. No project was more memorable than the one back in Mozambique where his now estranged daughter had been bitten by a snake. It was the very same

Danny Carruthers that drove like a bat out of hell to get Ebony to the nearest medical facility in time for Dr Bush to work his magic. Whilst a part of him remained thankful towards him and respected him for the hard-working team player he was, there was now a part of Jerry which now resented him. Danny after all, had held onto his job afterwards and by the looks of things had been promoted since. Additionally, the closeness by which he and Moira seemed to work and the banter they seemed to share often caused pangs of jealousy and feelings of suspicion for Jerry that their relationship was not strictly professional and their relationship was a little more in-depth than a simple platonic one. He looked after himself physically and was often seen to be walking around the camp with his top off most of the time. He had seen that this had not gone unnoticed by Moira and was suspicious of the looks she gave him sometimes.

Jerry finished off the first of his cans and tossed it over the back of the sofa in the loose direction of the bin. It missed. He unsteadily made his way to his feet and staggered his way to the bedroom. Once there, he fell to his knees by the side of his bed and reached underneath, seeking a small cardboard box he knew was located under there somewhere. He soon located its upturned edge and pulled it out towards him and began to look inside. It was littered with photographs which he had taken from the house with Moira's blessing when they split up. She had made it clear that she had no desire to keep them at the time. He grabbed a handful and began leafing through them one by one, discarding each one on the floor randomly as he finished with it. He stopped at one. A photograph taken some years ago of himself and Moira, their arms around each other whilst on one of their many expeditions together. They both looked so happy and well suited at the time. He focused his gaze on Moira. Her long slender figure fully in view on the picture, her short black hair tied back in a bun revealing the most kissable neck he had ever had the privilege of putting his lips against. He was not sure if what he was feeling for her now was love or just a simple lust. He looked at her again, then back into the box where another photograph caught his eye. Again, it was of Moira. This time taken at home in their very own garden. With the look of a supermodel, she lay there on the grass in a pair of shorts and a bikini top. He now completely ignored all the other photographs. Leaving the box where it was, he took the one picture in hand and sat down with it on the sofa, staring at it as he opened a second can with his other hand. He stayed like this for a few moments, aware of an increased level of sexual arousal building up within him. It was certainly pure lust he felt, as he began thinking about what it would be like to have her one more time. His inhibitions were beginning to disappear as he began to contemplate the idea of getting in contact with her again. With another series of large gulps from his can came another thought. The thought that after all this time apart, she might even consent to the idea of one night together. Maybe she missed him too. A few more moments of looking at the photograph lead to an urge to pleasure himself which he quickly indulged in, sliding his free hand down his trousers. The climactic sensation he sought came in moments and sitting back in satisfaction, his decision was made. She could only say no after all.

Chapter 13

168

t was one month into term and Ebony's anxiety had settled a little. She no longer dreaded her trips to and from school. Her mother's work schedule had eased somewhat and so she now picked Ebony up two days out of the five, even driving her to school at least one day a week. The days on which she had to work, Ebony would now meet Diana outside the school gates upon arrival and the two of them would maybe go to the canteen for a quick bite to eat before lessons. They would even take their breakfast outside and sit under the big tree a while and rest if the weather permitted. They both seemed to share that unexplained degree of lethargy in the morning and half an hour sat in the sun seemed to help.

There was still the problem of Alexa and her friends to cope with and at times, she still caught Ebony unawares. This was particularly true during lessons they shared when at least one of the girls would try to land Ebony in trouble in some shape or form. It was only when she was alone. It seemed that whenever Ebony was with Diana, they never came close They covered their tracks well and with their parents being governors for the school, they hid behind this influence to make themselves almost immune to prosecution from the tutors. Such special treatment meant teachers often turned a blind eye to their activities within the school grounds and they were automatically included in any degree of extracurricular activity they chose to participate in, even at the expense of those with both greater talent and enthusiasm. It was a situation that angered Diana and she had told Ebony that this was one of the reasons why she would always try to be there to protect Ebony from them.

The basketball squad, which Ebony now found herself to

be a part of was no exception. Despite the inevitable presence of all three of them for a very important team trial session later that week, Ebony was confident of her chances of making the college team for the forthcoming inter-state competition. She had always been quite a gifted player but recently her game play had seemed to have gone up another level. She seemed much more agile, much more accurate with her shooting and certainly much more dominant on the ball than she had ever been. She was a little sad that her mum would have to work on the day of the tournament but was buoyed by the fact that Diana had promised to be in her corner on the day if she made the team. Since they met, it struck Ebony that Diana seemed to have an in-built sense to know when she was needed. She had thwarted several attempts from Alexa to isolate Ebony and the frustration on Alexa's face was often evident. So much so that Ebony now firmly believed Alexa despised Diana far more than her.

That afternoon brought about a double period of Physical Education as per Ebony's time table and with it, perhaps a last chance for one of Alexa's group, Natalie, to jeopardise Ebony's chances for the trial the day after. Alexa herself had been put into another group. Due to her physique and desire to participate, her group seemed to centre around those who did not care much for sporting involvement, only being seen to make any degree of effort when the tutor was in close proximity. She was lazy since she knew that she would be picked for the team if she wanted to.

Soccer was the chosen activity for Ebony and her elite group that afternoon. Ebony noticed that her and Natalie had been put on opposing sides for the match. As they joined their team mates, the two of them exchanged glances from across the half way line. Whist Ebony's was one more reminiscent of curiosity and to some extent, paranoia, Natalie's was one of sinister intent. The game started in a scrappy manner, the teacher issuing instructions left right and centre to encourage more of a structured flow and better play by both sides. Ebony's first few touches were good ones, finding team mates with precise passing and avoiding tackles when in possession. Both herself and Natalie appeared to have been allocated defensive roles, meaning the likelihood they might confront one another within the confines of the game would be significantly reduced. This was to change when, during a final interval and based on her performance so far, the teacher approached Ebony, asking her to move much further up the field and get into more attacking positions, perhaps again with a view to considering her for college representation when the time came.

Ebony sportingly clapped as a shot from a team mate was well saved, resulting in a corner kick for her team and the first chance for her and Natalie to be stood shoulder to shoulder in the penalty box. Natalie's opportunity had arisen. As Ebony took up a position to wait for the ball, from behind, Natalie pulled her own team mate back in order to swap positions with her. Seeing that the sports tutor was more focussed on the taking of the corner itself, Natalie quickly raised her elbow up towards Ebony's face, targeting a malicious blow to her cheek. Ebony yelped, sinking down to her knees in shock at the impact. A small spatter of blood from the impact had found its way onto both the face and neck of one of her team mates, who turned her head in horror, her loud reaction giving the impression that she had been the one struck by the hit.

The incident immediately got the teachers' attention as she walked over to investigate, calling a halt to the game as she did so. She wasn't aware of Ebony at first, who was knelt behind the crowd of players, her mouth filled with blood which now cascaded down one side of her chin. The hit had caught her squarely on her upper jaw and touching it gently, Ebony sensed that a certain degree of damage had been done, particularly to her tooth, which now sat very loose within her upper jaw. It was only after the other girl was sent to clean herself up that she noticed Ebony on all fours, spitting blood onto the floor.

She took a quick look at Ebony's face. The left side of her cheek had swelled. Although in pain, Ebony was not crying. She just stayed in one position, adjusting to the shock, her hand massaging her jaw. The teacher turned to the group.

"Right! You lot go and join Miss Heath's group for now. I'm going to take Ebony inside and get her checked out."

Slowly, the crowd dispersed, with Natalie propping up the rear, a look of sheer pride and satisfaction on her face. She glanced over her shoulder twice more, before making her way over to Alexa to boast her achievement, playfully skipping as she did so.

The teacher gently grabbed Ebony under her arm in order to help her back to her feet. Instead of accepting the teachers' gesture of help, Ebony, still on all fours, backed away slightly.

"Come on Ebony." The teacher encouraged. "We need to get you inside to the nurse straight away and have that checked out."

"Give me a minute." Ebony pleaded, her arm raised to

indicate that she was well enough to remain there and collect her thoughts for a second.

Looking down at the floor, her vision was understandably a little hazy. She considered what she might now look like as a result of the injury even though any degree of pain had quickly subsided. Although the teacher had not approached her in order to try and help her again, Ebony could easily detect her presence. Her tracksuit had that fresh changing room smell that Ebony could sense in the air.

With her vision clearing slightly, Ebony regained her feet unassisted. The teacher then led her quietly back to the departmental office, calling for the nurse as she did so from her phone. Ebony had no desire to see the nurse. Instead, she just wanted to go home; or at the very least to be alone a while. Her mother or her new best friend Diana were about the only company she would welcome at present.

The nurse arrived within minutes, evidently keen to do all she could. She softly tried to move Ebony's hand away from her mouth, where Ebony held a blood-stained tissue pressed against it to stop the remainder of the bleeding.

"Please don't." Ebony insisted, her voice slightly muffled by the tissue she held to her lips.

She backed away, with a solitary shake of her head.

"I think it's best if I take a quick look Sweetheart." Said the nurse implying her best bed side manner voice. The nurse leaned in again to get a closer look by again reaching for Ebony's hand gently.

Sensing the nurse was not going to give up, Ebony reluctantly removed the tissue she had placed on her mouth.

Instinctively, the nurses' hands drew closer which caused Ebony to back away once again.

"Do not touch." Ebony ordered, more forcefully than last time. There was almost an anger in her voice this time. She could feel it welling up inside her. However genuine the nurses intentions were to settle her; they were having the opposite effect.

"Ok." Said the nurse, backing off slightly, her hands raised as a gesture of surrender. "May I just have a look with my light?"

Ebony nodded weakly, watching the nurse's every move, ready to take further action should she attempt to go back on her word. She did as she promised and in turn, Ebony co-operated as best she could, holding her mouth partially open for her to look at from a close but safe enough distance for Ebony.

"It looks like you will need an emergency dentist Ebony," The nurse diagnosed, placing her small light back on the desk and reaching for the phone. "I know one who I think will be able to see you this afternoon."

Not waiting for Ebony's response, the nurse was soon talking to a gentleman on the other end of the phone, enquiring as to his availability later that day. She soon hung up, a happy smile on her face.

"He can see you in about an hour. He is a friend of mine, so I always call upon him when I need a favour from him. You will like him Ebony."

She passed Ebony the address and with the assurance from Ebony that she would not go alone, wished her good luck, asking to see her the following morning.

Much like going to the nurse, Ebony despised the idea of visiting the dentist. Amongst much more prominent ones of late, a long-standing nightmare existed of being pinned down in one of those green revolving uncomfortable chairs, its surface covered in that plastic protective cover that emitted the strangest of odours as she lay on it. Also, there was the big alien like spacecraft as she saw it as a child, with it's three-pronged attack of dazzling light capable of blinding any human being. Ebony's imagination had led her to believe that if you sat there long enough, this contraption that would rest just a few feet above your face was big enough to suck you into an alternate dimension, never to be seen again. It was at this moment that she would often wake and run into her parents' room for comfort. It had led to an irrational fear of dentist surgeries. She realised though, that there was a need for treatment, or at least to have it looked at and tidied up a little.

She was also aware that if she didn't go of her own accord, her mother would insist on taking her there herself, frantic with worry that she had suffered some extent of permanent damage. The school day wasn't far from finishing and so after slowly changing back into her uniform and placing her blood-stained games shirt in her bag, she made her way through to the main foyer in the school reception area and up to the third floor where she knew Diana had her last class for the day.

Diana was one of the first out of class and seeing Ebony, offered her a friendly hug, willingly offering to accompany Ebony to the dentist as a source of moral support. Ebony's mood lightened once again from Diana's smile and the two of them made their way out of school and down the road towards the assigned address scribbled on a piece of notepad. As they set off, Ebony began to recount what had happened. She did not need to say who had done it. Diana seemed to know. As they exited the school gates, Diana made both Ebony and herself a promise that they would find a way to get revenge on the three of them.

"I agree." Responded Ebony. "But how?"

"Leave that to me Ebony. I'll think of something."

It took around ten minutes to arrive at their destination, nothing more than a regular looking house with a small sign above the door indicating that the owner did indeed operate his practice from inside its walls. As they entered cautiously, it was noticeable that there was no reception as there would be at a normal practice. There were no signs up advocating good dental practice or adverts related to the promotion and protection given by varying mouth care products like you would see plastered over the walls of a normal practice surgery. It was just a normal house, evidently with an adapted room somewhere geared towards administering treatment. They sat on an armchair together and waited patiently for a moment, wondering if they should make their presence known in some way to whoever was in the house. As they were about to do so, the visible door at the end of the hallway opened and a man peered out.

"Hello." He shouted down the hallway. "You must be Ebony. I'll be right there."

"Thank you." Acknowledged Diana on Ebony's behalf.

Moments later, the man emerged, shuffling his way slowly down the corridor to greet them.

"So which one of you can I help today? The nurse at

school told me I might be able to have a look at your mouth after an accident."

"This is my friend Ebony. She is a little upset at the moment but hopes you can help her" Diana replied on Ebony's behalf, her hand resting gently on top of Ebony's in support.

"Shall we have a little look then?" He asked gently, focussing his gaze on Ebony. "Follow me."

They both stood, then began to follow the man into the room from which he emerged a moment ago. The layout of the room was what Ebony had expected. Unlike the rest of the house which appeared purely residential, the room resembled every other dentist surgery she had visited. The plain white walls, the shiny floor surface, even the faint sounds of a local radio station from a small stereo on the desk. The chair at least did both appear to be and feel far more comfortable looking than she had expected. She settled on it as best she could, still wary of the dentist's every move around the room as he prepared his little tray of tools to begin his examination.

Sensing her fear, he began his examination very cautiously, holding nothing but a small magnifying glass and a torch and began to look into Ebony's mouth which she opened nervously for him. It didn't take him long to diagnose the problem.

"There looks to be a problem with this tooth here." He explained, pointing it out on a small chart which he handed to Ebony. "It's been broken and will need to be taken out, so it doesn't cause you any more pain or an infection in your gum."

It wasn't the news Ebony wanted to hear but with Diana stood close by her side, as well as the reassurance that the process would be over with quickly and relatively pain free, she soon found herself giving him her approval to proceed. He began to prepare the local anaesthetic and as he reached into her mouth to apply it, an all too familiar feeling came over Ebony once more. The feeling she had felt a short time earlier. The state of mind whereby she wanted nobody anywhere near her. Her pulse began to race and she could feel the blood in her body begin to simmer. If he did not finish what he was doing quickly, she would react in some way that would stop him. But how? He was after all, almost nose to nose with her and in quite a dominant position with regards to moving sharpened tools around within her mouth cavity. A wrong move to get him to stop might cause her even more damage. She felt a reassuring hand on her leg which momentarily settled her. It was an impeccably timed intervention to stop her lashing out at him in self- defence even though he meant no harm. Beneath closed and watering eyes, she suffered the emotional discomfort. Although closed, her eyes ached in a way she had never felt before, as though someone was pressing down on them and squeezing her eye balls in a pincer movement, yet she did not open them. She daren't' in case of what they might reveal. Whatever was happening with her eyes, she knew enough to realise that their appearance when looking into them may have somehow changed. They felt alien to her, What was not alien to her was this aching sensation she felt, It had happened a lot recently. Every time her emotions were on edge. When she had looked at herself during this time, what stared back at her was not something she wanted to share with anyone else.

With the last extract of the tooth removed, the dentist began to check the other side of Ebony's mouth. It was then that Ebony felt a strange sensation within her gum. It was more of an ache than a pain and one she could only liken to that of the teething process from when she was young. Something deep within the confines of her upper jaw was slowly moving, edging its way downwards, millimetre at a time into the void from which her broken tooth had been extracted. This was unexpected since at Ebony's age, this was most definitely her adult incisor that had just been removed. No human would have a third tooth there to replace it. With the dentist now focussed on his final check of her bottom row of teeth, she took the opportunity to run her tongue up between her cheek and gum to sense for the movement. It was slow but it was very deliberate and whatever it was that was about to emerge, it would show itself within the next minute or so. She was eager for the dentist to stop before he discovered this strange turn of events.

"That's about it." He announced. "Just one last check to see if I've missed anything."

His upturned finger went straight back into Ebony's mouth and directly to the sight of the sensation Ebony was feeling. Slowly using the tip of his finger to check inside the tooth cavity, the tip of his finger brushed against something very sharp. So sharp that the slightest touch easily penetrated the surface of both his glove as well as the skin on the tip of his finger. He pulled it back in haste.

"Ouch" He said quietly, shaking his hand then examining his sore finger. Beneath the surface of his glove, a minute speckle of blood emerged.

"I'll ask for you to be given an x-ray Ebony if that is alright with you. I was sure I had it all but maybe there is still a small bit of the root buried deep up there. If so, come back and we will be sure to get it out. But for now you can go."

Ebony slowly got to her feet and softly thanking the dentist for his efforts, took her bag off Diana and walked out into the hallway again. The dentist did not reply. He was too occupied rinsing and nursing what was now a very small yet painful wound on his finger tip which was beginning to swell.

The two girls began to amble their way back down towards the main street again and towards the bus stop, during which time, all Ebony seemed to do is show her appreciation and thanks for Diana agreeing to come along for the support. All Diana seemed to do was to stop telling Ebony to apologise.

"What are friends for?" Diana replied on a number of occasions. "I'm sure when the time comes, you will do the same for me." She added confidently.

"Of course I will. You have fast become my best friend. Almost like a guard or something. I just seem to feel safe and secure when we are hanging out together."

"I'm glad." Diana added, smiling that infectious smile Ebony had come to associate with her. "That was my intention."

They waited for a moment or two then a bus turned up. It was time for Diana to go. They exchanged a quick friendly embrace and then Diana climbed on board, ensuring to sit by the window so she and Ebony could wave to each other as the bus pulled away. Both were keen to get home in spite of how much they enjoyed each other's company. It had felt like a long day. Ebony was pleased therefore, that within minutes of Diana leaving her, her bus turned up also. Thankfully it was far emptier than the school one.

Diana got off at her usual stop, just on the other side of a small park which left her a short pleasant walk down the meandering pathway that lined the stream. On the other side, tall apartment blocks hid partially behind scattered trees. The trees had blossomed and so it hid away the eyesores of the apartment buildings. This made the park a far more pleasant place to be at this time of year. Coral was a very regular visitor and would often be spotted following the tracks on one of her regular runs. The one main pathway formed a circuit so it was commonplace to see her numerous times passing by the same spot before returning home.

Diana preferred a much slower pace. She even stopped on a bench a while to rest before the final leg home. She was no runner. She could see her destination in the distance, peeking through a series of tall, long branches of trees that danced in the breeze. After a few moments, she picked her bag up again and continued her short journey. She was also very thirsty and craved a plentiful helping of Shesha's special concoction to quench her insatiable thirst. The images began to tease her mind of a very tall glass filled to the brim of her favourite drink and her taste buds were almost dancing by the time her building came into full view.

As usual, she entered the building from round the back. Both the bottom and first floor were almost vacant, thus what used to be the main entrance to the building had been boarded up long ago. Herself, Shesha and her sister were the only residents of the building. The entrance lay off the main street and through a gate in a gap in the railings. It was very secure and the first measure of security to overcome was the huge padlock on the iron gate. There was an art to unlocking it, but Diana had been shown exactly what to do and so entered the gate without an issue. From there, she walked down the narrow pathway, lined with weeds from overgrown patches of grass which she could not help but trample on as she made her way round to the back of the building. With the height of the building itself, its tall three-sided walls offered a high degree of privacy at both the rear and the side of the building. A feature that played a big part in Shesha choosing to purchase and renovate the generous interior space to meet his own requirements. Once up a couple of steep steps at the rear of the building and Diana came to a second door. A non-descript heavy wooden door which Shesha kept double bolted. He always insisted that it be re-bolted each time someone entered the building behind them. He was meticulously protective over both the people and possessions within the building. As a result of having the building to himself, it meant of course Shesha could expand onto the lower floors should he choose to. It was clear he had intended to do so and the moment he retired marked the start of such a development. He had already put two of the rooms on the first floor to good use and planned to do more in the near future.

As Diana bolted the door behind her as instructed and made her way slowly up the stairwell, she caught sight of one of the room in question. It remained locked and out of bounds. Whilst she was curious as to its contents, she was far too respecting of Shesha's wishes and instructions to stay clear and never enter. He had told her it was his project and she would learn of it in due course, a process by which her sister was now undertaking. Coral had been in the room on a few occasions but always at Shesha's side. Whatever was in there was a sight to behold as Coral did not quite seem the same girl after emerging from behind its doors that very first time. The light sound of talking and the shuffling of feet seemed to indicate that someone was in there at present and so Diana continued up to the second level of the building and opened the door into their plush and spacious living quarters.

A note in the kitchen confirmed her suspicions. Both Shesha and Coral were in the first-floor room engaging in a 'lesson' as the note described.

By the time the lesson was over and Shesha returned to the second floor, accompanied by a very tired and drained looking Coral close behind him. Diana had already fallen asleep on the sofa. On the table next to her was a large drink container and a glass, the container drained of its contents. On it was a small label with a large letter 'D' which Shesha had scribbled on, before leaving it in its usual place in the refrigerator. He would do this sometimes when he had put together a specific concoction for one of them dependant on its individualised contents, telling the girls that they sometimes needed different medicinal ingredients at different stages and whatever was in them was put together purposefully for them and them alone. Diana never questioned it. Some blends were nicer on the palate than others but that was to be expected and whilst she had her favourites, she enjoyed all the blends of flavours that Shesha had lovingly put together for her.

Seeing Diana asleep, Shesha turned to Coral. Her eyes were closing too and was also in need of sleep.

"You must rest too daughter. You have worked hard and

what you have endured will make you tired." Shesha advised, pointing towards the living room door.

She didn't hesitate. Shesha was right. Coral was exhausted to the point of feeling slightly nauseous and she yearned for a long rest. With a small peck on Shesha's cheek, she slowly made her way to bed.

"I will wake you later when I assure you that you will feel very much refreshed."

The voices had caused Diana to stir and her eyes half opened to see Shesha sat in his usual place by the window and none too surprisingly, with book in hand. He glanced over at her.

"Good evening daughter."

"Hello uncle." She replied with a waking yawn and a stretch.

"How is the plan progressing regarding our young friend?" Shesha asked, putting his book down on his lap to listen.

"Things couldn't be better uncle. We have very much bonded and I have made every attempt to keep her out of harm's way as you asked. There are a small group of girls who seem to have taken a liking to bullying her a bit but they will not touch her with me close by."

"I knew I could trust you with this task daughter. Please continue to do as you are doing. You have a way with people. That is part of your gift. I would think it will not be long now before she will confide in you with regards to more serious and personal matters. At which stage of course, I shall begin to intervene."

"Of course uncle." Diana replied. I shall remain by her side to help her as best I can."

Chapter 14

ohn and Eve had scheduled a nice relaxing night in front of the television. It was their favourite viewing night with back to back programmes, all of which they enjoyed. Tea had been prepared much earlier and sat in the slow cooker ready to be served as and when they felt like doing so. In the fridge to accompany it was a large bowl of salad, prepared by John with pride as most of its ingredients were fresh from his very own garden.

The only issue seemed to be getting Eve off the phone long enough to come and sit with him. Whilst he loved to hear about and spend time with the family, he wasn't one for discussing the smallest of issues for hours down the telephone. On the other hand, no matter seemed too trivial for Eve to discuss at length. He could often overhear her talking to some relation or other, mostly Moira, with a deep concern in her voice about the smallest of things. When he focussed on listening more intently to what was being said, it would often turn out to be something along the lines of advising Moira to use a different fabric softener if the one currently in use seemed to be leaving grease stains in the clothes. The usual motherly advice.

Finally, Eve bid whomever she was speaking to goodbye in order to join him.

"I was just about to call you love. Our programmes are starting." John said with a touch of impatience in his voice.

"Yes. I'm sorry about that. That was Colin down at the bowling club. He was just telling me the greens are in a mess. Some foolish boys have been tearing across them on their scooters or whatever those things are and have torn it to pieces. He is upset as there was supposed to be a tournament there this week."

"Mhm." John nodded in acknowledgement without even taking his eyes off the screen.

"Then before that was our Moira." Eve continued, not seeming at all bothered that John's attention was now firmly fixed on the screen rather than her. "She was saying that our Ebony had lost a tooth in a little accident at games."

She gazed up at him, expecting a response. There was none.

"John. Did you hear me?" She asked sternly, knowing full well he hadn't.

"Yes Eve love." That's a shame about the bowling thing." He replied, trying to summon up some sympathy. "Bloody fools!" He added.

"Did you hear what I said about Ebony. About her accident?"

"Lost a tooth you say? I'm sure she is fine. These things happen playing tough sports. What was she playing?" He asked, trying ever more desperate to show a little more interest amidst the distraction from the television.

"Moira did not say. I do worry about her playing all these things though. I think Moira should have a word with her don't you?"

"Yes love." Said John laughing.

"What's so funny?" She asked, looking up from her magazine.

"Oh. It's just the answer this idiot gave to a question he was just asked. It was so obvious too."

She smiled a half- hearted smile.

"What a plonker." Continued John, talking to the television in response to what he heard. He now switched his full attention back to the programme, shuffling in his seat for extra comfort. His attempts to draw Eve into watching the programme with him seeming to fail.

"Ebony has made a new friend by all accounts though. Supposedly a very nice young girl who is helping her really settle in. She even went to the dentist with her to have her tooth seen to."

"That's another easy one. Dakota." Shouted John, barking his answer at the television with self- satisfaction.

She looked up from her magazine and shook her head at him. She watched for a second or two as he grew more animated, frustrated by the lack of evident knowledge shown by the on-screen quiz contestant.

"Dakota. Dakota" He repeated, now stood up with his hands on his hips awaiting the contestant's response.

"Ohio" The contestant responded.

"Oh my god!" Screamed John. His hands now on his head as though he had just missed an open goal in a World Cup Final.

"Settle down love" Eve instructed quietly. You will be having kittens at this rate."

John began to slowly take his seat again, happy that the contestant had no more questions to answer. Both his, and John's ordeal was over as quickly as it had started.

"Anyway. As I was saying." Continued Eve, making the most of a quiet brief interlude between John's over enthusiastic antics. "Maybe you could speak to Ebony about this sport thing love."

After sharing a couple of programmes of mutual interest later on, they grew tired and finally retired to bed. As they climbed the stairs and headed to the bedroom, Eve made one last attempt to persuade John to bring the subject up with Ebony next time they spoke.

"I will. I promise." Said John puffing up his pillow and placing his head on it as a hint to Eve to say no more about it.

"Goodnight love." He whispered with a yawn as he heard her slip into bed by his side.

"Sweet dreams." Came her reply.

Chapter 15

This was the day Moira and her team had been waiting for for quite a while. Three months of preparation had been leading up to this day and as Moira gulped down her final drop of tea and finished off her breakfast, the nerves and excitement had already started to build. Ebony had already left for school with her house key on the understanding that she may return to an empty house later, as well as her mum's sincere apology that she would be unable to watch her in her basketball tournament after school. She promised to ring Ebony as soon as she could to find out how she had gone on, as had her grandad. This could well be a very exciting and fulfilling day of achievement for them both.

Moira had plenty of time to get ready. She was not meeting Danny at the museum until eleven o'clock. It was only quarter to nine. Her dress suit hung neatly over the living room door and she felt ever so eager to put it on straight away with an irrational fear that if she did not get dressed and leave soon, she would be late for her rendezvous. It wasn't as though they needed to be there early either. They had spent the previous afternoon together there, along with a couple of other members of the team setting up the exhibits. As for the luncheon which was to follow, that had been well and truly taken care of by the efficient hospitality staff of the museum. Her and Danny had worked hard to get to this point, and this was to be the day to sit back and enjoy the fruits of their labour and celebrate with colleagues and trustees that had made this day possible. She was due to make a short speech to open the new exhibits to the public and thank a few people, none more so than her team of experts and those who had invested heavily in the project. This was perhaps the only element of the afternoon she had any real nerves about. After that however, it was party time. Enjoying the free-flowing drinks and an elaborate buffet was the sole plan, surrounded by the impressive collection of specimens which the museum had generously offered to house on a permanent basis. Desperate to pass half an hour or so, she reached for her phone. Pulling up Danny's name, she began messaging him.

HOW ARE YOU FEELING DAN X. She typed with a smile.

A reply came back within seconds which made her chuckle.

I'M SHITTING BRICKS. WAS UP AT 6. HAD TO GO TO THE GYM TO TAKE MY MIND OFF IT A WHILE. SURE IT WILL BE THE BOMB THOUGH!! TAKING A SHOWER. SEE YOU THERE SOON XX

Moira read one portion of his message to herself again.

...TAKING A SHOWER...

She placed her phone back on the table and sighed. It was the sort of sigh that someone would give when daydreaming of a celebrity heartthrob whilst gazing at their picture. She had a picture of him in her head, soaked from head to toe in soap suds, his masculine frame sporting his artistic collection of tattoos, one of which stretched across his torso. She sat there a moment, her chin resting in the palm of her hand, her elbow resting on the kitchen table, smiling.

A knock at the door suddenly broke her train of thought. She was not thankful for it as she would have been happy to sit for a while with the images of eroticism that danced in her head. She opened the door to the postman who then handed her a series of non-descript irrelevant leaflets which quickly found their way into the trash. She looked at the kitchen clock again. Another ten minutes had passed.

"Sod it." She said to herself, rising from the chair and making her way upstairs to select the rest of her attire for the day. After some deliberation between two choices, she finally chose. She lay it out on the bed neatly and systematically began to get dressed, taking care not to inflict the slightest crease in her clothes as she did so. By the time she had emerged downstairs again it was quarter to ten. Happy to be a little early, she grabbed her phone, rang a cab and shut the door behind her, waiting eagerly on the front porch for the car to arrive.

Across town, some three blocks away from their intended venue, Danny was just adding the final touches to his appearance. He was feeling a little more relaxed now and was finding the process of applying a handful of styling cream to his swept back hair somewhat therapeutic. With a few deliberate sprays of aftershave, he too was now ready. He carefully gathered his things, placing them neatly into his gym bag and left the plush surroundings of the changing gymnasium rooms behind him. As he exited the building, he looked up towards the sky. Showers had been forecast for later in the day and his hope was they had not arrived prematurely to tarnish his spotless image as he made the short walk down to the museum. He wanted to look his best.

The entrance to Central Museum sat well elevated above street level and necessitated having to negotiate a series of steps. Danny began climbing them slowly, taking care not to over exert himself at the risk of the emergence of any unwanted sweat patches. He even stopped for a moment half way up as the climb stopped and the stairs unfolded out into a small courtyard area, highlighted by an impressive waterfall monument. The water feature itself was encompassed by a series of benches, offering a valuable and strategic resting place for those heading up to the museum some two hundred steps further up. It had become a well-known venue to meet dates and partners could often be seen sat there together enjoying each other's company, some a little more graphically and elaborately than others he seemed to recall from nights out on the town.

As the distant sound of the town hall clock signalled half past ten, Danny entered the main foyer of the museum, heading nonchalantly down the corridor to the wing where his exhibits now proudly stood. Greeted by a few familiar faces along the way, he smiled as he pulled his gym bag from off his shoulder and carried it down by his side, ready to jettison it into the nearest corner he could find once he entered the museum wing. A convenient coat stand had been erected just outside the door for visitors attending today's event. This was the perfect place for it. He placed his bag down on the floor, hiding it under some coats and with one deep breath, walked into the designated area where everyone was to gather, not quite knowing how many people might be waiting for him at this early stage of the proceedings.

He first spotted Moira in the distance, looking elegant and beautiful as always. She was smiling as she shook hands and shared a conversation with a gentleman who also looked familiar. It was the Curator of the museum. He was quite an imposing character and on the few occasions Danny had spoken to him, he came across as a little cold and judgemental. However, watching Moira with him now, she seemed to have him in the palm of her hand. Her blend of charm and sophistication, along with a little bit of flirting and persuasiveness at times, had no doubt had a big influence in securing their success here at the museum and having them host this event. It was with that in mind that rather than approaching her now, he would leave her to it. Besides, he had spotted a waiter carrying a tray of champagne flutes a moment earlier. He had been used to tracking and capturing some of the rarest exhibits seen in the world of nature recently so finding a smartly dressed waiter in a tuxedo carrying drinks shouldn't be that hard.

They did not actually catch up with one another until after Moira's speech and the formalities. A long-awaited embrace and a friendly kiss on the cheek from Moira was their first interaction, which resulted in a look of desire cast towards her. They stood staring into each other's eyes for a moment, lost in a mutual look of lust for each other. She smiled shyly as she pulled away slightly. Looking around, the crowd was beginning to grow thin, thus prompting a suggestion.

"Say Moira. How about as soon as the powers that be leave, me and you make ourselves scarce and carry on the celebrations somewhere else?"

Moira had had a few glasses of champagne by now and any inhibitions had long since vanished so the invite was nothing but appealing.

"Definitely." She said. "I can think of a much better way to celebrate than this."

"Besides." Danny added. "That curator has all the warmth

of a snow pee. He seems to like you though. You seemed quite close to him before. You're such a flirt."

"I was wasn't I?" She joked sensing Danny was trying to engage in a similar sort of accusational banter. What can I say Dan? He does have a huge..."

She paused for a second and smiled cheekily at Dan ....walllet."

They both began to snigger together like two school children having played a trick on the teacher, attracting one or two looks from other guests.

"You are a bad girl Moira Maher." Danny replied, now trying to keep a straight face.

"Yes I am aren't I?" Maybe I can get naughtier later?" She suggested with a shy smile.

Dan only smirked with approval. They were both eager to escape what had become a very boring end to proceedings and within half an hour, they were in a car which Danny had been provided with, heading for much more comfortable surroundings for a drink and a far more intimate celebration.

Dan selected one of his favourite bars in town. A quaint establishment where they served very good cocktails and where the ambience was just what he was looking for. As the car pulled up outside, Moira looked over the road at the large neon sign indicating the entrance to a very familiar pool bar. The very same pool bar that brought back so many memories from the past of her and Jerry. She suddenly developed a slight reservation about going into an alternate venue so close to it, even after all this time. She was however, in good company this time and quickly shook off the negative feelings in order to follow Dan in, not wishing to disclose anything to him or suggest another venue that they might go to instead. She certainly wasn't to know that Jerry himself had become a frequent visitor there once again.

She settled down at a small table, deliberately choosing a seat with her back to the window whilst Dan went for the drinks. Despite its immediate proximity to the pool bar opposite, the place Dan had chosen seemed very nice. Moira did not really get out to socialise much these days, yet she wondered why she had never spotted this place before. It was ironic then, that as Dan sat down opposite her with drinks in hand, that he should ask the question he did.

"What do you think of this place?"

"Seems nice. I have never been here before, but I recognise the area." She answered, not wanting to give too much away.

Dan handed her a drink. It was a large glass with several straws and the liquid inside was a deep red colour, fading to an orange further down. It was a cocktail that Del-boy himself would be proud to be served.

"We only need to stay for one or two then I'll drop you back off at home." He said reassuringly.

"It's fine Dan honestly." She replied.

She took a sip of her cocktail, it's refreshing taste pleasing to the palate. She seemed to relax again then, as the conversation started to flow easily once more. Dan's dry humour and her flirting soon had them laughing again and before she knew it, she had gotten through three cocktails and an hour and a half had passed. They were both very much caught up in the moment.

It was not surprising therefore that none of them spotted a lone, yet familiar figure from across the way, staggering his way to the window ledge in the bar opposite. Jerry staggered for a moment, gathering just enough focus and co-ordination to place his drink on the ledge, using his elbow to keep him upright. He was nursing what the barmaid could only assume to be about his eighth pint of the day. A pint undoubtedly bought on borrowed or hustled money. Although he was well used to more now and his body had learnt to tolerate alcohol to a point where he would often collapse in a corner. He was close to that state now. His head would drop, then rise in order to take gulps from his glass. As he deliriously scanned the view, he caught a glimpse of someone who looked vaguely familiar through the window opposite. For a moment he couldn't believe his own eyes. His vision was not clear in his condition and through both the double vision he now had as well as the poor lighting he had to contend with from inside the bar opposite, he was not positive yet that the person he now stared at was who he thought it was. He would have to wait till he came outside to be one hundred percent sure. He was feeling alert all of a sudden and now, exhibiting the behaviour of someone on a surveillance mission or a stakeout of sorts, he sat watching this persons' every move. As it happened it did not take long for Jerry's patience to be rewarded. Not only that, he felt optimistic that he might also get a look at the female company he was keeping as well. A vague outline of the back of her head was all he had to go off for the moment.

They were soon to be seen moving towards the exit of the bar and Jerry slid himself along the ledge by the window in order to get a better look. It was a position which now allowed him to use the length of a long curtain to conceal himself behind should he need to. He pulled it across to partially cover his body, peering round it for another prolonged stare.

"It is as well." He said to himself in surprise. "It is my old friend Dan."

He let go of the curtain but stayed in position. A part of him was very keen to wonder into the street outside and shout hello as Dan came out, thinking it would be nice to surprise him. He was about to do this very thing when he suddenly noticed who he had for company.

"I should have known it." He cursed between clenched teeth, grabbing the curtain again with a clenched fist of anger. "That little bastard is with my Moira."

His mood had now changed in the blinking of an eye. The idea of making himself known in a civilised manner had quickly passed as a surge of jealousy so strong, stronger than he had ever felt before, had now taken hold of him. Not only that, he now felt cheated and betrayed. A man he trusted. A man he worked with who he deemed honest and a friend to them both, had most likely been sleeping with his wife the whole time they had worked together. That was Jerry's assumption now anyway. That was the drunken paranoid conclusion he had come to and it would need a persuasive person to make him believe otherwise. As far as he was concerned, all the pieces fit and here before his very eyes, was the concrete evidence needed to confirm his suspicions.

He watched as Dan put his arm round her and gently ushered her to his car which had now pulled up for them outside. She willingly climbed in, grinning. He then watched as Dan strode round the other side with a cocky swagger and a smirk and climbed in next to her in the back seat. Jerry staggered back a step or two to hide himself behind the curtain once more as the car moved off.

Jerry returned to sit by the bar, taking his now warm half empty glass of flat beer with him. In a rage, he slammed it firmly down on the bar top, almost shattering it. The barmaid, hearing the noise wondered over. It was Nicola, beginning her shift for the day.

"Another one Jerry love? You look like you could use something a bit stronger." She hinted, as she pulled out a shot glass from under the bar.

With a quick look about, she poured him a shot of whiskey and placed it on the bar in front of him.

"I shouldn't be giving you that really." She began whispering, leaning over the bar to get closer to him, revealing the top portion of her breasts over her low-cut top, hoping he might look up to ogle. "You want to come by after I finish work Jerry?"

He didn't answer. His whole body was swimming in a sea of anger, rage and discontent from which no flirtatious act nor indecent proposition could save him from. He gazed up just enough to clock the glass of whiskey which sat before him and after a moments hesitancy, drank it down in one swift motion. The speed at which he threw his head back to drink it obviously disorientated him for a moment, causing him to stumble backwards into, then almost over, a bar stool behind him. Through his half-shut eyes, Nicola noticed a look of evil vengeance she had never seen in him before. She had looked into those eyes many times and this was the first time they portrayed any desire to do something menacing. He staggered to the door and pushed it partially open, looking back at Nicola before exiting. He knew exactly where he wanted to go. She was first to speak addressing him with a worried plea.

"Go home Jerry. You have that look in your eye to say you are going to do something you might well regret."

"Might shees you... shoo... soon." He slurred. Then, disregarding Nicola's advice, he left.

He stepped into the daylight, squinting. Swaying slightly this way and that, he allowed himself a moment to get his bearings. Confident with his decision on where he was heading, he set off stumbling towards the corner of the road. He was not heading towards his flat as Nicola had pleaded with him to do, but in the opposite direction. His intent was to track Moira down and at least get an explanation for what he saw. Perhaps he could obtain the truth from the horse's mouth rather than just speculating. So it was that he slumped down on a bench at a nearby bus stop, not even bothering to check the displayed timetable and waited impatiently for a bus to arrive.

As Moira pulled up at the house, her phone rang. She fumbled around for it frantically in her handbag, its tone growing louder as she sifted through the objects that obscured her view. Locating it, she noticed Ebony's name on screen. She pressed the answer key and put the phone to her ear.

"Hi Ebony Sweetheart. How is the tournament going?"

"We won mum. I was just going to go out with my friend Diamond to celebrate with a burger and a milkshake if that's ok with you?"

Moira smiled.

"Yes. That's fine. You two girls have fun and celebrate. Be home by nine though please."

Moira quickly hung up and turned her attention back to Dan who waited patiently sat by her side for her to finish.

"That was just Ebony. She and a friend are off to celebrate their win at the basketball which means I have got a bit more time to spare before I make tea if you want to come in for a coffee?" She asked nervously, whilst confidently anticipating what the reply might be.

"Love to." Dan replied instantly, undoing his seat belt and opening the car door.

Having received the invite, he quickly trotted round to the other side of the car to help Moira get out, politely opening the door while she sifted around for her house key.

"Madam." He jested, doing his best impression of a chauffeur, offering his hand to help her out. She took it welcomely, re-introducing that spark of energy between them brought on by the mere touch of each other. Dan didn't let go of her hand as they negotiated the pathway together, as well as the several porch steps. As Moira reached the top step, she stumbled forward, her toe catching the lip of the top step. Despite the fair number of drinks that Dan had consumed, it seemed his reflexes were still sharp. He caught Moira with both hands to prevent her falling. She looked up at him, a little embarrassed, yet grateful.

"At the right place at the right time as always." She remarked.

She leaned in to kiss him. He kissed her back. Not a friendly best friend kiss like many times before. This one was far more passionate, stemming from a deep desire they shared for one another. It was evident from the way they held each other that this moment had been something they had both yearned for since way back.

After what seemed like an eternity embracing each other, Moira eased away slightly, her lips parting from his, yet still with her hand resting gently against his chest.

"I best get that kettle on." She said trying to unlock the door. "Too many prying eyes and all."

The door seem jammed and after a couple attempts, rather than persisting with it, she gestured for Dan to follow her round to the back door which led directly into the kitchen. He followed as she led the way round and through the side gate, warning Dan to be wary of the small collection of rusty tools that lay up against the wall.

"Sorry Dan. I really must get around to throwing them. They've been there since me and... well, they've been there a while."

After a moment of uncomfortable silence, they were entering the kitchen where Dan sat at the kitchen table while Moira fussed around with her coat and then filled the kettle in order to make both herself and Dan a welcome sobering beverage. He watched her every move in admiration, whilst sensing a little anxiety and nervousness from the speed at which she was attempting to go about things.

"Just relax Moira. Do you want me to leave?"

She turned to him quickly in response to his question, knowing full well he was aware of the change in her body language.

"Don't be silly." She replied. "Its just been a little while since I had a man back to the house and he wasn't here to fix the drains or something."

"I know." He responded in empathy. "But hey. It's just a coffee right?"

"Right." Came the reply, though not a very self-assuring one.

Across town, a twenty- five-minute wait for a bus finally brought its reward. As Jerry endured the ride, every little activity or sound around him seemed to anger him further. Even the likes of a soda can which rolled across the floor this way and that every time the bus lurched around a corner, was a source of tremendous annoyance. Behind him sat an elderly gentleman on the phone, evidently confirming his whereabouts to a loved one who was expecting him home. By the sounds of the conversation, his arrival had been expected a while back and Jerry was aware of the decibel levels creeping up in the conversation between them. It took every shred of remaining patience not to turn around and hit the gentleman. After all, he was trying to use what was left of his reason and logic to determine how he was going to handle the situation when he arrived at Moira's house. He did not have long. The bus was approaching her neighbourhood quite fast and he would be disembarking within the next five minutes. He did however conclude that he needed some form of plan of action or pre prepared speech of sorts. He was not even sure they would be there but it seemed a good place to start searching.

As Jerry got off his bus, across town, Ebony was just getting on hers, her hands full with her school bag and a generous sized trophy as a result of the vote to award her with most valuable player. She clutched it proudly with one hand, using the other to bid Diana farewell through the dust- stained bus window. She reached into a side pocket of her bag, pulling out a set of headphones and her Mp3 player. Switching her music on, she sat back to relax a moment and reflect on her triumph, thinking all the time how her mum will react when she sees it. She couldn't wait to get home. A nice bath, then most probably a celebratory tea, maybe even her favourite takeaway if she stayed awake long enough. An hour resting in the garden on a lounger now seemed even more appealing and as she stared up to the sky from out of the window, she was pleased to see hat there were no signs of rain for the rest of the evening. The clouds were parting and it looked like it was going to be a reasonably pleasant evening.

Back at the house, the sun's rays began beaming through the windows of the kitchen as Dan and Moira continued to chat over the last few mouthfuls of coffee, neither of them daring to discuss what was really on their mind. They were sat close together, both very much waiting in anticipation for the other one to make the first move, a gentle caress, another kiss would have been more than enough to instigate another moment of pent up lust. Dan swigged down the final mouthful of coffee and stood, making his way over to the sink to where Moira stood in order place his cup in the washing up bowl. Moira turned, sensing him close by.

"I guess I'd best...."

That was as far as his sentence got. She was suddenly pressed up against him, kissing him, making no secret about her intentions. She wanted him. Right then and right there.

She began to moan as he fully began to reciprocate her passion, placing his palm firmly on the side of her face, not allowing her to escape from an ever-deepening kiss. He began to slide his hands down the side of her body. First his right hand, then after stroking her cheek, his other hand followed. He was strong and it took very little effort to lift her from the floor and place her in a sitting position up on the counter at a height slightly superior to his. As he did so, she wrapped her thighs firmly around his waist. What was going to ensue was now inevitable. She quickly removed his tie in one fluid motion, tossing it on the kitchen floor. Her jacket quickly followed, disregarded without any degree of thought as to where it landed. She felt him begin to kiss the nape of her neck and down to her chest, unbuttoning her shirt as he did so. She loved the idea that his lips might wish to explore every inch of her

They were now so lost in the moment; they had no sense of awareness of anything else. The time passing by, the ever-increasing pile of clothes strewn over the kitchen floor, perhaps even the undetected creak of a garden gate opening around the side of the house was sure to go undetected. From the opening of the side gate, it appeared that at this most inopportune of moments, they were about to encounter a most unwelcomed visitor.

Jerry had crept round the back of the house and using the wall for support, peeked in through the corner of the kitchen window. The scene which confronted him quickly tipped his rage over the edge. Any thoughts of just going there to talk to them had vanished in the blinking of two drunken bloodshot eyes. His focus shifted for a moment, catching sight of something resting up against the wall. A small collection of old wooden handles and rusted garden tools. He recognised them as a small collection of his old gardening tools. Varying degrees of rust and degradation meant that some of their purposes were no longer clearly identifiable and that they had been sat outside a while. However one item had seemed to have braved the elements and withstood the test of time significantly better than the others. His old trusty spade or 'ol digger' as he called it. He reached for it with an evil smile, lifting it towards him to inspect it closely. It was heavily rusted but intact aside from a small corner piece which left a sharp jagged edge. He grasped the handle firmly and looked back through the window, hiding his face behind a plant pot on the window ledge.

Dan's shirt was all but removed and Moira's was soon to follow, now fully unbuttoned and pulled down around her elbows. Her head was fully back, eyes closed, savouring Dan's touch. Jerry watched, resisting the urge to enter until he caught sight of his hand slip under her skirt to reach for her panties. As she shuffled slightly to allow him access to remove them, Jerry made his move. Spade in hand, he slowly walked past the window and then reached for the door handle. The door was behind Dan, yet had Moira kept her eyes open, she would have spotted him entering and raising the spade above his head. As it was, there was no chance of warning him of the devastating blow to the back of the head which he was about to suffer. A large cracking sound filled the room as another part of the rusted spade broke off and embedded itself in the back of Dans skull. There was no scream of pain from him. There was no time to scream. There was the chance however, for Jerry to inflict a subsequent sickening thud as Dan's lifeless body first jolted forward into Moira, then lifelessly fell to the kitchen floor. By the time Moira could register what had just happened, Jerry was stood over Dan, spade raised again, ready to deliver a third and fatal blow. He turned it slightly, to make use of its remaining head portion, then quickly and brutally brought it down on top of Dans head with full force. It caught him on the side of his face and blood began to pump from yet another open wound. He was almost unrecognisable now from seconds ago, blood coating what remained of his handsome facial features along with his torso.

Satisfied the spade had done its damage, Jerry released his white-knuckled grip of the handle. The spade dropped to the floor, splattering yet more blood across the kitchen, this time up the wooden chair legs and staining the edge of the table cloth, quickly bathing it in crimson. Moira now realised the graveness of the situation, letting out a first scream of a blood-curdling series of screams.

"SHUT UP SLUT!!" Commanded Jerry, trying to raise his voice high enough to be heard, grabbing her with both hands as he did so. She quietened a little, still fighting for breath due to the shock of events. Jerry came at her again, the back of his hand raised high, ready to deliver a hard back-handed slap. It was a slap well deserved from his standpoint. She grabbed his arm, fighting tooth and nail for her survival. Had the situation been calmer, they both might have heard the faint creek of the garden gate being opened for a third time.

Ebony's Mp3 player had prevented her from hearing anything that was going on in the house. She sighed a thankful sigh that she was home, even remembering to come around the back on account of the front door being jammed. She looked behind her for a second as she was about to remove her ear pieces and reach the kitchen door. She could have sworn all the tools had been stacked neatly against the wall, rather than being on the floor, partially obstructing the pathway.

She did not know where to look first as she entered the kitchen; the blood that coated the entire surface of the kitchen, a partial view of a body lifeless on the floor, or her own mother beating off the advances of a strange intruder who was evidently beginning to overpower her. Ebony grabbed the first thing she could get her hands on. A heavy steel sauce pan. Mustering up as much strength as she could, dropping her trophy in the process, she hit the intruder across the shoulder blades. The impact wasn't big enough as to cause pain, but it provided the chance Moira needed to escape his grip and retreat to a position behind the counter. He turned and only then did the true horror of his identity become clear to Ebony.

"Hello sweetheart." Jerry uttered, his calmness eerie beyond comparison. "Haven't me and your mum told you its bad manners to interrupt?"

Jerry snatched the pan from Ebony, slowly raising it above his head

"Leave her alone Jerry. Please." Moira pleaded mercifully, taking an ill-fated step towards them.

Sensing her having come closer, he turned back towards her and using the pan he had just taken from Ebony, struck Moira hard with it on the side of the head, the shot rendering her unconscious. The impact sent her spiralling into the wall before hitting the floor, taking with her a picture from the wall which shattered as it landed. She now lay still, surrounded by shards of glass, one of which had caused a laceration to her forehead as a result of the impact.

Turning back to Ebony, he saw that she had moved, now cowering in the corner in a squatted position, her left arm having taken hold of the cupboard handle, her right attempting to shield her head as though ducking under a low flying aircraft with her hand resting on the back of her head. As he approached her slowly, Jerry suddenly noticed the trophy.

"Well well." He remarked with a creepy enthusiasm. "Aren't we the big achiever these days? Shame you are just too much like your mother."

As he took a second step towards her, Ebony began to sense that feeling again. Up to that very second, she had been fearing for her safety. Suddenly, this was no longer the case. Her eyes were open but her vision began to fade slightly, as though a mist had suddenly covered her eyes. Her eyes had begun to ache as they had numerous times before. From inside her mouth, she felt an intense feeling of pressure on her upper jaw. It was the funny sensation of movement she had felt from within her gum before. She began to rock slightly from side to side. Her pulse was racing so fast that she could feel her whole head throbbing in tune with the rapid beat of her heart. She felt she would have to defend herself now as best she could as her only avenue of escape was well and truly cut off by the looming figure of her father, now stood over her and with an intent to cause her harm. It was now or never.

She moved her head slightly up from behind her arm, calculating his exact position from his movement. For as long as he continued to move, he was clearly visible to her. Reaching up to his arms would not be the best option as he was still armed and chances are, he would have overpowered her easily. She was at waist height to him now, therefore his leg seemed to be the most vulnerable area to target her attack. He raised the pan slowly above her but it never even got above his head before he suddenly dropped it to the floor. What felt like a succession of needles were now easily penetrating the flesh in his thigh and a pain began to spread quicker than he ever thought possible. It was becoming so intense that any residual effects from the copious amounts of alcohol consumed earlier were gone in an instant. He began to shake, suddenly struggling to draw breath. His eyes began to spin with an onset of dizziness. As he dropped to his knees, gripping his leg with both hands, he took one last look towards his daughter, not quite believing it was her who had just incapacitated him so quickly. What stared back at him only vaguely resembled the daughter he knew. His last vision before his eyes permanently closed was that of a pair of serpent like eyes, dark green in colour. Her cheeks bones appeared now far more prominent suggesting something was underneath her cheek bones forcing them to protrude out from her face. Below her mouth, her chin dripped blood down one side and onto the floor. Ebony's mouth was partially open which had also allowed Jerry a last despairing glance at what weapon she had used to wound him. Fixed within her upper jaw, a very thin but evidently disproportionate tooth was barely visible. It was at least an inch and a half long and was a tooth far longer than what any human incisor should ever be. He did not have time to deliberate. His ability to draw breath had all but ceased. His body seized as he began vomiting violently. The poison within him was about to shut down his diaphragm, Within another few seconds, his entire cardio-respiratory system had failed. With no way of the messages to get from his brain to his heart muscle to tell it to pump, it stopped. Jerry was dead. This only left Ebony, kneeling in a pool of blood amidst a plethora of bodies.

After a moment or two of just staring down at her father's dead body with her serpent like eyes, her vision began to return to normal once more. Her heart rate dropped and a tickling sensation she felt in her mouth saw the fang retract almost as quickly as it had appeared. A mixture of blood and another substance, more bitter in taste, lingered on her taste buds. A moment ago, she had savoured it as though it were water from the holy grail itself. However now, feeling almost like her human self again, it was beginning to give an unpleasant aftertaste. With her grip on reality fast returning, a quick survey of the horrific scene before her made her want to escape. She wanted to be as far away from here as she could. Even if she could have explained the turn of events which had transpired earlier, she certainly had no desire to for now. Her plan was to at least escape the neighbourhood, then ring the police from a payphone somewhere secret. Whilst she was eager to seek medical attention for her mum and flee quickly from the house, she was conscious that running from the house in a panic would arouse too much suspicion. She had to remain calm for the moment. She could let her emotions pour out later. Swapping her blazer for her sports jacket which was screwed up in her bag, she got up and left, shutting the creaky garden gate behind her. She had checked her mum was alive at least and would send help as soon as she could.

As she walked around the side of the house, she was sure she heard something fall from her bag. In her haste to leave, she considered that maybe she had not fastened the zip properly. She allowed her self a brief look down but spotted nothing. She was not thinking straight at the moment and so thought maybe the noise of something falling from her bag was a figment of her imagination. Content nothing was missing, she continued her journey to the front of the house and down the driveway, without looking back.

Chapter 16

he cold sensation of an icepack on her swollen cheek was an abrupt awakening for Moira. She flinched in pain, screwing her eyes up in response. Her entire cheek was throbbing and it hurt to even make any facial expression to exhibit the pain. An unfamiliar series of bright panel lights shone down on her from above. It quickly became obvious she was no longer at home. With slow and painful turns of her head, she began to take in her surroundings. Sensing her confusion, a strange, yet softly spoken voice from nearby attempted to soothe and comfort her.

"You are in the hospital Moira. You took quite a nasty bang to the head. How do you feel?"

The nurse who had spoken suddenly came into view as she hovered above her head, comforting her whilst trying to examine her facial wounds.

"What happened?" Moira asked, flinching in pain again as she made the effort to speak.

"Well as I said." The nurse repeated. "You have quite a nasty cut to your head as a result of a fall of some kind and there may be a chance you have a small fracture to your cheekbone. Do you remember anything of what happened?"

As the nurse began her routine observations of Moira, Moira simply lay there, not uncooperative as such, more in a daze as she tried hard to recount the events of the incident. Seeing the frustration etched on her face, the nurse intervened with a suggestion.

"Try not to think about it now." She said fluffing up Moira's pillow and pushing her slowly backward again so she was once again lay down. "It's quite common after a head trauma like that that you will suffer a little bit of temporary memory loss but it will come back to you." She assured, removing the blood pressure cuff from her arm.

With that, the nurse left, alerted by two uniformed gentlemen who had made their way into the ward and were hovering near the nurses' station. She approached them to head them off.

"If you are wishing to speak with Mrs Maher, I'm afraid now is not the best time officers. She needs to rest for the moment and has no recollection as to what happened as yet."

The two officers looked at each other with a frustrated resignation, as well as a little surprise that the nurse seemed to know their intent. With a respectful nod and a promise of their return, they slowly left the ward, handing the nurse a small card as they did so.

Moira had overheard the nurse talking and had sat up again. Realising she wasn't about to be interrogated, she lay back onto her bed again in relief. She knew she would not be of much help to them today and could not face a series of upsetting questions. She clutched her ribcage, still sore from the impact with both the wall and the kitchen floor. She winced as her over- zealous movement sent a pulse of pain through her body. Moving was a bad idea for the time being.

As the evening passed and her headache subsided, her memory began to slowly return. Whilst nowhere near to the extent of being able to tell the story of what happened, she was now beginning to experience brief flashbacks, none of which were making much sense to her at the moment. She was beginning to get a strong impression that she was not alone when the incident occurred although the image of exactly who was with her was still lost within the realms of confusion and her state of concussion. She anticipated a long night as the effects of the temporary amnesia eased off and her recollections became more vivid. She swallowed in fear. A fear to suggest that maybe she will not want to remember what had happened when her memories came flooding back.

An hour passed until a nurse woke her from an unexpected period of slumber for the usual series of routine checks. Remaining silent yet co-operative, Moira stared upwards, not focussing on anything or anyone in particular. Even when the nurse lifted her band aid to check on her head wound which had caused her pain earlier, she barely flinched. She was beginning to remember things with a little more clarity now. The odd word here and there. She was at least certain now that she was not alone before she lost consciousness. There was also a plethora of none-distinguishable sounds. A glass surface being smashed, a faint thud and lastly, what could only be described as a loud cracking sound. Then she remembered a distinct smell. A stale smell so pungent that the memory of it was almost inducing a state of nausea. Her memories were well and truly gathering momentum. Despite her hesitation to do so, she remained lay back, allowing the thoughts and the emotions that surrounded them to surface. She became so focussed that she completely ignored the nurse who had entered her particular bay shortly afterwards to offer her refreshments and any additional painkilling remedies. By the time she had emerged from her daze, the ward seemed very quiet. Squeaky footsteps, distant murmuring and the infrequent moans of discomfort and pain from fellow patients were all she could hear. The curtain to her cubicle had been closed in its entirety so there was no way of knowing who was around to communicate with or where each of the sounds were coming from. The bed mounted call button was her only way of face to face conversation at the moment. She had no desire to disturb the nursing staff, so instead she turned to the radio that was part of the entertainment system accessible to her by her bedside to relieve the boredom. Placing the earphones gently into each ear, she slowly began tweaking the dial for a desirable station to listen to and pass the hours until she hopefully fell asleep again. Having recognised a well-known local channel with a DJ's voice she was familiar with, she settled back again to listen. She would have to endure a series of news bulletins however, before the music was to return to the airwaves.

"The hour's top local story then," Began the reporter. "Former Maxillofacial surgeon and now part- time dentist Robert Grant has been found dead in his home earlier on this morning. The alarm was raised when Mr Grant failed to answer the door to a customer who had attended his place of work for an appointment. Reports say the 64-year-old gentleman had been in good health recently, though he had gone into semi-retirement three years ago after discovering a heart defect. Police entered the scene, to find Mr Grants' body lay on the floor of his treatment room in his house. Whilst all indications seem to point to an acute heart failure being the cause of his death, minute traces of a poison of some kind have led to the local law enforcement officials to treat the death as suspicious. An autopsy is scheduled for tomorrow."

"Poor guy." Moira said, suffering a brief moment of survivors' guilt.

A brief weather bulletin followed, highlighting the possibility of a drastic downturn in the weather over the next few days and then with an all too familiar jingle, the radio turned its attention back to playing music, the majority of which Moira quite enjoyed. She even sang along under her breath to give her mind a rest from thinking about the events of earlier that evening, promising herself she would focus on that when, and only when, the need arose. The police would be back in the morning to talk to her but for now she would try to get some rest and hope the music would send her off to sleep.

It was ten o clock sharp when the two officers from the previous day returned to the ward to interview Moira. Any attempts from the nurse to delay or dissuade them from doing so this time would be futile. They had come looking for answers and seemed ever so determined in their demeanour to get them. The nurse showed them to Moira's cubicle and shifting the curtain aside, they both stepped in, each choosing opposing sides of the bed to stand on. Seeing Moira had spotted them immediately, they began to engage straight away with her in the usual expected introductory fashion. A somewhat false type of bed-side manner.

"Mrs Maher." The first of the officers said, offering an outstretched hand. "How are you feeling this morning? Last night must have been quite an ordeal for you."

Moira shook his hand with a faint nod of agreeance.

"My name is Inspector Chen. This is my colleague Lieutenant Mercer."

Mercer stepped forward slightly, bowing his head slightly as a sign of greeting, then stepping back once more having done so.

"We are a real pair of nice guys and we are here to help piece together exactly what happened to you last night." He paused a second as though ready to deliver the catch to the situation. "However in order to do so, we may have to ask you some really bad questions." He added apologetically.

They both removed a notepad and pen from their pocket, poised and ready to note down anything useful they might be able to use. Though it seemed as though Inspector Chen was evidently going to be leading the line of questioning, Mercer seemed the most eager of the two to listen. He was evidently a lot younger than Chen in his appearance and was most definitely less experienced when it came to handling cases and interviews, yet for some reason, his presence was more calming and Moira almost wished he had come alone, his body language suggesting a far less stern approach to that of Chen, who by now had procured himself a chair from behind the curtain and pulled it up close by her bedside.

"What do you remember from yesterday Mrs Maher? Let's start from early that morning." Suggested Chen.

Moira paused a moment, figuring out where to start. Her memory of events was far clearer but remained sketchy when it came to putting things in order of time and sequence.

"I remember waking up pretty early." She began hesitantly. "It was going to be a big day as we were celebrating some of our work going on display at the museum."

Chen was quick to jump in.

"You said 'our.' Who were you celebrating with?"

"I work with quite a large team sometimes. Some photographers, scientists and of course the people from the museum itself. I guess the main person I work with is... is... Oh god!" She suddenly shouted in terror.

"Mrs Maher?" Chen asked, keen to uncover what had brought about this sudden response.

Chen watched as she buried her face in her hands and began to weep. Chen looked over to Mercer who had already reached into his pocket and pulled out a handkerchief for Moira and handed it to Chen. Chen passed it to Moira, ensuring he touched her arm with it so she could acknowledge the gesture and carry on with her explanation after a brief interlude.

"Danny." Moira called out as if trying to summon him.

"Danny?" Repeated Chen inquisitively.

Mercer leaned forward and whispered something quietly to Chen who nodded as he listened to the information. It seemed Mercer had done his homework.

"I assume you mean Mr Carruthers?" Chen asked.

Moira nodded between sobs as she began to calm down a little from her outburst.

"I remember him being injured. I can see him now laying on the kitchen floor, his shirt covered in blood."

Mercer leaned in again, this time even closer to Chen to ensure Moira could not hear the message he was conveying. As he stood again, Chen let out a sigh.

"Right. Thank You Lieutenant."

"From what I have just been informed Mrs Maher, I'm afraid I have some bad news. It seems your colleague, a Mr Daniel Carruthers, died as a result of his injuries sustained at the scene. That is why we are here Mrs Maher. This is no simple accident with regards what happened to you and Mr Carruthers. This is being considered a homicide case."

Moira listened as Chen began to explain his findings. Everything from the blood-soaked pile of clothes and smashed picture to the presence of Jerry at the house and his suspected involvement in the case. Everything seemed to make sense to Moira after Chen had finished explaining how far he had got with the investigation so far. Everything but one thing. Something Chen now was looking to Moira to help him solve.

"With you unconscious and Mr Carruthers unfortunately having been fatally wounded at the scene, what could have possibly caused the death of Mr Maher? There had to have been another party involved in some way for him to have been found dead at the scene as well." Chen theorised.

Chen looked at Moira for an answer, playing the role of the dumb cop but deep down, he had a very strong incline as to who else was at the scene anyway.

"I'm afraid I don't quite remember that part of it Inspector." Answered Moira with a vague expression.

"Hmm." Chen replied. "Okay. We can come back to that I am sure"

Chen then stood, checking his watch. Behind him Moira caught sight of a brief nod and a smile aimed towards her from Mercer as a thank you for her co-operation.

"Well that's all for now Mrs Maher. We have plenty to be going on with. I have left my card with the nurse and if there is anything at all you remember in the meantime, I ask that you call me. We will of course be back within the next couple of days so please do inform us of your whereabouts as your house is still unfortunately inaccessible at the moment until our forensic team have completed their full investigation."

With that, Chen disappeared, Mercer closely in tow, leaving Moira to digest everything she had learnt over the past hour or so. There were still a few gaps in her memory which only the passing of time would fill. She began sipping a cup of tea brought for her by the nurse. Her hands had stopped shaking enough for her to grasp the cup safely now. It would not be long before the gaps could be filled and she could recall the chain of events from start to finish, should she choose to share them.

Chapter 17

bony continued to walk, not quite knowing where to go or when to stop. Her thoughts and feelings had made her oblivious to her surroundings. So much so that she had almost stepped out into the road in front of on-coming vehicles that beeped and swerved wildly to avoid her. The wind had picked up considerably and a chill in the air seemed to have prompted most passers by to select much warmer items of clothing than her. She had been left with little option but to change back into her gym gear as her normal skirt and blouse were soaked in blood. She had gone so far as to hide behind the bushes close to her house in order to change, stuffing her crimson-stained school clothes back in her bag. Ebony's skin may have been cold to the touch, dressed in her sporty tracksuit top and shorts but she didn't feel the cold. In fact, as she continued to eat up the miles of unfamiliar terrain some five miles from her house, she barely felt anything at all. She had just been through every single emotion that was thought to be possible in such a short space of time that her emotions were spent for the time being. She walked zombie-like, down street after unfamiliar street and over roads followed by more previously unencountered roads. It was only when the throbbing of her tired feet, accompanied by the shooting pain of an emerging blister on the sole of her foot, that she became aware of the need to rest.

Eager to find more tranquil surroundings than those offered by the road side, she surveyed the scene ahead for a suitable place to stop and take refuge. Whilst nothing but buildings lined one side of the street, she was able to vaguely make out a clearing up ahead on the opposite side of the street. It looked like it could be a small park of some sort.

Though the street lights did not offer much help in identifying what was actually there in the distance, it seemed like the best option available at the present time. She just needed to escape the noise. With aching feet, she trundled the last two hundred yards further down the sidewalk and then crossed to find herself confronted by a small park square. A memorial garden of sorts. Huge trees that lined the pathway blocked the majority of light from the street lamps which offered the gardens very little light and so any features within the square itself remained unrecognisable. Day was turning to night quickly now so only the outline of a large grey monument situated in the middle of the gardens stood out. Nowhere obvious to sit could be seen from where she was so it left her with little option but to venture further into the eerie depths of the darkness to find a comfortable place to rest.

The gardens seemed to offer only the one dimly lit pathway which ran around the back of the monument and away into the distance but there was no indication as to where it might lead. It was difficult to see exactly how far into the distance the pathway travelled in the fading light. As she slowly ventured down it, she felt her senses heighten again, in a very similar fashion to when she would venture outside into her back garden at home after one of her frequent nightmares.

"Not again." She cursed.

She looked around her in all directions. The only movement she could pick up on was that of the odd stray cat prowling about, the smell of which would quickly come and then subside. As far as people went, there was nothing to indicate that she was anything but completely alone. Then, she caught sight of what she was looking for. Appearing vaguely in the darkness ahead were the outlines of a couple of long park benches which offered her the chance to sit. Although it was almost dark now, their white colour reflected in the moonlight had made them just about visible. In both pain and relief, Ebony took the last few steps towards them and sat to rest, somewhat content with her decision not to press on any further. As if like a light switch, the moment she began to relax a little, all the events of earlier on that day came flooding back. Firstly, the image of Dan's contorted blood-stained body lying motionless on her kitchen floor. Her vision then switched to her mum sent crashing into the wall. Finally she pictured her father, her estranged and now evidently deranged father, who seemed quite maliciously prepared to follow up one murder with those of both herself and her mother.

Within the space of a few seconds, the emotional rollercoaster was in full swing. First came the feeling of confusion. Confusion which quickly transcended to fear. A fear that soon proved to be a catalyst for anger. Finally, the anger gave way to guilt as she looked back on her own actions. Then for some reason, the rollercoaster just stopped. Stopped dead. Not with the feeling of guilt that she had known only seconds ago. This feeling was different. It was almost a deep-centred, cold- hearted sense of what can only be described as satisfaction. A positive sense that she had done the right thing. It only lasted a second or two but it was enough to temporarily cleanse her soul and allow her to justify her earlier decisions in reaction to events. Decisions that lead to the demise of her own father. A sense that he deserved what had happened and had very much brought it on himself. Then, with the metaphorical roller coaster having stopped once, it was round the track of emotions for another circuit and the negative emotions quickly returned. This cycle continued for what seemed like an hour, though by now, the mere concept of time had been well and truly lost on Ebony. Each brief upturn in her mood brought about a feeling of justification, quickly followed by a downward spiral that brought about negative feelings and worrying questions to which she had no answer. Was her mother ok? What would happen to her now? Perhaps most significantly, what did she intend to do next?

She knew she needed somewhere else rather than a park bench to rest for the night and then take stock of things again and decide on her next course of action in the morning. The question was, where? Little did she know that the answer to her question was to momentarily appear in the form of a small gentleman who approached her quietly from the shadows of darkness, his eyes having been fixed on her every move for quite a while now.

Ebony leaned forward, rubbing her sore ankles which still ached from her long walk. She was blissfully unaware that the figure emerging slowly from the darkness had made his way very quietly towards her from behind. Even with Ebony's much heightened senses of late, for some reason or another, he remained undetected as he stood only a few feet away from her. He reached out a gloved hand and placed it softly on the bench just behind Ebony.

"That looks sore." The unfamiliar voice said softly and with empathy as he watched Ebony rub her ankle.

Despite the aches and pains she was experiencing and minus one shoe which she had removed to examine her blister, Ebony shot up from the bench, startled by the voice. As soft

as it was, it was still a shock to hear. She was certain she had
been alone all this time. Evidently not. That all too familiar
feeling of tension was fast building up inside her again and
she could feel her vision beginning to cloud as it seemed to
habitually do now in such situations. It was becoming clear
to Ebony that with each occasion she now felt tense, in a
situation where she might be under threat, these same changes
were happening, also that they were occurring quicker each
time. It was as though her body and mind were now trained
to react within an instant. Her fight or flight response was
as quick as it had ever been and seemed to be getting quicker
still. This is how she felt once more, hearing the voice of the
undetected stranger.

"Do not be afraid." The soft voice assured her, raising his
hand slowly from the bench, palms held up and open as a
show of peace,

Conscious of the visible changes that may be evident for
the stranger to see, Ebony's head stayed mostly down, instead
just staring out of the corner of her eye to see who the owner
of the faint shadow cast over her might belong to.

"All I wish to do is take a seat next to you for a moment."
He paused, looking for a sign that his request might be
acceptable to Ebony.

"My feet tire easily also." He added.

With her vision clearing again as her nerves settled
slightly, her level of anxiety dropped almost as quickly as it
had escalated. She raised her head and took her first proper
look at the man now sat down in front of her. She could not
see him clearly as yet. A combination of the dim light and the
collar on his coat pulled way up to eye level, along with what

appeared to be a tatty baseball cap obstructed the majority of his facial features. The only thing visible were his eyes, yet even these were not looking directly at her. Instead, his gaze seemed to be focussed on something further into the distance. This was in fact, another tactical ploy on behalf of the friendly stranger so as not to un-nerve Ebony in anyway with the intensity of a fixed stare. Whoever this person was, his body language seemed very much consistent with his words and his intentions. He did seem to offer no threat to Ebony so far.

"Do I know you?" Asked Ebony softly.

"Perhaps." Came the vague reply.

Both of them remained silent for a moment, Ebony thinking of another question to ask the stranger. Before she could think of one to ask, the stranger spoke again.

"However I do know a little something about you. Ebony isn't it?"

He took a quick glance at her to gauge her reaction to his question, hoping his knowledge of her name had not alarmed her too greatly. Her eyes had clearly widened in surprise, though she did not appear agitated or anxious. The stranger began to elaborate.

"My youngest, Diana, or Diamond as you might know her. She speaks very fondly of you."

Although she could still not see his face, she could hear the smile in his tone as he spoke, as though he took great pride in the mere mention of Diana's name.

"Your youngest?" Ebony questioned. You mean Diamond.....Sorry, I mean Diana is your..."

"Daughter. Yes." He interrupted.

"I don't understand. She said she lived with her Uncle." Ebony responded with confusion.

He chuckled slightly.

"I don't expect you would understand Ebony. At least not for the moment. Please allow me to explain."

Ebony moved in a little closer, but yet still not comfortable enough with him to take a seat right next to him. She was however, now very much interested in what he had to say.

"Diana is not my biological daughter. You could say I adopted her. I came across her some years ago after a family tragedy left her as an orphan. She was also quite poorly when I found her. I was able to use my knowledge of medicine to treat her and became quite attached to her during the process. I still take responsibility for her ongoing treatment. Without it, she would be certain to fall ill once more. Before I knew it, she had chosen to stay with me as opposed to the other options which presented themselves to her. With the necessary blessings and permission, it soon became a formality. I call her daughter as that is how I see her in my eyes. She refers to me as Uncle at my request. Not father. That would dishonour her actual father. I hope this helps you understand."

Ebony nodded enthusiastically, her level of interest bringing about an even broader smile from her new friend.

"So that would make you"...? Ebony asked, prompting him to reply with his name.

"For the time being Ebony, you may address me as Shesha."

"So what is it that is wrong with Diana" Ebony asked, her voice now coming across with a degree of self confidence in his presence. She now took a seat next to him as he began to explain.

"Do not worry Ebony. I know you have grown close. She remains completely healthy as long as she continues to take the medicine which I am able to supply her with. It takes time and effort to prepare it exactly right but if done correctly, she thrives and can be seen to achieve things she thought she never would."

"It sounds like amazing stuff you give her then" Ebony replied in amazement.

Shesha nodded modestly.

"Oh very much so Ebony. Very much so."

Ebony looked down to her pocket, feeling her phone vibrate from deep inside. She wanted to answer it but at the same time felt very much drawn into the conversation with Shesha. His presence was having a very calming influence on her and talking with him, learning more about her best friend, had Ebony hanging on his every word like a small child settling down to a bedtime story. After a few vibrations, her phone went silent once more, the screen returning to its blackened state.

"Maybe you should have answered that." Shesha suggested, looking away again momentarily. "It may have been your loved ones. Your mother perhaps, wondering where you are. They must be concerned with it being so late."

"I doubt it was my mum. She is in hospital."

I am sorry to hear of her illness. I hope she can return to full health soon." Shesha replied with sympathy.

"She isn't ill." Ebony quickly clarified. "She was attacked."

Ebony's voice began to wobble slightly, a lump appearing in her throat. She was struggling to get her words out and Shesha was quick to react to her change in mood.

"That is terrible. You mustn't talk about this now if it upsets you Ebony. Try to stay clear of such feelings as sorrow. Such emotions are, for the most part, wasteful."

Ebony ignored his advice, somewhat eager to tell her tale about what had transpired earlier. Fighting back the tears, she began to recount events as best as she could remember them as Shesha listened. As she got to the part where she had struck her father, her tears subsided and the tone of her voice grew softer. Her change in demeanour had not gone unnoticed.

"It appears you did what you needed to do by means of self-preservation and to protect your loved ones Ebony. That is nothing to be ashamed about. Your father seems to possess an evil twisted soul. Fate has a way of dealing with people in such ways." Shesha explained calmly.

Encouraged by his non-judgemental attitude, Ebony was warming to him fast and had the inclination that she could tell him anything. She continued to tell Shesha about the changes she had been undergoing recently and how they had affected her behaviour. Not the usual teenage changes that come about with the natural onset of adolescence. Instead, the changes of a much darker nature. Everything from the unexplained feelings of fatigue during the daytime, to the desire to inflict harm on others if provoked enough. She stopped suddenly as she overheard Shesha say something to himself quietly as he thought back to an incident in his not so distant past.

"Exactly what Diana was like" He whispered, finishing his sentence with a sympathetic sigh.

Ebony's tone changed to one of surprise.

"She underwent these changes too?" Ebony asked.

"Very much so Ebony. Luckily I was able to help her before she began to lose control of her emotions and actions in such a way. She still has these tendencies but I have been teaching her to manage them far more wisely. They no longer control her. The medicine helps with that too."

"You wouldn't know to look at her and talk to her" Ebony replied.

"Then it appears I have used the gift I was blessed with quite well. The exact way I intended. The gift to guide people with such a unique ability. An ability which you and Diana now seem to share in some form."

Ebony looked at him, keen to contradict his viewpoint.

"Gift?" She asked. "I would call it a curse. A curse that just caused me to do something every part of me would have never thought about doing…and to my own Dad."

Her voice was beginning to rise again in a mixture of shame and anger. Shesha turned side on to her and gently reached for her hands, encompassing them within his own as a gesture of comfort and reassurance.

"What you see as a curse Ebony, is merely just an uncontrolled gift. With that gift comes great benefits. Yet in the wrong surroundings and with no one to guide you, it will always lead to regrettable and unfortunate incidences such as what you tell me you have experienced recently."

Ebony nodded.

"I think I understand." She uttered, yet still with a somewhat vague look on her face.

Shesha stood, letting go of Ebony's hands softly, instead replacing that with a soft hand around her shoulder to which she did not resist.

"Walk with me Ebony. I want to tell you a story I told Diana soon after I first met her. It seemed to help her believe in herself and her abilities in a new light."

Keen to listen to Shesha's anecdote, she quickly got to her feet and with one quick shuffle of her foot to get her trainer to sit more comfortable around her sore heel, she began to walk besides him.

"There were once three men." He began as he slowly shuffled his way quietly along the pathway in the direction from once he came. "The men were very different in their personalities but all were friends. Seeking a better life than what was on offer, they set out on a journey together to find fame and fortune. They had little of neither money nor belongings to travel with. The one thing they did have in common was that they were all in possession of a gift of some kind, but with no knowledge on how to benefit from it. As luck would have it, they encountered a small empty bottle on an old market store which they agreed to purchase for means of carrying water. The bottle was dirty and one of the men decided to use his robe to clean it before they looked for an appropriate water source to fill it and share between them. The man rubbed the bottle vigorously in an attempt to get it clean. Low and behold, a magical figure appeared, a genie if you will. Having been freed from his imprisonment inside the bottle, he thanked the three men and offered them one wish each."

Shesha turned to Ebony who walked eagerly beside him, matching him step for step.

"Are you with me so far Ebony as this is where the story gets interesting?"

Ebony nodded.

Shesha nodded back in appreciation.

"The first man took barely any time to think before giving the genie his answer. He had always wanted to have a means of getting about more easily so he wished for a car. With a small gesture and a smile, the genie granted his wish and the three men now had a car to share to continue their journey. The man was overjoyed. This was something he was definitely going to enjoy.

The second man was a little more thoughtful as several items of desire came to his head. After a few moments, he decided on a financial award and in turn was granted enough gold pieces to live comfortably on for the rest of his days, relaying to the others about how he would use his new found fortune He was a man of so many ideas and dreams and he was ecstatic that most of them may now come true."

"…And the third person?" Ebony asked impatiently. "What did he wish for?"

"Well… Let me tell you." Shesha requested, slowly raising a finger in a request for Ebony's patience.

"The third man took the longest to decide. After congratulating the other two on their good fortune, he turned to the genie himself, certain his wish was exactly what he wanted. He leaned in close to the genie and made his request. 'My wish is for the finest quality paint brush money can buy'. The other two men ceased their celebrations in surprise, then after a moment, burst into belly aching fits of laughter. Believing that the other two were ridiculing him rather than respecting his decision, he decided their friendship should end and returned home, paintbrush in hand.

Shesha's tone now changed slightly. They had reached the end of the pathway and were back out on the main sidewalk. He stopped and turned to her.

"You wish to hear the end of this?" He asked.

She nodded once more without hesitation.

"I am close to my home now but you are welcome to join us for dinner. Besides." He added. "I feel you should not be wondering these streets alone at this time of night Ebony and are seeking solace in a safe place to at least take time to gather your thoughts."

Ebony nodded in acceptance, her enthusiasm suggesting she was keen for both somewhere dry and warm to rest a while, but also to hear the end of Shesha's story. He began walking again. She quickly followed.

"So, as it happened, fate brought them together again years later and they were able to recount their tales of how that one event had changed their lives. The first man who wished told the other two how much he had loved his car and how after so many years, he still did the same thing as he has always done for a living, claiming he was content with life. The second man had some exciting tales to tell, travels to far off places, buying a house and many musical instruments to fuel his love of music. Yet it became obvious that he played none to a high standard. They all had pride of place in his house and he would bang the odd drum or pluck the odd string every now and again. The third man, the one who had walked away, listened to the other two boasting with smiles ear to ear with regards to their exploits and shenanigans, even offering them his congratulations. They turned to him eventually to ask what he had done after they parted. 'I went home and painted a picture. Then another one…then another one' he said. Before I knew it, I had painted a hundred pictures. Do you see where this is going Ebony?"

Ebony looked at him with a blank stare.

"I think so." She replied hesitantly.

Ebony could see the wrinkles on Shesha's face as he offered her a sympathetic smile.

"The moral of the story is Ebony that everybody falls into one of three categories of people. The first man is unfortunate. For sure, he enjoys himself, yet he plods through life never realising his full potential. He never discovers his gift in its true essence and at some point, his car will cease to function. The second man recognises his ability and yet remains so misguided, his gift goes to waste. He knows not what to do to make the most of it and learnt nothing on how to use it with the help of the right resources. His life turns out to be wasteful and in time his money will disappear. It is the third man, the third man alone that we should strive to be. The one who recognises his gift and allows it to flourish."

"What happened to the third man?" Asked Ebony with intrigue.

The story stops there my child." Shesha uttered with a sigh of regret. I asked the same question of those who first told this tale to me. It took me time to realise that it did not actually matter that the story had no ending in this sense. Once he discovered and began to use his gift, his future was an open book. He could accomplish anything he wished."

"I see." Said Ebony, with a little more understanding than was previously evident.

"Don't ever be like the second man in the story Ebony."

Shesha preached. "My own gift is to help people like you and Diana and make sure everyone I help finds themselves in a position such like the third man did."

"I would like to learn what my gift is. At least not to feel so bad afterwards and not to feel afraid of it." She said, her head dropping and voice becoming slightly mumbled with shame and regret.

"You have Diana for that too. I will be here for you too should you wish it."

Ebony looked him in the eyes and with one tear running down her cheek, quietly whispered.

"Thank you."

"Now we must get inside. The weather is shortly to get much worse. I am expecting Diana will be home by now."

Shesha pulled up his collar again and led the way from the clearing at the end of the pathway, over the road and towards his building that overlooked the park from a scenic elevated view. As they approached, Ebony noticed that the only lights that were on were all on the top floor.

"This is your house?" Asked Ebony, stopping for a second to admire its size.

"It is." Shesha answered humbly. "Though we solely reside on the top floor. There is little to be seen anywhere else in the building so I ask that whenever inside, you do stay on the top floor as the bottom two floors are very unsafe and offer much danger should you choose to explore them."

It took Shesha a couple of moments to unlock and then relock all the doors which he had armed with numerous measures of security and it dawned on Ebony that what ever was in the building had much value, at least for Shesha.

She wondered what treasures might lie inside. She could be forgiven for thinking that Shesha did not look the rich type. His non-descript clothing, his quiet demeanour, did not exactly paint the picture she had in her head of a rich mature old man. In truth, Ebony was expecting to be guided towards a small bedsit where Shesha might live with nothing more than a bed, a toilet and a kettle. He really did seem that type. She could not be more wrong and as she ascended the wooden staircase in the darkened corridor, she began to get a vague idea about how much space even one floor of this building would take up.

The stairs creaked more and more under the weight of her feet as she approached the top. The top stair in particular creaked so loudly that Ebony felt scared for a second that it was about to give way under her. There would be no way anyone could reach the door which she now stood before without alerting somebody to the disturbance.

"Maybe that was his intention." She thought to herself as she waited for him to open the door.

The door began to creek slightly as Shesha gently pushed it open. In front of Ebony was a long corridor with several doors lining the walls at random intervals on both sides. The door nearest to her was slightly ajar and the sound of what appeared to be a television set at a modestly loud volume could be heard. Somebody was evidently in the room and with a possible view to enjoying a relaxing evening watching television. After stepping into the hallway himself and slowly removing his hat and jacket, Shesha turned to Ebony who was still rooted to the spot. With a slightly nervous look on her face, she slowly followed him in

"Do not be afraid Ebony. You are most welcome here. Besides." He added. "You must be in need of some refreshment by now. Not to mention a towel." He concluded with a smile as he watched the drips run down Ebony's forehead.

Taking her wet clothes from her, Shesha gestured with a welcoming hand display for Ebony to adjourn to the room where the television could be heard in order to relax. Ebony took a couple of small steps and touched the door gently in order to push it just a little further open. The television was huge. So huge that it took up the entire wall space on the far side. A huge window also now came into view with several strange looking artefacts which took pride of place on the window sill. Though slowly walking away down the hall and away from Ebony, Shesha still seemed ever aware of her reluctancy to enter the room.

"Diamond has been keenly awaiting your arrival Ebony. Best not to keep her waiting any longer than you have to." He called out, without even turning around.

He smiled to himself and then continued walking down the corridor as he heard Ebony push the door open and let out a faint scream of excitement as she spotted Diamond sitting there. An excited scream typical of two teenage girls who had not seen each other for a while and had just been reunited at a party.

Once the initial excitement subsided, Ebony began to confide in her best friend once again, expressing her confusion with all that had gone on, as well as the guilt for what she had done.

"You must stay here with us Ebony" Diamond insisted.

"I….I …don't know" She stuttered. I need to get home for my mum"

"I concur." Said Shesha, re-entering the room carrying both a drink and a bowl of what smelled like a very nourishing broth of some kind. A spoon protruded out from the side of the bowl and steam rose up from its contents. Suddenly, Ebony had never felt so hungry. The soup was too hot to consume straight away so Ebony's focussed switched to the drink which Shesha had placed before her on the table. She reached out for the glass and pulled it towards her. She examined its contents. It was almost transparent in colour and completely odourless. Swishing the glass slightly from side to side, Ebony could see that the contents were far more viscous than water. The texture seemed more consistent with the likes of a milkshake perhaps, or even a medicine of some sort.

Under a disguised stare from Shesha, Ebony took a cautious sip of it from the glass. It was like nothing she had ever tasted before. It had a strange flavour. Neither bitter nor sweet. Yet strangely, even the first sip made it very moreish. It was almost as though it was the exact taste she had craved for a long time but never discovered. She quickly began to finish the rest, only to be interrupted by Shesha.

"Not too fast Ebony. It is a drink best drank slowly in order to savour it properly."

"Ebony began to consume it much more slowly as advised, though every instinct within her body was telling her to gulp it down. Having finished it to a chorus of observed silence, she placed the glass back down on the table. Her lips tingled slightly as she looked up and smiled.

"Good isn't it? Uncle makes it regularly for us. He calls it our medicine. We have been drinking it ever since we met

Uncle. It keeps us well and very much strong and alert to face everything what tomorrow might bring."

"Very well said daughter." Shesha whispered with pride, stroking the back of Diamond's hair in affection.

"How do you make it?" Ebony enquired, still wiping the last remnants from her sticky lips.

"Ah." Shesha replied, raising his hand high, palm open. "I am afraid that is something I am unable to disclose. At least at this moment. Take solace in the fact that when you are in our company Ebony, it will never be in short supply."

Shesha and Diamond exchanged a brief glance and a wry smile so brief that it went undetected by Ebony, who was now very much focussing her attention on the appetising dish of soup which she had propped on her knee.

"After you have enjoyed your soup Ebony, Diana here will be happy to fetch you another glass."

"Yes please." Came Ebony's yearnful reply and as she placed her spoon back in the bowl, in between mouthfuls of soup.

She had soon finished and as she placed her spoon back in the bowl one final time, Diamond quickly, and as promised was soon back with another glassful of the strange but addictive new drink.

"Thanks." Ebony gratefully uttered.

"Don't mention it sister." Came the innocent reply. "I'm sure Uncle won't mind if you take some with you to bed later too."

This time Ebony did not offer any resistance to the idea of staying. She was fully resigned to it. In fact she now felt she almost belonged there. She began to relax as she finished off her second glassful and a warm feeling came over her. A sense of comfortable numbness. even her thought processes were clouded by the sensation. She felt nothing. For the first time today, she was very much at peace and any guilt or worry had quickly subsided. Now what she yearned for above all else was a good night's rest.

An hour passed and with her delicious soup well and truly digested, along with another couple of drinks, Ebony was very much ready for bed. Her eye lids felt like lead weights and as much as she wanted to stay awake, her resistance was proving futile. It was a shame as during the last half hour of chatting with Diana, Diana had told her much about her older sister, Coral. The more Ebony heard, the more fascinated she was to meet her. However unlike most evenings in the recent past where Ebony had tended to come to life of an evening, tonight was very much the opposite.

"Don't worry Ebony." Diana said, offering out her hand whilst standing over her. "You will get to meet Coral soon enough. But for now. You need your rest. Come."

She beckoned Ebony to take her hand, extending the other one in the same manner. Ebony took her hands gratefully and used the last of her energy to prise herself up off the most comfortable seat she had sat in for quite a while.

Diana led Ebony gently down the hallway, as a guide might lead a blind person. She stopped at a door further down the corridor and opened it silently. Ebony was almost asleep as she walked but could still make out the outline of a huge bed which formed the centrepiece of the room. It was much bigger than the bed she had been used to at home. The covers had already been turned down for her which made it even more inviting to climb into. In Ebony's case however, it was more a case of flop on as she didn't even attempt to get under the covers. In fact she was asleep the moment her head made contact with the pillow. Diana slowly manoeuvred the top cover from under her dead weight and placed it gently over her, covering her up to her chest. Having done so, she stood there a moment, watching over Ebony like a guardian as she fell into a deep sleep.

"Sleep my sister." Whispered Diana with one gentle stroke of Ebony's cheek. "Sleep. As tomorrow will be a better day and the first day of the rest of your life…with us."

Ebony slept soundly, her only movement being a slight adjustment of a pillow or to pull the covers up slightly as the outside temperature plummeted as the night turned into early morning. As she adjusted her position for the final time, she could have sworn she heard the faint sound of two girls laughing together, another door being slowly shut and a familiar creaking of a wooden step as someone descended a staircase.

Chapter 18

iana relaxed under the tree for the moment before returning to the school building. It felt a little strange sitting there alone but she remained content. She had become very much used to sharing her lunch break sat there with Ebony. She missed having her around at school, even though she only saw her during lunch and sometimes before and after school. She knew Ebony missed her during the day time too. In the short time the two had known each other, they had become inseparable. Now Ebony was staying with her, she consoled herself with the fact that whilst she could not spend time with her at school for the moment, she could spend most evenings with Ebony whilst she stayed with her and her sister.

Before entering the building, Diana reached into her pocket to pull out a small piece of paper. She unfolded it. On it was a series of digits making up a telephone number. A number given to her by Ebony herself. It was her mum's number. Ebony has asked Diana to send her mum a message to let her know she was well. She agreed, on the understanding that it should be brief. Ebony needed a little bit of time, away from those who knew her, or might be looking for her, to recover from the trauma. Diana knew that the best place to do that was with her, her sister and Shesha. It appeared Ebony was fast beginning to realise that too. She was keen to see her mother but recognised that where she was happened to be the safest place to be until the time was right for her to go home. It was easy to see that Ebony wanted to be there with them anyway. That desire grew stronger each time they were together. The more Ebony allowed herself to be cared for, turning to Shesha for guidance, the bigger the sense of belonging she felt. Though she had spent only one night with them, that sense of belonging was very much evident already.

The bell rang for the end of lunch. Diana stood and grabbed her bag deciding not to use the main entrance into school like most of the other pupils, instead opting for the back entrance. It would mean a much longer walk, past the sports field and up the hill but she did not mind. Rather that than getting squashed in the main corridor by hundreds of students all piling in to the main entrance in a bottle neck scenario. As she reached the entrance, a second bell sounded. A bell that signified the actual start of her lesson. She was about to be marked absent if she did not hurry.

As she opened the door and made her way down what was now an empty corridor, three familiar faces appeared. It was Alexa and her two friends, Kat and Natalie. They looked up to see her approaching, sensing the opportunity to tease her about Ebony's absence.

"Where is your little friend then?" Natalie asked as they approached.

Rather than allow her to answer, Alexa decided to answer for her.

"Didn't you hear girls? She is on the run. A bit strange how there were two murders at her house and she has not been seen since. Maybe our little Bony ain't quite the little sweetheart we thought she was eh?"

Alexa looked back at Diana. Her attempt to wind her up was not working.

"Wow Alexa" Responded Diana. Your English is coming

on well. That must be three sentences you managed this time. You keep up the good work."

With that, Diana offered the three of them a sarcastic smile and confidently strode past them, almost bumping shoulders with Natalie in the process. She was some twenty feet down the corridor when she heard Alexa shout.

"It is best she does stay away. The only person she should be running from is me. When I see her next, she is getting it."

Diana stopped. Alexa had triggered her anger. She turned to look at Alexa.

"Not whilst I am around Alexa. You have no idea what you are getting into. Leave Ebony well alone." She warned sternly.

The girls laughed, walking off to the end of the corridor and out the door, leaving Diana alone once again. She watched them leave, her blood still simmering until they were out of sight, then made her way to class for an inevitable telling off for her tardiness.

It was now after school. Rather than making her way straight home, she waited outside school for Alexa and her friends to come out. Remaining out of sight but staying within easy visual range, she followed Alexa home. She did not live far from school in a very affluent neighbourhood. Her house was huge, the biggest on the block and as Alexa opened the door with her key and went inside, Diana watched from a safe distance.

She watched the house for any further movement for a few minutes and then made her way back towards the school, a satisfied look on her face.

"Good. Now we know." She said to herself, rubbing her hands.

On her way back to school, she passed a small newspaper shop. On a stand were a series of tabloids from that day. The headline of one paper in particular caught her eye.

MURDER MAYER BE THE CASE

It seemed, as expected, it was all over the local news at least. She made her way towards the bus stop and as she waited for it to arrive, one thought came to mind. If Ebony did want to stay out of harm's way and wait till the story had died down, it may be some considerable time.

"Perfect." She said to herself, pulling out her pass as the bus approached from the distance.

Chapter 19

251

"Is everything ok Madam?"

Stephanie looked up from her desk as she placed the final items in the top drawer. It was her brand-new office desk to go nicely with her first ever brand-new office. Given very courteously to her as a result of her recent promotion to the position of Head of Sales and Purchasing.

"I was kind of hoping for the bigger office down the hall." She hinted to her secretary. "But beggars cannot be choosers I suppose."

The lady in front of her, assigned now to being Steph's new secretary smiled meekly back at her.

"Well if there is anything I can do to assist you in settling in, do not hesitate to ask."

"What does a manager have to do to get a much-needed cup of coffee around here?" Steph replied abruptly, taking full advantage of her secretary's generosity.

"Of course Madam. I shall see to it straight away."

She turned to leave but then quickly turned back to Stephanie again to see she had returned to the task of organising her desk, taking great pride in placing each item of stationary and her personal items in their designated positions.

"Here is your pass key Madam."

She handed Stephanie a card which contained both her photo and a series of numbers on it.

"This will entitle you to full access to all the company records as well as complimentary use of all the amenities that the management here are entitled to."

"Very good. Thank you. Just leave it here on my desk if you don't mind."

It seemed clear that despite the assistant's best intent

to impress Stephanie with the perks of her new position, Stephanie was for the moment, far too distracted with the aesthetic look of her desk.

Placing the card on the desktop, the secretary made her way out of the office, closing the door behind her, shortly to return afterwards with a fresh hot cup of coffee. Stephanie reached for it and sat back in her office chair taking stock of her new surroundings, not even thanking Charlotte, her secretary, for the drink. The comfort of the chair, along with the fresh aroma of a strong coffee brought a smile to her face. She sipped the coffee with a sigh of satisfaction, even going so far as to putting her feet up on the end of the desk. She felt at home and justified that her lavish surroundings were nothing more than what she deserved after her hard work for the company over the last few years. Whilst she anticipated a little bit of ill will towards her from former colleagues who might believe she had slept and manipulated her way into such a prestige position within the company, she did not care now. As far as she was concerned, it was her sales figures that brought her this promotion and not her physical one.

After having finished her coffee, she leaned forward again, placing the cup and saucer on the desk. She reached for the card the secretary had left for her and inserted it into the designated slot in the side of the keyboard of her brand-new office computer. The screen came to life instantaneously and within a few seconds began to display screens containing sensitive company information, only a small amount of which, she had ever had access to before. She noted quickly that the number of e- mails she was now receiving had substantially increased and the frequency by which they were appearing in her in box was not something she was used to. She began to work her way through them. Most of them at this stage appeared to be messages welcoming her to her new role and from those people she might well be working with in the near future introducing themselves to her. With a brief smile whilst skim reading each one, she quickly deleted them one by one.

She moved straight to one particular e -mail and skimmed its content with her eyes. Without even finishing it, she reached for her phone and began dialling, an impatient look on her face. After a few rings, her call was answered. The voice was one she recognised.

"You know why I'm ringing then?" She asked in frustration.

The reply was a hesitant one. The voice was a mumbled response of apology and evident embarrassment. What she was being told only angered her further.

"I ordered this almost three weeks ago with the assurance it would arrive as part of a shipment a week ago. Need I remind you," She added. "If it was not for our business, you and your so-called partner would be picking up rubbish off the streets of Beijing."

"I assure you. It is on it's way Madam." Came the stuttered reply in broken English.

"If it isn't with me in two days. You can stick your supply contract renewal up your arse. Do I make myself perfectly clear Mr Wong?"

"Yes..Yes." Came the humbled reply. "I chase up now."

Moira hung up, failing to even grace her call recipient with a proper farewell. She had another call to make after all. She began to dial again, this time rather than doing so from behind her desk, she was now on her feet and slowly moving over to the blind covered window that allowed visual access to the rest of the office floor. With her finger and thumb, she separated the blinds at eye level and took a strategic peek through whilst she waited for an answer. Everyone was going about their business as expected and the office floor appeared quiet. It was then a soft- spoken voice picked up.

"Yes. It's me." She confirmed with a discreet whisper. "The package will be arriving in the next few days. I will be delivering it myself first-hand to ensure there are no more delays. It won't be too long to wait now."

"Yes Madam." Came the simple response.

"How is the other part of our project moving along?"

"Things are progressing nicely Madam. All involved are doing everything asked of them to bring about the eventuality we had both planned and foreseen. I am certain you will be extremely satisfied with the outcome."

The calm and confident reply seemed to settle Moira and a wry smile began to appear.

"I will be in touch very soon to arrange an exact time and see what progress has been made. Keep me informed."

"Yes. As always Madam." "Came the humbled reply once more. "Good day to you Madam."

Moira hung up, content that everything was in hand. At least everything associated with this particular issue. She returned to her seat and summoned her assistant in order to help her with some of the more mundane tasks to hand. She was keen to put her secretary to good use and delegate where possible now she was in a position to give orders rather than take them.

The rest of the day passed by without incident. An increased responsibility did of course mean an increased number of calls that she had to take as well as a significantly larger number of orders she had to manage. However, there was nothing to test her and very little that she was not used to handling as part of her previous role. Perhaps the biggest change she noticed as the day drew to an end was that time passed by so much faster. There were no longer those long breaks in between tasks where she would find herself wondering out of the office for extended lunches or secret daytime rendezvous with love interests. She also knew that her regular shopping trips after work might have to be sacrificed, or at least limited until she had learned to manage her increased workload. Although today was not going to be one of them, she also expected that there would be many an evening where she would have to stay behind for meetings and to balance the company books and chase up recent purchases similar to the one she was so secretly dealing with earlier. For her first day in her new role though, a five past six finish made her feel she had got off lightly. It would have been earlier but for a troublesome client chasing up the whereabouts of a purchase they had made. It appeared that some were more difficult to track down than others and not everyone in the department was as efficient as she was in recording these purchases correctly within the company database. She hated incompetence, especially when it meant that it ate into her free time having to correct such errors. This particular error had now been dealt with, but one unfortunate subordinate was soon to be faced with a very unpleasant confrontation with her in her office the following morning. Her last thought as she picked up her car keys and phone from off her desk was how she would ensure that the aforementioned colleague would be under no illusions as to what the repercussions would be should the same incidence occur again.

Only a few workers remained on the office floor, all of which seemed too preoccupied to notice that she was leaving for the day. She would have waited for them in previous times to wish them a pleasant evening or maybe even to ask one of them if they might be impartial to a post work drink in the bar they all tended to frequent nearby. Things may well change now. She was their boss after all. It suddenly felt somewhat inappropriate to even ask them. So it was instead, that she chose to walk out the office saying nothing to anyone, focussing solely on getting home to relax in front of the television for the evening. That is assuming she was not going to be disturbed again as she had been the previous couple of evenings. Her somewhat distraught sister had been on the phone numerous times in an effort to track down Ebony or see if she had been at least in touch. She had not been seen nor heard of in the few days since the event and Moira's desperation was evident in her voice.

If it was not Moira, it was her mother expressing her grave concern for both Moira's and Ebony's welfare. Her mother did not know the whole story as to what had transpired but it had been impossible to keep it secret from her. It had after all become newsworthy in not only this state, but now neighbouring states also, as the search for Ebony continued. Her disappearance had become somewhat of a mystery. Stephanie was far more relaxed about the whole thing though. Whilst she did express her worry and concern for Ebony, she also held much more faith in the idea that Ebony had been able to make adult decisions for herself despite her tender years. She had a good relationship with Ebony, whereby the times they did get together, she saw a strength and a level of independence in her that her own over protective mother and grandmother failed to see. It was a trait she most admired in a girl of such tender years. Perhaps because it reminded her so much of a younger version of herself. So it was that she had calmly said the same thing over and over again to both Moira and her frantic mother when they had rang.

"She will be fine." Stephanie had told them both confidently. "You always underestimate her ability to look after herself, especially since what happened a few years ago."

It had fell on deaf ears. As she was sure it would do again the next time she rang. She had thought of just not answering the phone at all to either of them but that would have only made matters worse. Stephanie was about the only one who believed that wherever she was, Ebony was alive and well, or at least as well as can be with what she had been through. She was likable and made good friends easily. She was certain to be hiding out with one of them until things died down a little

As it happened, Stephanie's plans changed that evening, as she found herself jumping at the opportunity of entertaining some male company. Someone whose company she very much enjoyed, thus any phone calls or texts from pestering family members were very much pushed to the back of her mind. Maybe tonight, she would switch her phone off.

When she woke the following morning, feeling both empowered and content, she quickly noticed that she was alone. The covers on the other side of the bed had been put neatly back into place and the only evidence that she had shared the bed with anyone had been the indentation left in the pillow beside her own. It was still early so she figured that he must have left before daybreak and in a manner so subtle and quiet that it had not caused her to even stir. She smiled a satisfied smile knowing she would most definitely see him again very soon. This was becoming quite a regular thing and although the first time she slept with him had been with an ulterior motive, she had since realised what a great lover he was. Such is the case; she was no longer reluctant to accept any advances from him of any kind. She was definitely getting her cake as well as eating it and he was happy to help her out in any way he could. It was for sure, a mutually beneficial relationship that she had every intent on maintaining.

As she arrived back at the office for her second day, there was an added spring in her step. Not only had she enjoyed a very intimate night the night before, additionally, she had received welcoming news that the shipment she had chased the previous day was due to arrive later on that night.

"Should I collect it myself?" She wondered for a second.

It would mean a very late night again and she was not sure whether she would have the energy nor the enthusiasm come the end of the working day to travel the 250 kilometres journey to the port delivery centre and back again. Then, just as she seemed to have decided, her thoughts switched to the level of importance this package had. She did not want its arrival to be delayed any further. Both herself, along with other interested parties would not be happy with that at all. She also dreaded the thought of her highly sensitive fragile cargo falling into the hands of some rather clumsy delivery man who whilst on minimal wage, had little or no concern for the safe transit of the goods.

"Yes." She concluded The only way to be sure was to collect the package herself and then deliver it to its final destination personally.

Chapter 20

our days had passed since the incident. Three of them, Moira had spent in hospital. Now, back on her feet again, she had been discharged from hospital. She still ached and it would take time for some of her superficial wounds to heal completely but she was keen to get home. Or at least she thought she was. However as she stood on her own front porch, key in hand, she stopped for a moment. She developed a sudden urge to run. Not just to the end of the drive, not even to the end of the street, but much further. She wanted to be far away from the house. Perhaps it was the thought of what might confront her as she opened the door. Was Jeremy's lifeless body still lying there on her kitchen floor? Worse yet, was he actually still alive and waiting patiently for her to return, perhaps still wielding that sickening blood stained weapon with which he had committed such an atrocity? Though the police had assured her that neither would be the case, she could not help but feel that an unpleasant surprise awaited her on the one turn of the key.

Somehow she mustered up the courage to enter. She did not want to linger outside in case she attracted the attention of any of the neighbours. Neighbours who by now, would have been all too familiar with what had occurred a few days previous. Whilst there was no doubt in her mind that her neighbours had her best interests at heart, she was keen for some alone time. The only exception to this was Ebony. She was sick with worry as to her whereabouts. Everyone was on high alert to keep an eye out for her as she had not been seen for days. The police seemed to want to track her down for very different reasons to her mother. They still were actively searching for any clues as to her location, based on the assumption that she was still alive and well. Only a couple of short text messages from an unrecognised number was all that Moira had to go on to believe that this was indeed the case. Messages that as yet, she had not informed the police about.

She entered. Everything was silent. The only activity of any kind seemed restricted to the faint humming sound from the kitchen appliances and the flashing red light on the answering machine. She dreaded to think how many messages might be stored on that by now. The house felt both eerie and cold. Yet, as she hesitantly made her way into the living room and then subsequently, the kitchen, she was relieved to find no traces of how she remembered it looking when she saw it last. The floor was one again a brilliant white. The broken picture frame that had fell from the wall had been removed without any traces of glass left behind. Even the dirty footprints had been adequately wiped up from the carpet.

She stood at the entrance to the kitchen. Something in her mind was stopping her from entering but she couldn't quite comprehend what it was. She began to feel her heart race a little. Her breathing began to quicken and become louder. It felt like the beginning of some sort of panic attack. Before it could escalate, she closed her eyes, placing her palm on her chest. She inhaled deeply through her nose, held it for a moment, then exhaled again, expelling the air slowly through slightly parted lips. It seemed to work. Her heart rate slowed a little. After repeating this a few times, she opened her eyes once more and then stepped into the kitchen. She began filling the kettle from the tap and then flicked the switch. A good cup of high-quality coffee was just the tonic she felt she needed to feel more at home. None of that brown water with grit like they served her from the nurses' station.

"Now for the next task." She murmured with dread.

Grabbing her cup of coffee, she steadily made her way to the living room and over to her favourite seat by the window. She placed her coffee down carefully after a first welcome sip, on the nest of tables by the side of the arm chair. By reaching over to the other side of her chair, she pressed the button on her answering machine in order to listen to her stored messages. She even allowed herself a little smile as she began to estimate how many messages might await her, hoping one might be from Ebony.

"Twenty something." She guessed, waiting for the automated voice to confirm her suspicions.

"YOU HAVE ELEVEN NEW MESSAGES." Reported the robotic voice on her machine.

"Eleven." She responded. Not as bad as I thought."

She began to trawl through her messages. Predictably, several of them were from her mother with the others consisting mainly of reporters wanted to get a scoop on the story, two of them even going so far as to inviting her to a press conference to confront the local media to tell her side of the story.

For a second, she considered it. Then on further reflection, decided that it was not something she could face right now. She had not even told her parents the complete story as yet although the news coverage had done their part to put the fear of god into her mother. If she was not ready for that yet, there was no chance she could divulge exactly what happened to the whole state over national television in front of a series of flashing cameras and obnoxious news crew. Perhaps the upside to it was that she could use the opportunity to appeal for the safe return or news on the whereabouts of Ebony. There again, all those people that she knew and trusted were already looking for her. That would do for now. Whilst part of her longed for company right now, she also craved peace and quiet. It wouldn't last long. She knew once people knew she was back home, there would be all manner of visitors knocking on the door to ask after her. Whilst some would be genuinely concerned for her wellbeing, she knew some would attend with a different purpose.

It was with that train of thought and as she deleted the final message that she pulled on the cord which dangled down next to the windows edge. She pulled on it gently and the blinds began to rotate, thus darkening the room considerably. She flicked on the table light which bathed the wall and immediate surrounding area in an eerie yellow glow. It was not the most powerful of lights, but adequate enough for her to at least see her way around the living room safely.

Having turned on the television, she soon found herself drifting off to sleep. She was at least more comfortable now she was back home and in her favourite chair. She began to drift off again and the sound of the voices from the programme she had on began to grow quieter as her eyes began to shut. Her sleep did not last for long. She had forgot to switch the setting to vibrate on her phone and the loud ring tone now echoed around the room. It seemed so much louder in such tranquil surroundings. She answered it quickly, without even looking to see who the caller might be.

"Hello." She said quietly, rubbing the sleep from her eyes.

"Moira. Is that you sweetheart?"

The voice was instantly recognisable.

"Hi mum. I was just about to call you."

"I was getting worried. I haven't heard from you for a little while. I have left messages for you but you did not reply and you know I like to know you are safe."

Moira easily picked up on the concern in her mother's voice, with perhaps a little intent to instil a little guilt.

"I know. I'm fine though. Honestly. Just nodded off there for a moment relaxing on the sofa."

"Where on earth is Ebony? Has she been in contact? She has got me and your father worried sick."

"She is ok mum. I just spoke to her and she is staying with her new friend from school I told you about." Lied Moira, trying to sound as calm as she could. Little did she know that what she thought was a lie was actually very true.

The rest of the conversation consisted of the usual. Sue panicking about everything she could possibly panic about and Moira attempting to play everything down and assure her everything was, or will be fine.

"Stop worrying mum." Moira said for the third time.

There was only one thing that would possibly give Moira some respite from going around in circles with her mum and as her head began to pound and her muscles tighten with stress, it was a tactic she decided to resort to. Lying again.

"I have to go mum. There's the door."

Before her mother could respond again, Moira hung up. As she did so, her head almost immediately stopped pounding and she began to relax again. A five-minute interval between that call and the next one was barely a reprieve. She answered it once more, this time with a more enthusiastic tone.

"Mrs Meyer?" The caller asked.

"Yes. "She replied with hesitancy to the unfamiliar voice. Whoever it was seemed very happy with themselves that they had managed to get in touch with her.

"This is Sam Coleman from AR news. I left you a message yesterday and was wondering if…"

The phone began to give out a continuous loud tone. It soon became clear to Mr Coleman that Moira had abruptly terminated the call. He hung up and turned to his cameraman who sat besides him in the news van.

"We'll call round tomorrow. See if we can get more joy that way. I need this story."

The cameraman nodded in agreement as he took a large bite from his sandwich.

"You're right Sam. Its not every day we get to cover a double homicide." He replied with his mouth still half full.

"Are you aware of how disgusting that is Ron? It looks like you have some sort of eating problem." Remarked Sam with disdain.

"I don't have a problem Sam." Ron replied, taking another huge bite. "I love eating."

"You must love sharing too." Sam replied with sarcasm and pointing to his jacket. "Is your coat enjoying it too?"

Ron looked down at his jacket, picking up on what Sam had so rightfully pointed out. Without hesitancy, he took his index finger and scooped up the large dollop of sauce which had fell out the bottom of his overloaded sandwich and proceeded to place it in his mouth, savouring and sucking every last morsel of flavour he could.

"Thanks for the heads up on that one. Don't want to waste any part of this baby."

"I can see that." Sam replied, turning his attention away from Sam before he began to feel nauseous.

"So what's our next move on this?" Ron asked, crumpling up the sauce stained and partially soggy tissue which encased his lunch.

"Let's head down to the precinct. I want to get in that detectives' face about what happened with the other two people that were there. Besides, I think he knows a lot more than he is letting on."

"Good thinking." Replied Ron. After carelessly disposing of his screwed-up ball of tissue out the window of the van, he fired up the engine and pulled away from the sidewalk.

Chapter 21

bony woke up alone from a deep afternoon sleep. She felt warm and comfortable with the sweater that she had borrowed from Diana. She slowly stood and made her way toward the bathroom. The house was indeed empty and peaceful.

She suddenly felt a strange tingling sensation on her left arm. It was unlike anything she had felt before. It was not pain, more of a burning itch. Instinctively she began to rub it with her other hand. She rubbed softly at first, but that only seemed to intensify the itching sensation. She rubbed harder and faster through the material of her sweater. The same sensation seemed to be spreading as now her right arm began to tingle also.

By the time she had walked down the hallway to the bathroom, she was scratching all over in a frenzy of discomfort. Even her neck and face were beginning to exhibit the same symptoms. She felt like her skin was on fire.

Thinking she was perhaps overheating in some way, she quickly removed her sweater, allowing it to fall to the floor. Not noticing the abundance of white skin like flakes which stuck to the sweater as it lay on the floor, she looked with horror into the bathroom mirror.

She had thought that a slight discrepancy in her vision when she had woke moments ago was due to the fact that she had slept heavy. This was quite common practice for her since staying here. However it quickly dawned on her from her own reflection in the mirror that it was far more than just a touch of sleep in the corner of her eye.

With her vision diminished, she leaned into the mirror for a closer look. Her eyes were no longer the colour they were.

That bright twinkle had gone. Instead they appeared opaque and to some extent lifeless. She looked at herself through what appeared to be some sort of heavy fog. A fog that not only appeared to hamper her ability to see clearly, but one that seemed to be growing thicker.

Bringing her initial panic under control, she slowly reached for her eye with her fingers. As she drew close to her eye lid, she pressed her finger and thumb together tightly, with the intent on using the nails as a pair of makeshift tweezers.

She was all but touching the very surface of her eye now but it did not seem to bother her. It was as though she was in some sort of automated trance, carrying out a procedure she was used to doing on a daily basis, similar to removing a contact lens. With a slight adjustment of her hand position, she focussed her attention on the outer corner of the sclera. She intricately began to manipulate it with her nails until she had what felt like a thin layer of film-like skin between her thumb and forefinger. She slowly began to tug on it, peeling it away from the eye itself. Despite it being loose in parts, it was still quite tough to remove and though there was no pain, in fact no sensation at all, it pulled on her eyeball as she carefully and deliberately moved her fingers past her nose to complete the process.

The layer of skin fell from her finger and into the wash basin. She blinked a couple of times and using a tissue, carefully wiped off a small trail of blood which had slowly began to run down her cheek from the far corner of her eye where she first began her extraction. Looking into the mirror again, she smiled. Her vision in that eye was perfectly clear once more. The shiny surface of her newly exposed sclera was brighter than ever. After repeating the process with equal purpose and dexterity on her other eye, she began to focus on her arms. No longer were they smooth and olive in colour. They were now rough to the touch, blistered with small milky bubbles like a tourist peeling excessively after a long day in the Mediterranean sun.

Forming her hands into a claw like position, she began to scrape down the entire length of her arm from the top of her shoulder down to her hand. To her delight, a layer of skin came clean off in one smooth motion without even a rip or a tear. Underneath was anything but ordinary human skin. What she revealed was a silky and scaly patterned surface likable only to the serpent nemesis that had become such a prominent part in her life. However rather than fearing it, she appeared to be rejoicing in her discovery. She examined her arm with pride, rotating her elbow to view it from all the angles she could manage. She was shedding skin and at an alarming rate.

Looking back in the mirror, her appearance had now changed beyond recognition. Her pupils were no longer spherical. They were oval and green in colour. Her now forked tongue protruded out of a pair of pursed lips, tasting the air. She opened her mouth to look inside, letting out a light hiss as she did so. As her mouth opened, a pair of needle like fangs dropped into place from her upper jaw where her normal incisors used to be. She felt a solitary drop of honey like liquid drop from the sharpened end of each fang and onto her bottom lip. Not wanting to waste it, she quickly licked it up with her tongue and savoured the taste of her own secretion. Her cheek bones now were also very prominent and a small pulsing gland emanated from beneath them. Suddenly, as she stared at her reflection, the mirror slowly began to crack. The cracks were subtle at first but spread fast across the surface from each corner and in towards the middle. The half human, half serpent that was once Ebony covered her face with her scaly arms as the glass shattered violently, with shards of glass heading straight for her face.

She sat up suddenly. She was breathing deeply in response to her dream. It was evident she was alone again, as she was in her dream moments previous. Only this time, on the table sat a small note stuck to the surface. Next to it was placed a tall refreshing glass of her new favourite drink. She reached over for it, very much thirsty and in need of some refreshment. She glanced at the note as she did so. It simply read:

BE BACK SOON. S. XX.

Having quickly demolished the contents of the glass, she was at a little bit of a loss as to what to do with herself. She found herself wondering around the hallway, then without thinking, opening the main door which led to the downward staircase outside. Driven by curiosity, she slowly descended the staircase. She remembered the room on the floor below and how she had been very much discouraged by Shesha not to go anywhere near it. Every time she asked Shesha or the girls about it, they would quickly and deliberately change the subject, It was the only thing Shesha himself seemed to be very secret about. The girls were forbidden to talk about it much too. Promising herself only a quick glance to satisfy her curiosity, she continued down the stairs.

She followed the rail round as she reached the bottom of the stairs and noticed that the corridor grew very dark up ahead. Only a faint bluish glow from a small window pane within the confines of a large door offered any degree of light for her to navigate her way successfully.

She walked slowly towards the door, her heart skipping a beat with every step she took. It was fortunate that the see-through portion of the door was low enough for her to peer through though it did seem to move higher and beyond her reach with every step she took towards it. As she reached the door itself, the bottom edge of the glass was level with her forehead. She would have to stretch up onto her toes and perhaps even action a series of small jumps if she wanted a proper look inside.

Standing on her tiptoes offered only a limited view. What appeared to be a series of mounted cupboards on the far wall was about all she could manage to see. She took her first jump, stretching every sinew in her neck as she did so. A series of large glass tanks lined the walls both left and right. They sat on units which stretched around the entirety of the room apart from a small corner of wall space towards the back. It was the lights fitted inside these tanks that were creating the blue glow she witnessed from outside the room. A second jump now revealed that of those containers she could see, which she estimated to be somewhere in the region of twelve, the majority of them were not empty. She jumped a third time, this one a little higher than the previous attempts to see what was inside. Depending on which one she looked at, something was either moving or lay inside them. They were quite hard to make out in some of the containers. Whatever they were, most of them blended in well to their background. One more jump confirmed her suspicions, especially when she caught sight of a long, coiled tail resting against the back of one of the containers. They were snakes. Some were evidently bigger than others and they subtly ranged in colour from a bright green in one tank, to a black and yellow combination sported by another. There was undoubtedly a wide variety of species and she was now even more curious and eager to get a closer look. A look at the door itself seemed to indicate there was no actual key lock. This surprised her a little. She had been placed on trust not to enter but now she felt a subconscious calling from inside the room itself to proceed.

With her hand now squeezing the door handle, she wrestled with her conscience one last time. All it would take for the door to open would be the small matter of pressing down on the handle. Shesha had done so much for her though. Would it be fair to disobey the one rule he had put in place during her stay? It was a dilemma and for a second or two, her grip loosened on the handle, then she placed it back. It was too hard to resist. The voice inside her which told her she must enter was beginning to overpower. She tightened her grip again on the handle and carefully pushed downwards. The door opened easily. Easier than what she had expected. She slowly pushed it open to get her first look at the entire contents of the room.

She was correct in her estimation. Twelve large containers dominated the space within the room with six on either side. They sat neatly next to one another and although they were not fixed into the wall in any way, they appeared to be lined up with perfect symmetry. The glass casing for each container was crystal clear. So clear in fact that for a moment, she questioned as to whether the tanks even had casing on them at all. Only the solid black lids fixed around the perimeter of each one could confirm this without actually touching the glass surface itself. She looked around, still stood at the threshold of the doorway. The room was immaculately clean. The floor, which consisted of small square white tiles, reflected the light brilliantly from the fluorescent tubes located in each of the tanks making it appear almost illuminous. On the far wall, a series of overhead cupboards could be seen. The ones she caught sight of at first. Each one was no bigger than a standard medicine cupboard. She would have to open each one, should she dare to do so, for they offered no visible way of viewing their contents from outside. The doors were solid, each with their own silver knob fixated half way up. There were no labels of any kind on the cupboard doors, so if it was that they were full, she figured the contents were in regular use and someone must be very familiar with what was in which cupboard. There were after all, a significant number of units. She counted them quickly in her head, pointing to each one with her finger as she did so. There were ten in total, separated into two rows. On the counter top below sat a very interesting and peculiar contraption. It was something she could only liken to a scene from a film or a cartoon where a kind of mad scientist had used items of laboratory apparatus, with the means to conducting some form of crazy experiment. Whilst set up intricately with a combination of stands, clamps, tubes and varying sizes of conical flasks, there was no apparent activity happening. All the items of apparatus that could house some form of liquid or powder were empty Whatever Shesha had set this up for, had either already happened, or was due to happen in the very near future.

She took her first couple of steps into the room, standing in between the first two tanks. As she drew level, each of the snakes inside seemed to notice her, offering her a prolonged and milky-eyed stare. One of them even moved closer to the glass, its forked tongue tickling the surface. They could sense her presence. Of that there was no doubt and they were watching her every move.

She took another couple of steps forward, the snake adjusting its glance slightly to track her movements. She was close enough now to notice that the apparatus was perfectly clean, consistent with everything else in the room. On discovering this, she theorised that whatever experiment this had been set up for was to take place very soon.

"What was Shesha into?" was the question she now began to ask herself. The snakes she understood. She knew he had a fondness for snakes and based on her own recent experiences, it was evident he had learnt a lot about them. Perhaps now she realised why. He had many of his own to learn off and possibly even experiment with to some extent. Looking around at the snakes, none of them appeared agitated or mistreated in any way and were kept in the perfect environment for them to thrive. It looked like they were almost his pets of sort. However, this was a different story. The chemistry-type set up just did not seem to fit. She wanted to know more but remembered she should not even be in here so it was not like she could approach him to ask what it was all used for. She would have to figure it out herself.

She took the final few steps needed to be within reach

of the cupboard doors. She slowly reached up for one of the door knobs and squeezing it lightly, gave it a light tug to open it. She had partially opened it and was about to get a closer look at its content when a faint noise from behind her startled her. She spun round, letting go of the knob to the cupboard. As it slowly closed again with a light squeak, Ebony realised she was no longer alone in the room. She stared in surprise at Shesha as he looked at her, his eyes so wide, but not really giving anything away. They were almost bulging out of his head. He was flanked by the two girls who towered over his small figure. She expected to see a look of disappointment or perhaps anger on his face but that was not to be the case. Instead Shesha offered her a weak smile and a slight nod of his head. A nod that seemed to indicate that he had very much predicted this would happen at some point soon. The girls, behind him also gave her the same look although no-one spoke for a moment or two. Ebony felt slightly reassured by the response she was getting, though still felt wracked with guilt for disobeying him. Eventually Shesha broke the silence.

"We knew you would find your way in here very soon my dear Ebony."

"I'm so sorry." Ebony replied. "I don't even know why I did it." She added.

"That maybe true Ebony. It is lucky for you that I do know why you came in here today. In order to learn more about your gift, you must also understand it. That is why you are in here."

Ebony just nodded. What Shesha was saying did make perfect sense.

"I am guessing you felt a luring sensation from deep within you, a craving of sorts that you just could not overcome?"

Ebony nodded once more, almost as if she had been placed into some sort of obedient trance, overcome by Shesha's ability to read her thoughts and emotions with such accuracy. It was not the first time

"Good girl. I'm proud of you. It says your gift grows stronger by the day. You will soon learn to control it. It just takes a little bit of time. Now that you are here Ebony, its time to learn a little more about what you see before you. Are you ready to learn?"

Ebony nodded enthusiastically although the expression on her face had not changed from one of looking shocked and overwhelmed.

For the next hour or so Shesha explained to Ebony all about his past, his love for snakes, and the purpose of his laboratory style set up. At the end, he turned to her, placing a reassuring hand on her shoulder.

"Do you have any questions for me now Ebony?"

"So you used to be a Chemistry Professor where you used to live?" Asked Ebony.

"Correct." Came his reply.

"…And all this equipment is to make the medicine my sisters need to stay well?"

Shesha nodded, happy that she was taking all this in and understanding it.

"So the snakes are used to make anti venoms for people who get bit and you make them for hospitals like the one that treated me?"

"That's right Ebony. Like I said." He added. "My purpose

has always been to help people and I often need lots of supplies which are contained in this room. These are the errands I often send the girls on to collect. This is how I can afford this beautiful home we have and all my equipment."

The two girls, who had stayed with her, nodded.

"I think that is all I need to say now Ebony and I can see this information is a lot to take in. Why don't you go upstairs and pour yourself some juice? You will need your energy in order to help me with a few things. Now that you know what goes on in here, I can see there is a need to teach you more."

Ebony smiled and then made her way out the door and back along the corridor towards the stairs. As the girls gestured to follow her, Shesha stopped them.

"Daughters." He said quietly. It appears our beloved Ebony is progressing faster than we thought. Now she knows all about this, I see no reason to delay the next step in proceedings. It would be foolish to wait any longer. The time has come and to wait would only bring about more questions and more confusion for her."

The girls nodded in agreement.

"Then you know what you must do?" He asked, looking at them both in turn.

"Yes Uncle. We know." They uttered in unison, sharing a smile.

"Very good. I will be looking to receive a very important delivery in the next day or so. At that time, that is when we shall do what needs to be done. I think it best you prepare for it. She is ready."

The girls nodded again with a contained excitement.

"Go now." Shesha instructed. "Ensure you rest fully as

your strength will be much needed for later. Besides, I have my beloved friends to feed."

Both girls leaned forward to give him a gentle kiss on each cheek. Then, side by side, they walked out the door, hand in hand, closing the door behind them. They climbed up the staircase and joined Ebony back in the living room, all sharing a welcome drink together whilst Ebony asked them more about their past. Their bond had become strong, yet the events of the next twenty-four hours were to bring them closer still.

Chapter 22

er first lonely night had passed and Moira woke up to a quietness she had not experienced for a long time. Normally by now she would have dropped Ebony off at college and been on her way to work. But of course, present circumstances had led to Ebony not being around and her employers had very graciously given her a period of one week to get back on her feet and use her time to track down the whereabouts of her beloved daughter. She was understandably frantic with worry. However nothing positive could come of panicking. Instead she forced herself to devote her time and energy into searching for her as well as spreading the word as far and wide as she could as to Ebony's unexplained and prolonged disappearance. She understood why Ebony would hideaway somewhere, taking solace in the fact that the two to three messages she had received had assured her of Ebony's safety. She was so used to Ebony turning to her in times of trouble so it stirred feelings of sorrow and an underlying emptiness that she sought comfort at the hands of another during this challenging time. At least she knew that whoever she was with was obviously proving to be great help in guiding Ebony through this. Otherwise, Moira was sure Ebony would be home in an instant. So it was, that for the reason of not being hounded by the police or the media, Moira reluctantly had decided to give Ebony the time and space she needed. She would come home when the time was right. As far as the police investigation went, Moira would just play along, co-operate and answer their questions as best she could. As far as the messages went that had been sent to re-assure Moira of Ebony's wellbeing, the police were on a need to know basis. For the moment, she concluded, they did not need to know. She was hoping for another one very soon.

Heading downstairs to the kitchen, she fixed herself some toast and a cup of coffee. She knew that she did not have much time. She was expected at the police station at ten and it was already quarter to nine. She took her usual seat in the living room by the window, in order to have her breakfast, intermittently peering around the corner of the blinds. To her surprise, the street seemed devoid of activity. There was no plethora of journalists hanging round on the lawn trying to get a sneak peek or news vans parked up on the street. She guessed that might happen at some point though. The news companies were not going to leave someone they knew to be involved in a homicide alone for long.

"Good." She thought as she peered left and right. "Freedom. At least for the time being."

The freedom she was thankful for did not last long. In fact, it lasted as long as it took her to get showered and dressed. As she dried her hair in the bedroom, she caught sight of a white van which came trundling into view and pulled up at the end of the driveway, blocking the exit from the driveway in the process.

She watched tentatively from her bedroom window as two gentlemen exited the van, one from each side of the vehicle. They seemed in somewhat of a hurry. The second, man, the smaller and fatter of the two quickly ran around to the other side and opened the large sliding door to the main component of the vehicle. He pulled out a large camera and hoisted it up onto his shoulder. Following the first gentleman closely, they made their way up to the porchway and rang the bell.

Moira was not quite sure if she should answer or not. She had been advised to leave the handling of the press to the police, or at least not speak to them without a member of the investigating team present. There was no-one with her from the police at the moment and if she was going to get down to the precinct, she would have to confront them to an extent in order for them to at least allow her the chance to leave. She left her bedroom and then stopped at the top of the stairs. A thought came to mind. She pulled out her phone and using the card that the detective had left her whilst in hospital, she began dialling her number.

"Chen's office." Came the reply.

Moira recognized the voice.

"Hi there. This is Moira." She replied.

"How can I help you Moira. Aren't you coming to see me shortly?"

"It is about that that I am ringing you now." Moira replied.

"Is there a problem Moira?" The lieutenant asked, his tone now one of raised concern.

"You could say that. I have two members of the press banging on my front door as we speak. They seem quite determined to speak to me as they have parked across my driveway and blocked me in. Any suggestions?"

Mercer was quick to respond, as though responding to an emergency. His voice now came across a little stern as he gave Moira instructions.

"Here is what I want you to do Moira. Do not answer the door. I will send a car for you and they will bring you to me. Not to mention assisting you by getting rid of those arseholes at your front door. Thank you for letting me know."

With that, Mercer hung up. Just before he did so, Moira could hear him barking out orders to someone in the background. She just had time to make out the first few words before the phone went dead.

"Someone get around to the Meyer house…." She heard.

Downstairs, the two journalists waited for Moira to answer the door. The man holding the camera seemed to be growing impatient.

"This is useless Sam." Ron stated pessimistically. "It's pretty obvious she is not going to answer." He added.

"Well I am not giving up just yet. Why don't you make yourself useful and head round the back? Maybe she left the back door open or something," Suggested Sam, pointing to the side gate as though he were training a new puppy to follow his instructions.

Lowering his camera, he placed it on the porch next to Sam and slowly ambled off to inspect the rear of the house as instructed. The gate was locked, yet despite his chubby fingers, he manged to slip one of them through just far enough to lift the latch up inside. It was loose and gave way quite easily to the slightest pressure. The gate creaked as he pushed on it slightly, its hinges all but worn away with rust. He pushed it slower in a feeble attempt to lessen the noise. When it was opened wide enough, he lid through the gap sideways, brushing the back of his jacket up against the brick wall of the house.

"Well that was easy." He said to himself proudly. "Now to do some snooping around."

From his pocket, he pulled out a small digital camera. He

was poised to take a shot of anything or anyone that might add some substance to this case. There was nothing much to go on. No broken windows, no forced entry, no dead bodies lying on the lawn that he had hoped for to break the case wide open. He hung around for a minute as he did not want it to seem as though he had just took one quick look before returning to Sam. He had to at least make it look somewhat of a thorough snoop around. As he turned back toward the gate, something did catch his eye. Something the size of an envelope lay before him on the ground. He reached down for it. It was soaked through and dirty but a quick wipe off from the leaves and dried on dirt, then the discovery of a fine zip along one side, revealed what it was that he had found. He eagerly opened the zip and examined it's contents, Two or three pens, a pencil, an eraser and an item of makeup were all that was inside. It was a pencil case. He wiped its outer surface once more with his coat sleeve in the hope of seeing something that might identify the owner. Sure enough in the bottom corner, under careful examination, two faded letters were now visible. They were hard to make out and Ron had to squint heavily to identify them.

"E.M" He said to himself... Who could E.M be?"

With that thought, he made his way back round to the front of the house. Sam was still there on the porch, peering through the letter box to look for signs of life inside, pleading with Moira to come and answer the door.

"Check this out." Ron said enthusiastically, pulling the dirty stained pencil case back out from his pocket. Sam looked at him with a puzzled look on his face.

"It's a pencil case Ron." Sam said, stating the obvious.

"Yeah I know. What a great find eh? It was round the back near the gate. My guess is that it must have been dropped in somebody's haste to escape."

"Ron." Said Sam, raising his voice in frustration and disbelief. Here we are, trying to get an exclusive with the woman who is a suspected murderer in a double homicide case, whose daughter is missing for the best part of the week, and your overjoyed at finding a dirty pencil case in her back yard. Its hardly worthy of the six o'clock news is it?"

Before Ron could reply. Sam continued to chastise him in his usual manner.

"I'll tell you what to do Ron. Take your little pencil case back to the van with you and I will join you in a minute. Then I can drop you at the hospital on the way back to the office so the contents of the pencil case can be surgically removed from your colon."

Ron sheepishly picked up his camera and returned the pencil case to his jacket pocket before heading back to the van. He placed the camera back inside the van and slid the door shut. Sam had finally given up waiting and came down to join him, opening the passenger side door.

"Come on." He said to Ron in haste. "We will try again later. I'll be damned if I'm going to let this story go."

The van slowly pulled away, making its way slowly to the end of the avenue. Having returned to her bedroom, Moira watched it go with a sense of both delight and relief. She was only sorry though that the police car did not arrive before they left. Maybe they could have persuaded them not to return.

No sooner had the van disappeared around the corner at

the top end of the street, than a car came into view from the opposite direction and pulled up outside. An officer in full uniform got out of the car and made his way up the driveway to the house. Moira made her way downstairs to open the door and welcome him, a little disappointed it was not Mercer himself.

"Good morning Mrs Meyer. I was told you had some rather intrusive reporters hanging around the house. I see that is no longer the case."

"Yes." Moira replied apologetically." I am sorry that you just missed them. Looks as though I could have made it down to the station in time anyway. If you want, I can drive down myself?" She offered.

"No. I think it would be safer for you if I took you under the circumstances. You are the key witness in this case after all and so we need to keep you safe and away from the reporters until we can find out exactly what happened. Those journalists are ruthless if they suspect anyone of anything sinister." He added.

Moira locked the door behind her and followed the officer to his squad car. She glanced up and down the street as she climbed in, paranoid that she was being watched by someone. Thankfully, that seemed not to be the case and they were soon underway.

Arriving at the station some twenty minutes later, she was welcomed into the detectives office by Chen with a handshake and a weak smile of appreciation for her attendance.

"Take a seat Moira. Can I get you anything? A cup of coffee or tea perhaps?" He asked politely.

"No Thank You" Replied Moira. "I'm fine."

"Right. Well then." Replied Chen, sitting down behind his desk and opening the file of case notes in front of him.

"We completed the autopsy yesterday on a Mr Jeremy Meyer who you state to be your ex-husband. The tox screen brought back some interesting results Moira. Some of which are consistent with what you reported."

Moira sighed quietly with content, happy that Chen could see she was attempting to co-operate with the police and that her story of events seemed accurate so far.

"Mr Meyer was found to have had a very high levels of alcohol in his blood and the observations made on his liver did indeed indicate he had become a heavy drinker which explains a lot about what fuelled his rage and jealousy in attacking you. The coroner indicates a significant amount of cirrhosis in his report."

"I see." Acknowledged Moira, wiping a tear from her eye as she felt a little pity for him for a brief moment.

"However there is one thing we can not seem to get to the bottom of Moira and we hoped you might be able to shed some light on it."

"What is that?"

"Well, not only did we find alcohol traces in his system but there was something else which came up."

He paused for a moment as he checked his notes once more. "It appears that at some point around the time of the attack, Mr Meyer ingested a lethal and very acute dose of a poison of some kind. The internal examination revealed how at some point; Mr Meyer suffered a complete shut down of his respiratory organs. Do you keep any poisons of any kind in the house Mrs Meyer?"

"None that I know of." Moira replied, a little confused and shocked at what she had heard. "I have your average cleaning products under the sink, such as bleach, but that is about it."

"Well..." Continued the detective. "I can assure you this was no form of bleach that did this. Even if it were bleach, it would have meant swallowing a much larger amount to cause such damage. Even then, the damage would have been to his stomach and not his lungs and heart. So".. He continued. "We are not quite sure where this fits into the events which transpired as it throws into question our original belief that Mr Meyer was hit with something in self defence and that is what caused his death to occur. You say your daughter was there at the time, correct?"

Moira was now beginning to feel uneasy and felt like this was turning more into an interrogation rather than a friendly conversation to establish a few facts.

"Yes... I...I... think so." She replied hesitantly." At some point maybe."

"Would she know where to locate any poisons of such kind to use to defend herself. Perhaps maybe she had somehow injected Mr Meyer with something which could have caused such a reaction at the time?" Suggested Chen.

". Injected him?" She asked in surprise at his accusation "I'm sure Moira wouldn't have known where to get her hands on something like that." Retorted Moira in strong defence of her daughter.

"I guess we will not know that until we track down her whereabouts will we Moira?"

"I guess not." Moira replied with a sympathetic shrug.

"Well, in light of current findings, I am left with little

option but to put out an APB on your daughter. She really is the only one now who can shed any light on this. The solving of this case rests on finding her and bringing her in. It is becoming harder to see her as a totally innocent victim in all this."

Moira was not kept much longer and left under strict instructions that any contact from Ebony should be directly reported to him, no matter how insignificant it may be. With that promise made, Moira made her way out of the station, feeling somewhat betrayed by Chen's words. She quickly declined a lift home in order to clear her head and do some essential shopping.

Later that night, Moira opted to tell her parents a little more about what had been going on. For obvious reasons, she chose to play down events and come up with her own version of the story to tell her mother. At least that would buy her some time while her search for Ebony continued.

Chapter 23

Ebony had been up all night. She really had turned into somewhat of a night owl now and like Coral and Diana, spent most of the day resting when the opportunity presented itself. The weather had improved significantly over the last couple of days and she had made the most of every ray of sunshine, lay in the back garden on the grass, storing up her energy for the fun she was to have later that evening. The girls had promised her an evening never to forget and so the need for rest beforehand was paramount. She lay still, though her mind raced as to the possible things her sisters had planned for her. It was Coral's birthday so Ebony figured it would be something very special. She was almost salivating with excitement.

Once again, she had been left alone at the house, left with the one instruction not to enter the room on the first floor, for today at least. Shesha had a very special surprise waiting for later and did not want anyone to catch sight of it until it was ready later that evening. Although intrigued, Ebony swore that this time, her curiosity would not get the better of her and she would follow his instructions to the letter. Her intent was to remain outside for as long as the good weather lasted. Whilst she would have appreciated the company of Diamond and Coral right now to wile away the hours, she had accepted the fact that they had to go out on what Shesha had described as a very special errand to bring back some goodies for later.

The hours seemed to drift by slowly. Every minute seemed to last an eternity. It was six o'clock in the evening now and the sun had moved to the extent where its warming rays no longer bathed the garden in sunlight. The temperature was beginning to drop and an increasing chill now began to descend on her. The change in temperature prompted Ebony to retire inside. She slowly got to her feet and gathered the few belongings she had took outside with her. Shutting the heavy outside door behind her, she made her way up the stairs. She stopped briefly on the first floor, thinking she could hear murmurings of sorts from down the corridor. She then remembered that she was alone in the building, though everyone would be expected back shortly.

She shook her head, believing she was hearing things and began climbing the remaining stairs up to the second floor. She strode down the hallway towards the kitchen. To her surprise, Shesha was already there. Ebony watched as he began pouring the contents of a large clear jug into a tall glass.

"Good evening Ebony." Shesha said quietly. "I trust you are well rested."

He turned to look at her.

"Yes I am. Well rested and now very hungry." She added, wondering how he had got back into the building without her noticing.

Shesha smiled. He stared at her a moment and then picked up the glass from the counter, offering it to Ebony.

"A feast beyond your wildest dreams awaits you Ebony. As we promised, tonight will be a memorable one for you. One you will look back on fondly. However, before you eat, I want you to drink this?"

Shesha remained where he was, gesturing to Ebony with his eyes by focussing his attention on the glass he held for a second, then back to Ebony. His tone was somehow different to what she was used to. It was far more persuasive in tone yet remained its usual quiet self in terms of it's volume. It seemed he was quite adamant that Ebony should do as he asked and his eyes suggested there would be no doubt she would conform.

"What is it?" Ebony questioned.

"Your powers are growing Ebony. Growing stronger even than those of your sisters. It means your gift is ready to be used in the best way possible. Your sisters are worried for you though. They managed to persuade me that it was time that you began to take your very own medicine like they do. Only by taking this can you be just like your sisters and learn to control what happens to you and stay healthy like Diana. You want to be closer to your sisters, don't you?"

Ebony nodded. Something strange was happening and it made her feel a little uneasy. Yet at the same time, listening to his voice, she had but one desire. She reached forward slowly with her hand, taking the glass from Shesha. She moved it slowly up to her mouth. As the rim of the glass touched her bottom lip, she inhaled the aroma of its contents. Whilst the smell was familiar to what she had been accustomed to when drinking Shesha's magic potion of sorts, the odour given off was significantly stronger than what she had been used to. She took one final glance up towards Shesha, noticing that his hand was extended out towards her, the tips of his fingers touching the glass as he gently coaxed Ebony to tip the glass upwards, thus pouring its contents into her mouth.

"That's it." He exclaimed, as she began to swallow. "Drink."

She began to consume the contents faster, taking huge gulps as the liquid poured down her throat. She was drinking so fast that she couldn't even savour the taste as she normally would. As she took her final mouthful, Shesha removed his finger from the bottom of the glass, which she then lowered. She looked at the glass. The colour of the residue which stained the side of the glass was a little darker than what she usually had drunk. As she examined the glass, she realised why. The taste suddenly hit her. Whilst there were similarities between what she had noticed previously and what Shesha had encouraged her to drink now, what she had just consumed was far stronger in taste. With the strength came an added bitterness. A bitterness that now was really reacting with her taste buds. She closed her eyes a second, shaking her head in reaction to the flavour. The after taste was far less pleasant than what she expected. Before she could comment on the experience, a strange sensation overcame her. She felt her vision begin to dissipate slightly and a warm rush pulsed through her veins.

"How do you feel Ebony?" Shesha asked, watching her responses with those wide eyes of his.

Ebony took a prolonged blink. As she opened her eyes, the rush faded and though she was fully conscious and in control of her body movements, she could no longer feel herself moving. Her body had entered a phase of complete numbness.

"I... I... feel...."

She had not even finished the sentence when the bodily sensation changed once more. What came over her now was a craving. A craving so strong, it felt impossible to resist. What that craving was for, she was not quite sure. All she was aware of was the need to satisfy it. She looked up at Shesha. With her head still slightly bowed, like a servant to a master, she spoke once more.

"I feel ...good." She replied.

"Then come." Said Shesha, walking past her and out the door, beckoning her with a bony finger to follow him downstairs. Your surprise is waiting. As are your beloved sisters. I am sure you are hungry."

Ebony shuffled along the corridor, in a manner characteristic of a sleepwalker in the dead of night. A tiny part of Ebony still feared what was about to happen. There was certainly an element of apprehension. She was however, driven by desire. She could sense something close by that she yearned for. A taste in the air was driving her senses crazy and though a part of her subconscious seemed to be sending her a message to not give into temptation, resistance seemed futile and her desire to proceed was the dominant force which drove her to follow Shesha downstairs.

Shesha opened the door to the laboratory which Ebony had now of course discovered. She was no longer interested in the contents of the room itself. The numerous snakes, the plethora of instruments, did not even attract her attention. Her focus was centred on tracking down this scent that hung in the air. It was closer still now. So close she seemed to be able to taste it as her tongue rubbed across the roof of her mouth. It seemed to be coming from beyond the laboratory itself. Perhaps from behind the wall somewhere. Was there another room beyond the confines of the laboratory? It was a question which Shesha quickly answered.

He reached up. Twisting the small knob of the end cupboard, Ebony soon heard a small whirring sound. A section of the wall began to slide upwards, slowly revealing another doorway. It was a very old door, bolted and padlocked. It was obvious the door was part of the original structure of the building and although it seemed to function, it had never been replaced or treated.

"Ah. You are here." Said Shesha looking pleased.

"Yes Uncle. We are here." The sisters replied simultaneously.

Ebony did not even turn around to see both Coral and Diana behind her. She was still obsessed with the source of the scent she detected. It was making her drool. As she waited with Diamond and Coral for the door to reveal itself in full, Shesha moved to the side and then excused himself.

"I shall leave her with you girls. Enjoy the feast. I shall return very shortly and as you know. I will not be alone."

With that, Shesha left the room leaving Ebony in the capable hands of Coral and Diana. They both put her arm round her shoulder.

"Feast time Ebony" Diana announced happily, reaching for the door. "Close your eyes." She added.

"Coral began to chuckle playfully as she moved directly behind Ebony, she reached up to place the palms of her hands over Ebony's eyes in a manner similar to what every mother does when revealing a Christmas present to their young child.

The door opened and Ebony walked in, guided by Coral behind her. Once inside, Diana closed the door. That scent was so strong now that Ebony knew it's source was in the same room. Ebony had not experienced a sensation like it before. She did not quite know exactly what she was craving but yet she seemed to be aware of exactly how to precure it

"Join us now Ebony. "Coral whispered in her ear. "Join us

in using our gift to do good. To help rid the world of all that is bad. The journey starts now sister…. Surprise!"

With that, Coral took her hands away from Ebony's eyes. She looked around the room for the first time. It was quite dimly lit. Almost like a dungeon room. Just a handful of orange lights around the room, emitted a warm orange glow, a glow barely strong enough to see to the other side of the room. Around their feet, numerous rats playfully ran, squeaking at each other as they did so. The scent she detected changed as the rats passed. Her tongue rubbed the roof of her mouth again as she tried to identify it. It was the scent of ammonia and other forms of waste that these rats must have spent most of their time rummaging round in. Thankfully, it was not the scent belonging to what Ebony was craving. As the rats scurried away, the desired scent grew strong again. Her eyes suddenly focussed on what was on the other side of the room. Someone was there. Someone besides her and her sisters.

Across the room, the outline of what appeared to be three human females came into view. They were whimpering, sobbing even, in apparent fear. Ebony hung back as Coral and Diana approached them. They appeared to be young females, even school age, their identities hidden for the moment under hoods that were placed over their heads.

"Don't worry." Diana said, kneeling down close to the girl nearest to her. The sobbing girls' hands were bound tightly together and attached to a large metal hook on the wall. The same was true for the other two girls also, all of them becoming far more vocal in expressing their fear now, begging for their lives or a reason as to why they were being held captive in such a way.

"You will be freed very soon." Diana assured them.

She then looked back at Ebony. Her appearance was no longer that of the baby -faced teenager she knew. The skin on her face was scaly and greyish in colour. Her eyes had rolled over to white and a pair of small fangs, like hypodermic needles protruded from her upper jaw. She quickly pulled off the hood from over the girls' face. As she looked up at Diana, the girl screamed. Diana moved round to the second girl, who was crouched up against the wall, trying to create as much distance between her and the screams of terror next to her as she could. It was pointless. There was nowhere for her to go. Diana then removed her hood. She did not scream, though as Diana looked deep into her eyes, she could see the terror as tears streamed down her face. So overcome by terror that a small puddle of bodily fluid began to form as drops of urine began running down the inside of her bare legs. Coral then removed the hood of the third girl. She looked up. Not at Coral who stood close to her, but past her and directly at Ebony in the distance. She seemed to be holding it together a little more than the other two girls.

"This one is for you Sister." Coral said. She pulled on the girl's hair to force her head back. Ebony could hear her breathing heavy, attempting to disguise her fear, masquerading it as false aggression.

"What are you freaks?" She asked between clenched teeth. "When I get out of here, I'm going to kill you. Especially you." She added, looking in Ebony's direction.

Ebony had stepped forward out of the darkness. She now recognised all three of them.

"Don't threaten my sister." Warned Diana. "She is at her

most dangerous when she feels threatened. As you are about to discover."

"Dangerous?" The girl replied. The girl now recognised as Alexa from college. "She is nothing but a wimp. Isn't that right…Bony?"

"Your courage is admirable." Coral hissed. "Although it is very much misplaced Alexa."

Coral now also looked very much like a snake when it came to her facial features. Her eyes were almost black and her skin, rather than being a grey colour like Diana, was a deep red in colour. It was only when up close to her could she be seen properly.

Diana looked up at Ebony. She was sweating profusely and though trying not to watch what was happening, couldn't help herself but to look out the corner of her eye. She could feel herself being drawn in closer towards them. She took one step forward and looked over at Alexa.

"Shall we free them now?"

"Yes." Ebony replied, feeling an all too familiar ache within her mouth, more specifically emanating from her top jaw.

Diana smiled. She turned her attention back to the girl closest to her.

"Leave Natalie alone you bitch." Alexa yelled.

Diana smiled. Then she lunged her head forward at Natalie, sinking her teeth in time and time again into her bare shoulder. Natalie let out a high-pitched yelp. One of extreme pain as Diana began to feast at will on her skin. A trickle of blood slowly began to run down the girl's arm and then another down the front of her body towards her chest. Then another, this time down the back of her shoulder.

The more times Diana thrust her fangs into her, the faster the blood began to flow. Natalie began to quieten slightly, very much accepting her fate rather than resist. She had lost too much blood to resist. Then Coral lunged at the girl sat in the middle, feasting on her abdomen, leaving Alexa till last. By the time Coral had took her third bite. Natalie sat slumped back against the wall, almost lifeless after the attack inflicted upon her. She suddenly lurched forward, holding her stomach. Diana stepped back, looking so unbelievably satisfied. She smiled as the blood dripped down onto her t-shirt from her chin. Her appearance had returned to its full human state as she watched with pleasure as the last agonising moments of Natalie's life unfolded before her. Natalie began to heave, then after a few seconds, vomit violently. After apparently expelling all the contents of her stomach over the floor, Diana watched as blood began to run down Natalie's face. It was coming from both her eyes and nose. A trickle at first, then it began to pour out at speed. Inside her, her blood had lost its ability to clot and with the venom now punching holes in the pores in her skin, it could escape her body at will. With the blood almost drained from her body, she began to turn cyanotic as her struggling blood starved heart took its last couple of beats.

Kat, the other of Alexa's protégés, was quickly to follow. She gasped for breath as the poisons which pulsed through her bloodstream now began to shut down her lungs. With one or two last gasps of air, the neurotoxin had taken its full effect, freezing her diaphragm and stopping her lungs from functioning. She too was dead. Coral stood up and joined Diana by Ebony's side.

"Always save the best till last Ebony." Coral joked.

Ebony felt the hands of both Diana and Coral on her back, gently nudging her forward towards where Alexa was sat cross legged on the floor. Ebony stepped forward and leaned down over her, mouth open wide, revealing her own set of sharp fangs, the second of which had now grown back since they last came face to face. A nagging doubt in her mind occurred, the same sub- conscious doubt she had before this started. The question of should she do what she was about to do. She knew that if she went through with this, she would never be the same person again, if indeed she could even class herself as a person now. Barely six inches from Alexa's body, she paused a moment. Alexa did no such thing however. With her hands and feet firmly tied, the only weapon she had at her disposal was her head. Seeing Ebony's slow and hesitant approach towards her, she leapt upon the one opportunity that she had to strike, catching Ebony's cheek with her forehead. Ebony stumbled back slightly, dropping to her haunches, now very much enraged by Alexa's desperate actions. That was it. That was what was needed to push Ebony over the edge. She no longer felt human in any way. With lightening speed, she almost threw herself on top of Alexa, impacting her with such force and strength that the rope which connected Alexa's tied wrists to the iron support on the wall snapped instantly, taking the wall mounted hook with it.

Diana and Coral looked on in pride as Ebony ravaged her victim. As they did, they heard a voice from behind them. They knew who it was. Shesha. As promised, he had returned and was not alone. Stood by his side was a special visitor who had arrived just in time for the main event. The two girls parted slightly to allow a clear line of view for Shesha and his visitor to see.

Ebony had far from finished. She attacked the body with unrivalled ferocity. Ferocity that even her sisters seemed surprised at as they watched. This was what Ebony had craved. Finally, her craving was being satisfied. As she continued, she felt as though her last shred of humanity had disappeared. Whilst she finished off her victim, striking her continuously and even after Alexa's heart had stopped, she could hear two voices in the background. One of them was clearly Shesha.

"You must be proud now?" Asked Shesha quietly to the woman stood by his side. His voice just oozed content and pride.

"Yes. Of course, I am." Said the female who emerged from the darkness beside him. I am as proud as an Auntie could possibly be."

TO BE CONTINUED…..

Printed in the United States
by Bookmasters

Printed in the United States
By Bookmasters